D1642733

HER MISSING DAUGHTER

D S BUTLER

Deadly Obsession
Deadly Motive
Deadly Revenge
Deadly Justice
Deadly Ritual
Deadly Payback
Deadly Game

Copyright © 2018 D. S. Butler
All rights reserved.

This book is a work of fiction. Names, characters, places, and incidents are either products of the author's imagination or used fictitiously. Any resemblance to real persons, living or dead, is entirely coincidental. No part of this publication can be reproduced or transmitted in any form or by any means, electronic or mechanical, without permission in writing from the author.

http://www.dsbutlerbooks.com

HER MISSING DAUGHTER

A mother murdered.
A daughter missing.
A family with secrets.

On a hot August day, Abbie's best friend is murdered and her
goddaughter, Sienna, disappears.
Abbie is desperate to find and protect Sienna, but unanswered
questions haunt her every move. Has Sienna run away? Or has
someone taken her?
Just when Abbie thinks she's on the right track, there's a twist
that changes everything.

**Who killed Nicole? Where is Sienna? And who is still hiding
secrets?**

For my readers - thank you for your support!

PROLOGUE

SIENNA

I'D ALWAYS BEEN close to my mother, but when things started to go wrong, the situation spiralled fast. I didn't see it coming. I couldn't stop it. How could I? I was only fifteen.

I thought I had all the answers.

I was wrong.

I keep going over things in my mind, trying to pinpoint the exact moment things shifted to the point of no return. I'd like to rewind time and go back and live it all again. I wouldn't make the same mistakes. It's easy to see where I messed up now. Looking back, everything is crystal clear, but I didn't see it coming.

Not until it was too late.

People look at me differently now. They talk in hushed whispers when I enter a room. It's pretty bad. I can't imagine what they'd do if they knew this all started because of something I did.

But they don't know everything. They don't even know the half of it. No one does.

CHAPTER ONE

THE DAY my friend was murdered, I was five thousand miles away.

Nicole Carlson was my oldest and closest friend, but on the day her life ended, I hadn't given her a second thought. Why hadn't I sensed something? At the very least I should have felt a shiver of apprehension or a pang of sadness at the exact moment she passed.

I didn't, though. I was too wrapped up in the events of the day and hadn't paused for a moment. I didn't think about her, at all. Not once.

I'd been working for the Trela Health Foundation Charity in India, and we were setting up a new project, which kept me frantically busy. After I found out, I tried to remember what I was doing at the precise moment she died. I tortured myself, wondering if I was counting out pipettes or stacking bottles of reagent or some equally mundane, repetitive task as Nicole's life faded away.

The phone call came at one a.m., and I knew straight away it was bad news. No one rings at one a.m. with good news, do they? I thought it had something to do with the project, though. My first guess was someone had a medical emergency in the village.

The unrelenting, chirpy ring from my cheap mobile phone woke me from a deep sleep. I'd had one too many glasses of whiskey before I went to bed and regretted it as soon as my eyes opened. I don't usually drink much, but Bettan, one of our local suppliers, had brought a case of whiskey on his last visit. Because it had been such a long day, I thought the whiskey would help me sleep. The incessant rain drumming on the tin roof of our temporary Foundation building, accompanied by the night crickets' chorus had given me many sleepless nights so far this monsoon season. I thought whiskey might blot it all out. I'd tried just about everything else, including earplugs, meditation and music.

We had been tasked with setting up a new Trela Health Foundation initiative just outside a small village seventy kilometres south of Kochi. Our plan was to offer the local community advice on healthcare issues, particularly focusing on education. We had the funding in place, but as it was a new initiative in the area, I only had one person helping me. A very green behind the ears young man called Rich Michaels. He was a twenty-one-year-old American, working for the Foundation on his gap year. He wanted to get into politics eventually. That made sense. I could picture him wearing an expensive suit, striding down the halls in Washington. He never looked completely comfortable dressed casually in his baggy T-shirt and cargo pants. He worked hard, but he had a nervous character and didn't like making decisions without direction.

As our team contained a grand total of two people, it meant a lot of the work fell to me. I didn't mind. I liked being busy. It kept my mind off things and made me feel like I was making a difference.

When the telephone rang, I sat bolt upright in bed. Being woken by the phone in the middle of the night never bodes well, and my heart thudded as I reached for the light cord beside my bed. It didn't work.

I didn't use it much, preferring the lamp in the corner of the room, because the main light in the middle of the ceiling had a fan attached to it, which made the fitting swing in wide loops around the ceiling. I was terrified the whole thing was going to fall down and electrocute me one of these days.

With a groan, I pushed back the sheets and staggered out of bed. I reached down to switch on the small lamp, but again nothing happened. It took me a second or two to realise the generator wasn't working.

I cursed in frustration and headed towards my mobile phone, which was glowing with a faint green light and vibrating on the table by the window. I'd never been able to see well in the dark, and with the heavy monsoon clouds blocking out the moon, the room was pitch black. When I was almost at the table, I stubbed my toe on a chair leg.

I swore loudly as I picked up the phone. "Hello."

I didn't recognise the voice on the other end of the line, and my first thought was that it had to be a wrong number. I reached down to rub my sore foot, and facts started to filter through to my sleepy brain. The person on the phone was speaking in English… Or was that a Scottish accent I detected?

They repeated their question. "Am I talking to Abbie Morris?"

I nodded and rubbed my eyes before realising I would actually have to reply. "Yes, that's right. I'm Abbie."

There was a pause on the other end of the line, and it annoyed me more than it should have. My tensed muscles relaxed. So it wasn't bad news after all. What sort of person would call in the middle of the night unless it was important? If this was some sort of telesales call, I was going to give her a piece of my mind.

"I'm terribly sorry to tell you this," she said, and my stomach responded with a somersault.

I pressed a hand against my chest. My first thought was that she was phoning to give me bad news about one of my parents. They had left the UK to emigrate to Australia over ten years ago now, and though I saw them as often as I could, it wasn't enough.

But it wasn't my parents.

"It's Nicole," the voice said. "Something awful has happened. She's dead."

Maybe it was the fact I'd only just woken from a deep sleep, or it could have been because I'd never thought of Nicole as being vulnerable, but it took time for those words to sink in.

She couldn't mean *my* Nicole. Not the Nicole I'd gone through secondary school with. Not the Nicole I'd shared fun things with, like sleepovers, and watching Dirty Dancing three times in a row, eating whole pints of ice cream, and not the Nicole I'd shared teenage tragedies with, like over-plucked eyebrows, unrequited crushes and the hideous combination of violet lipstick and blue mascara. Not the Nicole who'd moved to Southampton with me so we could struggle through our nursing degrees together, balancing studying with frequent nights out and too many vivid blue Jucy Lucy cocktails. She was so vivacious and full of life. It just wasn't possible.

"I'm sorry? Are you talking about Nicole Carlson? Are you sure?"

There was a strange shuffling noise on the other end of the phone, as though the woman was covering the mouthpiece with her hand. Finally, she replied, "Yes, Nicole Carlson. You were good friends, weren't you? And you're Sienna's godmother?"

At the mention of Sienna's name, the horror of what this woman was telling me hit home. Sienna was Nicole's daughter. This wasn't a mistake. She was really talking about *my* Nicole. It felt like all the air had been sucked from my lungs. I groped around wildly, trying to find the chair and then sat down heavily. How could this have happened? Had she been ill? I'd spoken to her the day before yesterday, and she hadn't mentioned anything.

I hadn't been back home to the UK for almost five years. In fact, the last time I had returned, it was for Nicole's wedding. She'd fallen for a rich, successful man and joked he was going to keep her in the manner she wanted to become accustomed to. We kept up-to-date with Skype and FaceTime video calls, every week, but it was never the same.

I realised I hadn't spoken for some time and could hear the steady breathing of the woman on the other end of the line.

"Can you tell me how it happened? Was it an accident?"

The woman drew in a sharp breath and hesitated before answering. "It was no accident."

I shook my head in confusion. Her voice sounded bitter and angry.

My eyes were slowly getting used to the dark now, and I looked down at my toe and saw the injury had drawn blood.

I had so many questions, but I didn't know which one to ask first. "I'm sorry… I didn't get your name."

"I'm Angie," the woman said, irritation lacing her voice. She spoke as though I should know who she was, but I couldn't place her name or her voice.

"I work for Mr and Mrs Carlson," she added eventually.

Realisation dawned as I remembered a short, firecracker of a lady who had worked as their housekeeper. Shortly before she got married, Nicole had confided to me she would prefer to get a cleaner from one of the local agencies, but Angie Macgregor had worked for Steve for more than a decade before they got married, and he wouldn't even consider letting her go. Nicole said Angie was as efficient as a sergeant major and just as stern. I'd only met her on a couple of occasions and only briefly.

"Thank you for letting me know, Angie. Do you know when the funeral will be held? I'd like to come back for it. How is Sienna doing?"

"I don't know," Angie's voice wavered, and I felt like an idiot for asking such a stupid question.

Of course, Sienna would be distraught. I needed to get back to the UK and help her as much as I could. We'd spent a lot of time together when Sienna was a little girl, but I'd left the UK when she was only ten, and the last time I'd seen her was at Nicole and Steve's wedding. She'd only been eleven. Of course, she was older now, but I couldn't help picturing her as that little girl, who would be lost without her mother.

"I really think you should come back straight away," Angie whispered. "There's no time to waste."

"Excuse me?" I blinked in confusion. What a strange thing to say. What did she mean by that?

I heard another voice in the background, and Angie muttered, "I'm sorry. I can't talk now."

Then the line went dead.

CHAPTER TWO

I SAT IN THE SMALL, rickety chair staring at my mobile phone for a long time. How could Nicole be gone? It didn't seem possible. Maybe the phone call had been a bad dream. Maybe I was still asleep and in the middle of a nightmare.

The throbbing pain in my foot told me otherwise. I was definitely awake.

Functioning on autopilot, I stood up and gingerly slid my feet into a bright green pair of Crocs. Not exactly a winning fashion statement but practical when I needed to go walking outside in the mud. The generator was kept in a separate building next to our accommodation.

It was just next door, but I paused in the doorway, scanning the dark, water-logged ground for snakes. Then stared into the thick bush that surrounded the clearing. I had a torch shoved into my back pocket and pulled it out, shining it toward the trees, looking out for any reflections from the eyes of creatures lurking amongst the towering plants. When I was sure it was safe, I made a run for it, dashing across the clearing, muddy water splattering my legs.

The door was only a few feet away, but by the time I got there, I was soaked through. The rain was incredibly heavy and unrelenting, and I couldn't wait for the monsoon season to come to an end.

It took me ten minutes to get the generator up and running again, and when I got back to my room and stripped off my soggy nightclothes, I heard Rich's soft snoring through the thin walls separating our sleeping quarters. When he heard I would be returning to the UK, leaving him in charge tomorrow, he would freak out.

I rubbed my hair dry with a towel and tried to plan how to break the news.

As we were on the edge of the village, we weren't yet connected to the main electricity supply and had no Internet service. I wanted to get online and check out flights back to the UK, but I didn't want to venture to the village at this time of night in the dark on my own. We weren't far from Chimmini Wildlife Reserve, where panthers and tigers roamed. I'd never seen one as they were very elusive, but there had been reports of a panther sighting close to the village last week. They liked to hunt at night, so I wasn't taking any chances. I'd wait for daybreak and then head over to the village and book my flight.

There was no way I was going to risk bumping into a big cat. Bumping into the chair leg had been bad enough. I winced as I looked down at my injured toe. I tried to clean away most of the blood with disinfectant. It wasn't easy. I was a fully-trained nurse, but it was never easy working on yourself, and I was no contortionist.

I dumped the disinfectant-soaked cotton wool ball in the bin and washed my hands. His complete lack of medical experience was another reason Rich was going to be upset tomorrow. He was what the Foundation referred to as technical support. In other words, he was the general dogsbody of the camp, helping to set things up, communicating with the locals and keeping a close eye on the budget. He was a good communicator, though. Certainly better than me. He spoke six languages, while I relied mainly on hand waving and gestures.

It was a miracle the Foundation had accepted my application. They preferred multilingual employees, but timing had been on my side when I'd applied. Someone had left them in the lurch, and I offered to step in. I gave them the usual spiel in my interview. I wanted to make a difference…to help people…to make the world a better place. But I have to admit my motives weren't entirely unselfish. I'd desperately wanted to get away from the UK and couldn't pass up a fresh start in a new country.

I didn't fancy sticking around with everybody staring at me, gossiping and perhaps even laughing behind my back.

I'd needed that change of scenery after I'd been jilted at the altar. Yes, I was a cliché. Technically, I hadn't actually been at the altar. I had been left shivering outside the church, waiting to make my entrance, calling my childhood sweetheart on my Dad's mobile, trying to find out what was causing the holdup.

Humiliated in front of my family and friends, I was too embarrassed to face anyone and asked my Dad to tell the congregation there wasn't going to be a wedding. That wasn't even the worst of it. Later, I found out Rob had been having a yearlong affair with his secretary. Cliché stacked upon cliché. I would have laughed if it hadn't hurt so much.

Through it all, Nicole had been amazing. She'd kept me company as I ranted about all the years I'd wasted on a no-good scumbag, and she'd helped me out by eating her share of the chocolate ice cream when my anger turned to melancholy. She set me up on blind dates, including one with Steve's business partner, Toby.

Her heart was in the right place, but I don't know whether it was Toby or me who was more embarrassed by her matchmaking. With absolutely nothing in common, we endured Nicole's multiple clumsy attempts to bring us together until I finally put an end to it. Toby seemed a nice enough bloke, but he wasn't for me.

Nicole hadn't wanted me to go to India, but when I'd made up my mind, she'd supported me one hundred percent.

Nicole Carlson had been a good friend, the best. But now she was gone. I would never be able to repay her kindness to me, but I would be able to help Sienna. I would do everything I could to help her. I owed it to Nicole.

CHAPTER THREE

I WAITED for the tears to come as I sat cross-legged on the bed looking at my injured toe. The bloody thing was probably broken.

But no tears came. I still couldn't believe she was really gone. I only had that strange phone conversation to go on. Maybe Angie had memory problems or was unstable. She hadn't been young when I'd last seen her and she was five years older than that now. Deep down, I knew I was fooling myself, though. I had no reason to doubt Angie's word.

I leaned back against the thin partition wall then shivered as I saw a cockroach scurrying across the floor.

I reached down and grabbed one of my bright green Crocs and threw it at the large insect with all my might. My coordination skills had never been brilliant, and instead of hitting the cockroach, I hit a lamp, sending it crashing to the floor. I put my head in my hands and groaned as I heard movement from next door. After a moment, there was a quiet knock at my door, and Rich whispered, "Are you alright in there, boss?"

"I'm fine," I called out. "I just dropped something. Sorry for waking you. Go back to sleep."

The last thing I wanted was to talk to Rich about what had happened. I wasn't really a sharer. I preferred to keep things to myself until I'd had time to process them.

But tomorrow, I would have to drive myself to the airport and get a flight back to Heathrow. I got up and began to pack.

* * *

THE FOLLOWING MORNING RICH WAS CHEERFULLY WHISTLING IN THE shared room we used as the living area. It had a small sink, coffeemaker and a toaster as well as a small portable heating element we used as a stovetop. It wasn't exactly the type of kitchen where you could whip up an amazing meal, but we never had time for that anyway. Rice and vegetable curries and stews made up our staple diet.

"Morning boss." He grinned, poured a steaming mug of coffee and held it out to me.

"Morning," I said, taking the coffee and wondering how to break the news to him.

"What's on the agenda today?" he asked.

"Actually, there's been a change of plan. I had some bad news last night."

"Ah, I knew there was something wrong; you look terrible. Did you get any sleep?"

"Thanks for that," I said dryly.

He looked horrified. "Sorry, I didn't mean that… I just meant –"

I held up a hand. "Don't worry about it. I'm just pulling your leg. But I am going to have to go back to the UK so that means you're going to have to step up."

He smiled. "Of course, no problem at all."

I raised an eyebrow, thinking he was taking this better than I'd expected and then I realised he hadn't thought things through.

"It will be a little while until the Foundation can send somebody else out to cover me, so you're going to be on your own for a few days."

"What? I can't be here on my own. I've only been doing this job a couple of weeks. What if I get robbed or what if the locals decide we aren't welcome here because…?"

I put a hand on his shoulder. "Relax. They won't even know I'm gone. The Foundation will send somebody else out as soon as they can."

He scratched his head. "Well, maybe I should leave as well. Isn't there something in the rules about having more than one person on the site at a time?"

"We need you to stay. If people realise that the site is empty, they will come and help themselves to our supplies." I looked around, at the barren, temporary shelter we'd created. "Not that there's much here worth taking at the moment, but they won't know that. They might think we've got medication or things they can sell on."

He placed a hand on his forehead and groaned. "I don't know if I can do this."

"You'll be fine."

We stood in silence for a few minutes as I sipped my coffee and then he said, "But I don't have any medical training. What if one of the villagers gets ill and comes here for help?"

"Then you'll have to tell them we're not open yet and direct them to the District Hospital."

We were setting up a programme for the screening of intestinal parasites along with educating people from the surrounding villages on how the diseases were spread and how they could minimise the chances of getting an infection. Sometimes this was as simple as wearing shoes. Villagers tending the land would go to the toilet at the side of their plot rather than walk back to use the new facilities in the village.

Some of the elders didn't trust the modern toilets and preferred to use the pits.

As they intended to eat the vegetation they harvested from the area, this created a vicious circle, and it was our hope that we could minimise the spread of infection through education.

We would have a portable lab eventually. Some of the supplies were here already and others would be on the way. Reagents, microscopes and a centrifuge. We didn't need much else and could operate on a minimal budget. But with no medical training, Rich wouldn't be able to do much while I was gone.

The rain had finally stopped after continuing all night, and the sun was starting to creep higher in the sky and warm the land, creating a muggy, humid mist.

I sipped my coffee and did my best to reassure Rich.

"When do you have to leave?" he asked, a frown puckering his usually smooth forehead.

"Today," I told him, wishing I could have given him a little more time to get used to the idea. Nicole's funeral wouldn't be for a few days at least, but there was something about the way Angie Macgregor had delivered the news over the phone that made me feel I needed to get back quickly.

I was worried about Sienna. I hadn't seen much of her over the past five years, except in the background when I talked to Nicole on FaceTime or Skype, but I couldn't help remembering her as that little girl with big blue eyes and light coppery brown ringlets, although to Nicole's horror, she'd recently started straightening her hair, informing her mother she couldn't stand her natural curls.

Sienna would have Steve to comfort her, her stepfather for the past five years. I wondered how close they were now. They got off to a somewhat bumpy start, which I supposed was under-standable.

I put my cup of coffee down on the wooden bench in front of our makeshift home and stared out at the dark green vegetation. Anything could be hiding out there, and yet I felt safe. Nicole had been so worried that something would happen to me when I came to India. She insisted it wasn't safe and that I would have to ring her every week otherwise she'd never forgive me.

We made it a habit. On Friday nights she'd start on the wine early and call me at ten p.m. my time. It wasn't quite the same as meeting up in person, but it was better than nothing, and I looked forward to our weekly chats.

Through the video chats I'd seen Sienna growing up and noticed as each Friday passed, Steve played less and less of a role in their lives.

Sometimes I wondered if he resented me taking up his wife's time on Friday evenings. For the first year or so, if we were still talking when he returned from work, he would lean over Nicole's shoulder and wave at the screen. He never chatted for long, but he made the effort.

I couldn't remember the last time he'd done that. In fact, I couldn't remember the last time Steve had been at home when I was talking to Nicole. She'd said he was working longer and longer hours but assured me she was still happy.

Rich came back outside, chewing his lower lip nervously. He looked like he'd splashed some water on his face because the edges of his hair were damp.

He offered me a smile. "I'll be okay. I know I won't be able to do much when you're away, but I promise to hold the fort."

I grinned at him over the top of my mug. "I have every confidence you'll be great." I stood up. "Now, I need to get my things together and then I'm going to need a lift to the airport."

We both turned to look at the vehicle we'd rented. It was a fifteen-year-old, dilapidated truck, and I wasn't sure it was going to make it as far as the airport. From the look on Rich's face, he agreed with me.

"It will be fine," I said with more conviction than I felt and got up to walk inside slowly.

My toe was now red and purple, but most of the pain had gone. I was lucky it was just bruised.

It didn't take me long to pack. I'd learned to travel light during my time in India. I only had a couple of jumpers as it was cool here in the evenings. Although our base was on elevated ground, the days tended to be hot, and even the rain didn't offer any relief but just added to the humidity. We were at the tail end of the monsoon season. Soon the weather would improve, and hopefully, I'd be back in time for that.

I just had to get back to the UK for Nicole's funeral and make sure Sienna was okay. If she wasn't happy staying with Steve, I knew that Nicole's mother and sister would step up.

In fact, I knew they'd be only too happy to take over from Steve. I'd always liked Nicole's mother, but she was extremely full on. She liked to stick her nose into her daughter's business and didn't hesitate to show when she was disappointed in Nicole's life choices.

Case in point, when Nicole had fallen pregnant with Sienna during the final year of her nursing degree, Nicole's mother reacted as though it was the end of the world.

CHAPTER FOUR

I DROVE to the airport with Rich in the passenger seat. Our base was only sixty kilometres from the airport, but some of the roads around the reserve were not well-maintained. I navigated carefully around the largest potholes because the jagged holes had filled with rainwater, and every time the tyres dipped into one, thick, muddy water splashed upwards, smearing the windscreen.

After a few kilometres, the streaks of mud made visibility so bad that I had to pull over to the side of the road and pour one of the bottles of drinking water we kept in the back of the truck over the windscreen. I even wished it would start raining again.

As the water trickled down the windscreen, Rich thought it would be a great idea to lean over and turn on the windscreen wipers. I gasped as muddy splatters covered my white shirt, then shot daggers at Rich.

His eyes widened as he looked at me in horror. "Sorry," he called out of the window. "I didn't think the wipers would do that."

I bit back a sharp retort. It was on the tip of my tongue to ask him exactly what he thought was going to happen when he turned on the windscreen wipers, but I managed to keep my mouth shut. It had been an accident. I didn't want to part on a bad note.

I tried to wipe off the mud, but my attempts made it look worse, producing smears all down my shirt. When I climbed back into the truck, he apologised again.

"Don't worry about it." I fastened my seatbelt. "I know you didn't mean to cover me with mud."

The windscreen was also splattered with dead insects, but I tried very hard not to think about that.

The morning was already heating up, and as there was no air conditioning in the truck, we wound down the windows as low as we dared and continued at a steady pace. It was a balancing act. We needed the flow of fresh air to combat the heat, but we also wanted to keep the muddy water out.

Finally, we reached the main drag and took the highway towards Kochi airport. Rich twiddled his thumbs and every now and again shot me an anxious glance. "You *will* call them and tell them we need someone sent to replace you straight away, won't you?"

I nodded as I changed into a higher gear, thankful to have left the potholes behind. "I'll call them as soon as I've sorted out my flight. I promise."

He sank back against the seat but didn't look completely reassured.

After a moment of silence, he leaned forward and tuned the radio to a local channel, which played a quirky mix of Western music and Bollywood hits. As "Saree Ke Fall Sa" played in the background, I thought back to the phone call from Angie Macgregor.

It had unnerved me, but I couldn't say why. Maybe Steve had asked her to call me. That made sense. He'd be distraught and busy trying to comfort Sienna. I tapped my finger against the gear stick. There had been something about Angie's tone that struck me as odd. She hadn't sounded devastated or upset.

I mulled it over, and my hands tightened on the steering wheel when I realised why Angie's voice had sounded wrong to me. The tone of her voice hadn't been emotional or sad. No, her voice had been laced with fear.

A shiver ran along my spine. Why was Angie Macgregor *afraid*?

Having met her briefly, I imagined most people would be afraid of Angie Macgregor, not the other way around. If I were being unkind, I'd describe her as a battleaxe. Nicole would disagree with that assessment, though. After getting to know her, she'd grown fond of Angie and described her as a woman who knew her own mind.

I pushed my hair back from my forehead, already feeling hot and sticky. I couldn't wait to get inside the airport and be greeted by cool air conditioning.

After I sorted my flight, I'd use the waiting time to call and offer my condolences. Should I call Steve or Nicole's mother first? Or would calling be an unwelcome intrusion? Of course, I wanted to tell them how sorry I was and offer to help in any way I could, but I didn't want to bother them so soon after Nicole died.

I didn't even know *how* Nicole died. Angie hadn't offered the information, and I hadn't had a chance to ask before she hung up. Had there been a car accident? An illness perhaps? But no, I would have known if Nicole had been ill. There was no way she'd have kept that from me. Was there?

When I'd spoken to her the previous Friday, she'd seemed… normal. There was nothing to indicate anything was wrong or that she was ill.

I bit down on my lower lip as I turned onto the one-way system that looped around the airport.

The number of people and cars in the area was overwhelming, and for a moment, I longed for the peace and quiet of our base beside the nature reserve. The contrast was amazing, but that was India. Some areas were so populous you couldn't move without jostling into someone, and others were so deserted you could walk for hours without meeting a soul.

The airport was so modern and high-tech, it made me feel like I was entering a time warp. The village beside the nature reserve appeared stuck in time with one concession — everyone had mobile phones. The village had an electricity supply, but service was sporadic, and we frequently had outages, especially during the thunderstorms during monsoon season.

I pulled up beside the gate to departures, jumped out of the truck and avoided eye-contact with an official-looking man in a uniform striding towards me. Before he could say anything, I scooted around to the back of the truck and grabbed my holdall as Rich climbed over to sit behind the steering wheel.

I stuck my head in the passenger window to say goodbye. "Don't worry. Everything is going to be fine. Just sit tight, and somebody from the charity will be with you soon."

As I turned to walk away, he called me back. "Abbie, you are coming back, aren't you?"

I hesitated for a moment before nodding. "Of course."

As he pulled away from the curb, I turned and headed towards the airport's entrance, sidestepping the official, who barked something at me. I muttered an apology. Hoping he would assume I was a tourist who didn't know any better and let me off.

Inside the airport, I felt a rush of cooler air engulf me. There were people everywhere, and I took a moment to get my bearings. I apologised as I found myself caught up in a line of people queuing at the oversized luggage counter.

Like most people, I usually bought my airline tickets online. But as we didn't have the internet hooked up to our base yet, I'd hoped to book a flight at the airport. With a sigh, I took in the long queues at the airline desks, then pulling out my mobile, I made the decision to check online before joining the long, snaking line.

I logged into the booking site and quickly scanned the available flights. There was one today, leaving in three hours, a flight out of Kochi changing at Abu Dhabi. The changeover made it a thirteen-hour trip, but it didn't look like I had many other options.

I typed in my credit card details and purchased the ticket then passing the people waiting for service at the airline counter I walked up to the check-in desk. The woman behind the counter lowered her gaze to the muddy streaks on my shirt and her smile faltered.

"Any hold luggage today, Madam?" she asked in cool, slightly disdainful English as I handed her my passport.

"Um." I tugged open the zip on my holdall and rummaged around until I found a clean T-shirt I wanted to check my luggage in because the toiletries I'd packed wouldn't be accepted in the cabin.

I draped the clean top over my arm and put the holdall on the luggage belt. "Yes, please," I said, crossing my arms over my chest to hide the worst of the smears.

As soon as I'd checked in, I used the ladies' toilets to change into the clean T-shirt and threw away my muddy shirt. Then I called the Foundation and explained I would need a leave of absence. The woman I spoke to was understanding and promised to send someone to cover my position as soon as possible.

I still had a while to wait for boarding and decided to kill some time by grabbing a cup of tea.

Everywhere was crowded. As I stood in a line between a tiny lady who couldn't have been more than four foot ten and a strapping teenage boy who towered over me, I used the airport's Wi-Fi and logged into Facebook on my phone.

After, navigating to Sienna's page, I scanned her posts. I saw that she hadn't posted anything in the last week, but her wall was filled with posts from her friends telling her how sorry they were to hear about her mother's death.

It triggered a wave of grief that seemed to come out of nowhere. It brought it home to me. This was real. Nicole was really gone. My eyes flooded with tears and the back of my throat ached.

I blinked and rubbed my eyes. I would never see her again. My best friend. The person I could always rely on for anything.

It was so hot, and as the line lurched forward, I stumbled and braced my hand on the glass front of the display cabinet.

The tiny woman in front of me reached out, concern in her eyes.

I apologised and told her I was fine in broken Malayalam and then decided I didn't want tea after all. I left the small tea shop and headed back to the main concourse. There were seats but not enough because men were lying across them, sleeping. I decided to stand near the large windows that looked out onto the drop-off point.

Tears trickled down my cheeks as I stood with my back to the crowds. My mini breakdown drew a few strange looks. Passers-by probably saw me as a crazy tourist lady. Nobody stopped to try to talk to me, and I was thankful for that.

How could Nicole really be gone? Grief is selfish, and all I could think about in those moments was what was I going to do without my best friend.

I opened Facebook on my phone again and looked at Sienna's personal profile. She usually posted regularly. She had a passion for the environment and anything to do with campaigning against animal cruelty. I admired that about her, and I'd always liked her posts, but she hadn't put anything on social media for over a week.

Her timeline was littered with comments from her friends and this time I scanned through them.

Hey babe, let us know how you're doing.

Hi, I just heard the news. How awful. Call me if you need anything, hun.

Many more messages followed. But one thing stood out.

Sienna had not replied to any of them.

CHAPTER FIVE

THE FLIGHT to Heathrow wasn't much fun. I had a two-hour stopover in Abu Dhabi and spent the time pacing the small waiting area. As I'd checked in my holdall and forgotten to grab a jumper, I spent most of the flight shivering. I used the thin, scratchy blanket the airline provided, but I was still too cold.

My mind was a jumble of thoughts. Even if I had been able to sleep, the four-year-old constantly kicking the back of my seat made sure I didn't.

Organising the handover with Rich and the journey to the airport had kept me busy, but now sitting in the cramped seat, I had nothing to do but think and the pain of Nicole's loss began to build. I would never see my friend again.

For the entire journey, I was close to tears. The sadness was tinged with unease because I was still on edge after the strange conversation with Angie. That plus Sienna's absence from social media over the past week had unnerved me. It was understandable after her mother's death, but why before?

I was reading too much into things. It was probably just a coincidence and nothing to worry about.

When I finally arrived in Heathrow and collected my holdall, I headed for the section of cubicles dedicated to hiring cars. Charity work didn't pay a great deal, but I did have some savings as my outgoings hadn't been expensive while I'd been working in India. I suspected hire cars were more expensive when they were rented directly from the airport, but I didn't have time to investigate other options.

I yawned for the second time in a minute as I followed the bright yellow signs. Passing a coffee shop, I inhaled the scent of hot coffee, and it was too tempting to ignore. I hadn't been able to get any sleep on the flight, and a caffeine pick-me-up was just what I needed. Heading inside, I decided grabbing a takeaway would be the best option. The coffee shop was practically empty, quite a contrast to the tea shop in Kochi.

"Can I help you?" the barista asked.

"I'll have an Americano with a splash of milk to take away, please."

"Coming right up," he said, jerking his head and flicking his fringe out of his eyes.

I pulled a jumper from my holdall and shrugged it on as he busied himself making my coffee. I ran my hands through my hair and noticed a large flat screen high on the wall in front of me. It was running BBC News on a loop. The sound was off, but the picture caught my attention.

I froze.

There was a face I recognised on the screen.

Nicole.

"Oh, my God," I whispered.

I hadn't realised I'd spoken aloud until the barista said, "I know. Isn't it awful? It gives me shivers just thinking about it."

I was too busy reading the scrolling text on the screen to reply.

A thirty-five-year-old woman was murdered yesterday in Finchampstead, Berkshire.

My hands curled into fists, and my nails dug into my palm as I waited for more of the story, but the image of Nicole was replaced by a newsreader, who smoothly moved onto the next news story. As details on Brexit scrolled across the screen, I pulled at the neck of my jumper, suddenly feeling shaky and too hot.

"Is everything all right?" the barista asked, pushing the paper cup along the counter towards me.

With a shaking hand, I reached for the cup and managed to nod. "Thanks."

I needed to know what had happened. Nicole was murdered!

Carrying my Americano, I left the coffee shop quickly, dropped my bag on the floor and pulled out my mobile. I scrolled through the contacts until I got to Nicole's mother's number.

The call rang and rang, and just when I thought she wasn't going to answer, she picked up.

"Hello," she said. She only said one word, but I could hear her voice was thick with grief.

"Marilyn? It's Abbie Morris. I've just heard the news about Nicole, and I am so sorry."

There was a slight pause and then Marilyn said, "Oh, Abbie, it's just awful. Where are you? Still in India?"

"No, I'm at Heathrow. I just landed. Nicole's housekeeper, Angie Macgregor, called me yesterday. I just can't believe it."

"It's horrendous. I don't know whether to feel angry or just…" She broke off with a sob.

"I was just in a coffee shop and saw Nicole's picture on the television… Angie didn't tell me how she died and…"

"Can you come here now? We are all at Nicole and Steve's house.

Janet is here too. I'm so grateful. I can't imagine coping with this without her."

Janet was Nicole's sister. We'd never been close, but my heart went out to her as I imagined how she must be feeling.

"I'll get there as soon as I can," I promised. "Is Sienna…?" I was about to ask if Sienna was all right and then realised what a ridiculous question that was. Of course, she wasn't all right. Her mother had just died. "How is Sienna coping?"

I was greeted by silence on the other end of the line, and I wondered whether she was crying. Then finally Marilyn said, "Abbie I'll tell you everything when you get here. I don't want to talk about this over the phone."

"Of course, I understand. I'm going to hire a car and then come straight there."

After I hung up, I took a moment to try and catch my breath. I was shaking. If this was how Nicole's death was affecting me, I couldn't imagine how Marilyn was feeling or poor Sienna.

I'd seen the word *murdered* on BBC News. Marilyn said she'd tell me everything when I got there, but I couldn't wait that long. I visited the news websites but found no more information. According to BBC News, Nicole's death was a developing story. I walked down the concourse and sipped the hot coffee, barely noticing as it burned my tongue.

It seemed to take forever to fill out the paperwork in order to hire the car, and it was almost an hour before I was in the car and on the road.

It had been a long journey, but I was finally heading for home and getting closer to finding out what had happened to my best friend.

CHAPTER SIX

IT TOOK a little while to get used to driving the Honda Civic hire car, it certainly made a change from the large truck I was used to driving, but at least the roads had no potholes.

Before long I was on the motorway heading towards Finchampstead. It felt strange to be going back. Five years had passed since I'd returned for Nicole and Steve's wedding.

It was a sunny day, and the cars reflected the sunlight. I wished I'd grabbed my sunglasses out of my bag before I started driving, but it was too late to worry about that now. I didn't even want to stop at the services. I just wanted to get to Nicole's and find out what had happened to her.

I turned the radio on, but there was no news about Nicole on any of the main stations, and I was still too far away to get anything local.

I selected radio two, and the opening to "You're My Best Friend" by Queen began to play, I put my foot down, and flicked the indicator as I moved into the fast lane.

What had happened to her? Was it a random attack? A break-in?

I tightened my grip on the steering wheel. There was no point running through all the possibilities now. I was driving myself mad. Soon, I would get the truth from Nicole's family.

I wondered whether Angie would still be at the house. Would I get a chance to speak to her? I heard the cheerful ringtone from my mobile phone blaring out of my bag, but I wouldn't answer it while I was driving. Besides, it was my Indian phone, and the calls cost me a fortune over here.

I needed to get some cash and let my UK bank know I was back in the country and would be using my card. I'd need to book a hotel. It was only a slight detour to call in at Lloyds on my way to Nicole's. As I drove through the town centre, I saw there was some sort of renovation work going on. There were signs up everywhere and diversions. I started to wish I'd gone the long way around. I'd assumed this way would be quicker.

As I got closer to Finchampstead, the knots in my stomach grew tighter. Memories hit me from all angles as I got closer to the place I'd grown up. I passed the Chinese restaurant by the station in Wokingham – China Garden. I remembered they used to add something special to their chips, some kind of flavouring, and after a night out in Wokingham, Nicole and I would often head there for a bag of piping hot chips and then walk home, or walk to the taxi rank if we were feeling flush.

I could picture us as giddy seventeen-year-olds, lurching around on our heels like a pair of young deer that hadn't yet quite found their footing.

I pulled to a stop by the traffic lights and then looked across in the rearview mirror at the station behind me. That had changed. It was all new and modern now. I remembered taking a shortcut from school to the station, running through the cemetery and climbing over the wall at the back of the station car park. It looked like that way was blocked off now.

As the lights turned green, I accelerated and then saw someone I recognised walking along the pavement. Mr Farrow, one of my old teachers. I hadn't seen him for almost twenty years, and yet I recognised him.

I drove past glancing again in my rearview mirror. He'd hardly changed. I remember when I was at school I'd thought he looked old, but I guessed he was probably only fifteen years or so older than me.

He was the boy's PE teacher, so I'd never had any lessons with him, but he was a regular at the Queen's Head. As I drove along, I passed The Hope and Anchor and wondered if there was another town in England with more pubs than Wokingham. When I'd been growing up here, it seemed to me that Wokingham consisted almost entirely of pubs and Estate Agents. There were far more restaurants and shops here these days. As I drove past my old dentist, I wondered if I would see anyone else from my past.

There was one person I really wanted to avoid, but I doubted I'd be here long enough to run into my ex-fiancé and his new family. I turned down the radio and drummed my fingers on the steering wheel as I waited to turn right at the junction.

Finally, I managed to edge the car out into a line of traffic and sat stationary for a couple of minutes before the line of cars began to move.

All about me, everything was going on as normal. Everyone was going about their everyday lives as though nothing had happened. It was so unfair.

It took less than ten minutes for me to park and run to the bank. Luckily, the woman leaving the carpark offered me her pay and display ticket, which still had thirty minutes remaining.

Once I had withdrawn some cash and spoken to one of the clerks, I was ready to head to Finchampstead.

Nicole, Steve and Sienna lived in Yew Tree House on Fleet Hill in Finchampstead. The house and others in the area weren't cheap.

A little further down the hill was Finchampstead House. When I'd been in primary school, there had been some speculation that the Duke and Duchess of York might be buying the property. It came to nothing, but it was a source of thrilling gossip for a few months, and the mothers at the school gates loved to talk about the possibility of having royal neighbours.

Neither Nicole nor I had grown up in a house anywhere near as grand as Yew Tree House on Fleet Hill.

Oak Trees towered above the road, blocking out most of the sun, and the dark leaves of rhododendrons reached out towards the road. Only a few vivid pink flowers bloomed this late in the year.

I slowed the car as I neared the house. The ancient yew tree beside the driveway was dark and majestic. Yews were associated with graveyards and death. My anxiety increased as I passed beneath the wide boughs.

Luckily the large wooden gates were already open. The gravel driveway sloped downwards, and I couldn't see the house clearly from the road because of the trees and huge rhododendron bushes that lined the front of the property. But as I drove on, the house came into view.

The house was imposing. There was no doubt it was beautiful, but I found it intimidating. Behind the property, there were tennis courts and a huge garden. Although they had neighbours on either side, the large trees blocked them from sight and made me feel like I was in a secluded spot in the depths of the countryside.

There were four cars in the driveway already, none of which I recognised. I parked beneath a weeping willow, taking care to avoid blocking anyone in. Leaving my belongings in the car, I trudged across the gravel to knock on the door.

Yew Tree House was an odd mix of old and new. It was at least a hundred years old, but modifications had been made over the years. A huge window in front of the galleried landing and the double width oak door were recent additions.

When I'd first visited Nicole here, I'd assumed the house would have low beams, big open fireplaces and rough, lime-plastered walls, but instead, the interior was sleek and modern. Some of the floors were wood; others were high shine marble. The staircase was made of oak and glass, and above it, a huge chandelier dropped down from the ceiling.

I pressed the doorbell and waited.

The door was opened by a woman I judged to be in her mid-thirties, but I didn't recognise her. That threw me. An awkward pause followed as I tried to place her. Was she a friend of Nicole's I hadn't met?

I knew it definitely wasn't Angie. Angie Macgregor was in her sixties, and I would have recognised her.

In the end, I blurted out, "I'm Abbie, Abbie Morris, a friend of Nicole's. I spoke to her mother a little while ago."

The woman gave me a quick smile. Her chestnut hair fell in a perfect bob around her pointed face. She opened the door wider and took a step back.

"Come in. I'm DC Lizzie Camden, the family liaison officer."

I should have been expecting that. Of course, the police would be here. Nicole had been *murdered*. I took a deep breath and resisted the urge to get back in my hire car and drive away. Every cell in my body seemed to tell me not to enter this house.

I was being ridiculous. I stepped inside the hall. Everything was just as I remembered. My shoes clicked against the tiled floor. I kicked them off and leaned down to put them in the cupboard containing the shoe rack. As I opened the door, I blanched. Hanging beside the cupboard was Nicole's old wax jacket. She'd had it for years and only wore it for gardening and walking the dog... *Charlie.* I'd forgotten about Charlie.

Where was he? He usually greeted visitors at the door exuberantly with a lot of tail wagging and barking.

"Where's Charlie?" I asked the family liaison officer.

Her forehead puckered in a frown. "Charlie?"

"He's in the utility room," said a low, raspy voice.

I turned to see the grey, steely eyes and stern features of Angie Macgregor. "You came then," she said as I faced her.

"Of course."

I sensed she wanted to say something more, but she shot a quick glance at the family liaison officer.

"Will you be wanting a cup of tea, Abbie?" she asked as she turned to walk away.

"Yes, thanks. That would be great."

"While you're here, Abbie, perhaps we could have a quick chat," the officer said. She smiled at me. Lizzie didn't look like a police officer. She seemed too meek and tentative. "We're trying to talk to everyone who was involved in Nicole's life."

I tried to pay attention but was distracted by the retreating figure of Angie Macgregor as she walked into the kitchen. I wished I could follow her and go into that warm kitchen with it's cosy Aga and the old flagstones. I didn't want to talk to a family liaison officer. I wanted to go into the kitchen with Angie and then find Charlie.

But I was being ridiculous. If I wanted to find out what had happened to Nicole, the family liaison officer would be the best person to tell me.

"Let's go somewhere quiet, shall we?" Lizzie gestured for me to follow her and walked confidently into the living room. I felt a flicker of irritation at the way this woman was taking control and walking around Nicole's house as though she owned the place.

That was ridiculous. What was the matter with me?

As we walked through the sitting room, I noticed Nicole's

mother, Marilyn, huddled on the sofa being comforted by her daughter, Janet.

I stopped beside them. "I'm so sorry, Marilyn. It's just awful news."

Marilyn sniffed loudly and took a few shaky breaths. She was struggling to compose herself for my benefit and I felt guilty. If she wanted to cry, then she should be able to do so in peace. She didn't need to be bothered with platitudes right now. It wasn't as though I could say anything to make her feel better.

Nicole's sister, Janet, looked up at me and her eyes narrowed. She'd never been close to Nicole growing up. There had been a great deal of sibling rivalry between the two of them, although their contentious relationship had mellowed as they got older.

Janet was two years older than Nicole, and when we'd been children, I'd had some sympathy for her. Nicole was a sweet person and very likeable. She'd been popular at school, whereas Janet found it hard to make friends. Nicole flourished academically in her teens, but Janet had struggled and needed a tutor after school. It wasn't hard to see why resentment had built up between the sisters during their school years.

To be honest, I'd always felt a little sorry for Janet, even though at times, she'd been cruel to me. She'd teased Nicole and me mercilessly, she'd stolen Nicole's pocket money, and once when we were going to a concert, she offered us a lift to the station but actually turfed us out of the car two miles away so we'd missed the London train. Luckily, we made the next one and got to the concert only a few minutes late, but Nicole had been furious with her sister, and so had their mother. Janet had been grounded for a week.

All these thoughts were running through my mind as I stood in front of Marilyn, feeling helpless, wishing there was something I could do to ease her grief. In the end, I decided to do what Nicole would have done and knelt down beside Marilyn before wrapping my arms around her.

She sobbed into my shoulder as I hugged her tightly.

It was hard to decipher what she said because her voice was muffled by my jumper. I think she said something along the lines of, "It's not fair."

After a little while, Marilyn's crying grew quieter, and she pulled away, dabbing her tearstained cheeks with a tissue. "I'm glad you've come back, Abbie. Nicole would have appreciated it."

Before I could reply, I heard the family liaison officer behind me clear her throat.

When I turned, she said, "Let's have a chat in the dining room, Abbie."

Janet looked up sharply. "Why do you want to talk to Abbie? She doesn't know anything. She hasn't even *seen* Nicole for the past five years."

Her voice sounded bitter. I knew she was hurting so I didn't point out she was wrong. Even though I hadn't returned to the UK for five years, I had met up with Steve and Nicole in Thailand two years ago. They'd been on a two-week holiday and I flew in to join them for a weekend.

Images flashed through my mind, Nicole and I wearing brightly-coloured sarongs and sipping fruit-flavoured cocktails as we sat on sun loungers at the edge of the beach, watching the crystal clear water lap the shore.

I remembered it as though it were yesterday. I could almost hear Nicole's laughter as I described my attempts to change a tyre at the side of the highway in Kerala, almost getting myself arrested.

Lizzie looked pointedly at Janet, and I could tell she wasn't the soft, wimpy type I'd first assumed. "I'd like to talk to Abbie all the same. We're just gathering information at this stage."

"Information? That's not much use to us, is it?" Janet jabbed a finger towards the window. "You need to be out there, looking for whoever did this."

When she replied, the officer's measured, calm tone told me she'd dealt with many distraught relatives in the past. "We have a team of officers working very hard to find out what happened to Nicole."

"I can tell you what happened," Janet said. "Some nutter blew her brains out."

I felt the blood drain from my face, and for a few seconds, I just stared at Janet. Shaking, I stood up and turned to the officer.

"Nicole was shot?" I asked in disbelief. Shootings didn't happen around here. They were rare in the UK. Shootings were only reported as inner-city gang-related incidents, or occasionally suicides, but people didn't get shot in *Finchampstead*.

I shook my head. "What happened?"

Marilyn began to cry again, and Janet, obviously sick of talking to me, gave a snort of disgust, stood up and stalked out of the room.

I turned to Lizzie, waiting to see if she would answer my question.

"Yes, Nicole was standing on the bridge over the Ford on New Mill Lane when she was shot with a shotgun."

"What was she doing there?"

Lizzie shook her head. "We don't know yet. Nobody seems to know why she was there."

"Was she walking Charlie?" I asked, thinking of Nicole's black Labrador.

Lizzie shook her head. "No, she left the dog at home."

"Do you have any idea who did it? Was it an accident?"

She shook her head. "We don't know yet."

"Sienna must be devastated. Is she here?" I looked through the open doorway towards the stairs, imagining Sienna in her room, curled up on her bed, crying. She'd be listening to music. Since she was tiny, Sienna had always listened to music when she was upset.

The family liaison officer paused and then tilted her head to the side. "Sienna is missing, Abbie. She hasn't been seen since her mother's murder."

CHAPTER SEVEN

I STARED at the family liaison officer. Sienna was *missing*. Why had no one told me?

"I watched the news. They didn't mention Sienna," I managed to say eventually.

Lizzie gave me a sympathetic smile. "We haven't released that information yet."

Marilyn gave a loud sniff, and Lizzie said, "Let's go into the dining room. We can talk there."

I followed her into the dining room and sat down at the huge table opposite the display cabinet, loaded with spirits and crystal glasses. An ornate, silver candelabra sat in the centre of the polished wood. They never used this room. Nicole had told me they preferred to eat in the kitchen. The table was too big for just the three of them, and more often than not these days, Nicole and Sienna ate alone as Steve worked long hours.

I placed my hands flat on the table to stop them shaking. "Can you tell me what happened to Nicole?"

The woman nodded. "Yesterday afternoon, Nicole was shot. She—"

I flinched. I'd intended to keep quiet and let Lizzie tell me what happened, but I couldn't help interrupting to ask, "Did she die immediately? She didn't suffer, did she?"

The woman pursed her lips. I'd asked her a question she didn't want to answer. "By the time the emergency services got to the scene, it was too late to save her."

"And Sienna? Was she with her mother?"

My mind was racing through the possibilities. Maybe Sienna had been hurt… Maybe she'd been abducted.

"We don't know where Sienna is. There's no evidence to suggest Sienna was at the crime scene. We think it's likely the news of her mother's death scared her. She may be staying with a friend."

"But wouldn't she come back home to be comforted by her grandmother and Steve?" As I asked the question, I realised I hadn't seen Steve yet. "Where is Steve?"

"He's in the garden. Look, Abbie, I know you've been living abroad for a while, but you spoke to Nicole regularly, didn't you?"

I nodded.

"When did you last speak to her?"

"Friday night. About nine thirty my time, so about five p.m. here."

"Did Nicole confide in you? Did she seem worried about anything?"

"No, she seemed…normal. She'd had a glass of wine. She said it had been a tough week and she'd earned it."

Lizzie leaned forward, resting her elbows on the table. "Did she say *why* she'd had a bad week?"

I bit down on my lower lip. Nicole had been ranting about one of the mothers from Sienna's school. It was just her way of letting off steam, but I didn't want to tell the police officer about it. It felt disloyal.

"Something to do with Sienna's school, I think." I paused, feeling stupid.

The police were trying to find Nicole's killer. The officer sitting in front of me wouldn't think any less of Nicole for bitching about one of the other mothers at Sienna's school.

"She had a disagreement with the mother of one of Sienna's friends at school. The woman wanted Nicole's support on a petition and was upset with Nicole when she refused to sign."

"Do you know this woman's name?" Lizzie waited for my response with her pen hovering above her notepad.

"I'm sorry. She may have mentioned a name, but I can't remember."

"Do you happen to know what the petition was about?"

I tried to think. I should have paid more attention. "Something to do with the school, but I don't remember exactly."

She looked disappointed. "Don't worry. You might remember later. DI Clarkson is heading up the enquiry, and I think he'll want to talk to you at some point."

I pushed my hair back from my face and tried to focus. "Of course. Can I help with the search for Sienna? I guess you must have spoken to her friends?"

"Some of them. Steve and Sienna's grandmother managed to give us a few names. But no one has seen her."

The calm, matter-of-fact way she delivered the news, irritated me. "Sienna is only *fifteen*. I thought you'd have a search team out looking for her."

The Family Liaison Officer narrowed her eyes. "We are concerned about Sienna's safety, of course, but this isn't the first time she's gone missing."

I shook my head. What was she talking about? She must have confused Sienna with someone else. "I think you must be mistaken. Sienna had never run off. Nicole would have told me."

I was certain I was right, absolutely convinced, so when the Family Liaison Officer said, "Sienna has run away from home on two other occasions in the past six months, Abbie," it really took the wind from my sails.

Nicole always confided in me, so why hadn't she told me about something so important?

A shiver ran through me as I remembered the last time I'd been in this house. It had been the day after Nicole and Steve's wedding. I was flying back to India that evening, and Marilyn was staying at Yew Tree House to look after Sienna while her mother and new-stepfather were on their honeymoon. Sienna came up to me while I was packing.

"Do you have to go?" Sienna tugged on her hair and pouted.

I'd thought she didn't like the idea of being left at Yew Tree House while everyone else jetted off to exotic places. I'd stopped packing, sat down on the bed and patted the duvet beside me.

"Come and sit with me. I'm going to miss you." I pushed her light coppery curls away from her forehead. "I wish I could stay longer, but I have to go back to work. You'll have fun with your grandma."

Sienna looked down at her lap and didn't respond to my smile. She'd been quiet all weekend, but I put that down to the fact she was getting older. Now, I worried something was bothering her. "What's wrong?"

She shrugged. "I wish things didn't have to change."

"Sometimes things change for the better."

"Not this time."

I twisted around on the bed, so I faced her. "What do you mean? What's upsetting you?"

"Mum and I were fine. I don't see why we had to move in with *him*."

"I thought you liked Steve."

"He's okay."

I looked down at her sad face and thought I'd figured it out. "You know you'll always be the most important person in your mum's life, don't you? That won't change. The new house will take a bit of time getting used to, but soon you'll forget all about your old house." I hesitated. "Is there anything else? You can tell me anything. Steve… is nice to you. He doesn't make you … uncomfortable, does he?"

She shook her head impatiently, "He's fine. It's just not the same."

I hugged her then and stood up to continue packing. "I know, kiddo, but things can't stay the same forever. Give it a little while, and I bet you and your mum are happier than ever."

She watched me finish packing. When I left, she and Marilyn waved me off, but there was a look on Sienna's face that I'd put out of my mind until now.

She looked like I had let her down.

Angie Macgregor came into the dining room with a tea tray and gave me a meaningful look as she set it down on the table. I had no idea how to interpret that look. Did she want me to go and find her when I'd finished with the Family Liaison Officer so we could talk? We thanked Angie for the tea, and she left the room with one last glance over her shoulder.

After Angie closed the door, I poured some tea. My throat was parched. Lizzie shook her head when I offered her some.

"Do you think it was an armed robbery gone wrong?" I asked.

Lizzie shook her head slowly. "Nicole was still wearing an expensive watch, and her purse was in her pocket."

"Where was she shot?"

"The chest area." She traced her fingers along her breastbone. "But the head shots killed her."

I paused to take a deep breath. "And she was on the bridge over the ford?"

"Yes. New Mill Lane, do you know it?"

I nodded but couldn't hide my confusion. "Why would Nicole be there?"

My earlier theory that she had been walking Charlie had been wrong. The officer had already said she didn't have Charlie with her. I should have known that. It was a long walk from Yew Tree House, along a winding road that had no pavement.

"Do you know if Nicole had a connection to the place?" Lizzie asked, breaking my train of thought.

"Um, not especially. She did work there years ago. She worked in the kitchen when it used to be a restaurant. I think the New Mill has been converted into a private residence."

"Yes, some years ago."

"I can't think of any reason why she would go there alone."

The ford cut across the road, so there wasn't much through traffic. There was only a pedestrian bridge over the River Blackwater, and I couldn't think why Nicole would want to go there alone.

"Okay." The officer drew a line under her notes. "I know you've had a long day travelling, so we'll leave it there for tonight. You should get some rest. Where are you staying?"

I hadn't even thought about that. "I'm not sure yet, probably a hotel nearby."

I picked up the tea tray. "I'll take this to the kitchen."

I needed to talk to Angie Macgregor. She wanted to tell me something. I was sure of it.

Unfortunately, when I left the dining room, Marilyn called to me. I put down the tea tray and walked to where Marilyn stood with her daughter in the large hallway. Both wore their jackets and Janet jangled her car keys.

"Abbie, dear, where are you staying tonight?" Marilyn asked.

"I'm going to book into a hotel."

"Oh, that won't do, at all. You should stay with me, shouldn't she, Janet?"

Janet looked like she'd sucked a lemon. Clearly, she thought that was a bad idea.

"It's fine," I insisted, trying to defuse the tension. "I've already arranged something. But I appreciate the offer, Marilyn. Are you going home now?"

Marilyn sniffed. "Yes, there's nothing more we can do tonight."

"Do you think Sienna has run away? The Family Liaison Officer said she'd done it before, but Nicole never mentioned it to me."

"And why would she?" Janet asked, raising her eyebrows. "You were in India. There wasn't anything you could do to help."

I couldn't respond. Janet was right. Some godmother I'd turned out to be. Had Nicole not wanted to burden me? I'd left the UK, but I should have made more effort to remain part of Sienna's life.

"You're right," I said, and Janet looked surprised at my reply. "Where do you think she's gone?"

Janet glanced at her mother then back at me. "She's probably with that awful boyfriend of hers."

"Boyfriend? But she's only fifteen!"

Janet smirked. "Yes, and you were going out with Gary Stewart when you were fifteen, Abbie. I don't know why you're so surprised she has a boyfriend."

I was surprised because I was just coming to realise how little I knew about recent events in Nicole and Sienna's lives.

"What's her boyfriend's name?" I asked.

Janet handed her mother the car keys and said, "Mum, wait in the car, would you? I want to have a private chat with Abbie."

Marilyn hesitated, and I wondered whether she would refuse, but in the end, she said, "Goodbye, Abbie," kissed my cheek and walked out of the front door.

When she was out of earshot, Janet said, "I know you see yourself as some kind of heroine, riding in to save the day, but the holier than thou act doesn't cut it with me, Abbie. You know nothing about Sienna, and you've not seen Nicole for years. It is bloody inconsiderate of you to turn up out of the blue like this."

I was too shocked to reply immediately. Janet had just lost her sister, and her niece was missing, so I chose my words carefully. "I just wanted to help, Janet. I don't want to upset anyone."

Janet shoved her hands in her pockets. Her lips were so tightly pursed, they were almost white. She was barely holding it together.

I backed away and picked up the tea tray again. Before I made it to the kitchen, I heard the front door slam, and when I turned Janet had gone.

I carried the tea tray into the kitchen expecting Angie to be there, but there was no sign of her.

It was late. Maybe she'd gone home. I washed up the tea-things in the butler sink, hoping Angie would return, but she didn't.

I dried my hands and leaned against the kitchen counter. The room was large, but cosy at the same time. It was the room that most reminded me of Nicole - a collection of funny fridge magnets, a pile of magazines, a goofy photo of Nicole and Sienna, shoes beside the back door.

The flagstone tiles were cool and comfortable after the hot August day. The large farmhouse-style table dominated the kitchen. A Lesley Pearse paperback lay beside a duck egg blue cushion on the window seat, and I could imagine Nicole sitting in that spot in the sunshine, enjoying her book as Sienna listened to music.

I walked over to the small window nook and sat down. How had it come to this? How did I know so little about my friend and her daughter? I wished I could turn the clock back to Friday night. Had she hinted something was wrong? Had I overlooked something important?

Or did she simply not trust me enough to confide in me?

I looked out of the window and spotted a glowing light in the garden. I leaned forward, steaming up the glass with my breath. It was a bonfire. August wasn't the usual time of the year for bonfires. Who was out there and what were they burning?

CHAPTER EIGHT

I WALKED over to the front door to grab my shoes from the rack. The back door was open and led directly onto the patio. Closing the door behind me, I walked towards the glowing light and the heavy smell of smoke that wafted towards me.

Now that the sun had set, the temperature had fallen, and I shivered as the cool night air touched my skin.

A tall figure stood beside the fire. *Steve.* He stooped over, leaning heavily on a large stick. He used the stick to poke the fire, sending a flurry of tiny sparks into the air.

What was he doing out here alone? And what was he burning? I slowed as I got closer to the fire, wondering what to say to him. What *could* I say to comfort a man who'd just lost his wife in a horrifying act of violence?

When I was a few feet away, he turned and saw me. He watched me silently as I approached.

"Steve, I'm so sorry. I can't believe this has happened."

He turned back to the fire and gave it a vicious stab with the stick, producing another shower of sparks. "Thanks for coming back, Abbie. I'm sure Nicole would have been touched."

His words were polite, but his tone was emotionless.

"You must be so worried about Sienna."

He turned back to face me. His glasses reflected the flickering light of the fire. "I'm sure she'll turn up."

I was speechless. That wasn't the response I'd expected from Sienna's stepfather.

"I want to help in any way I can. I could go through Sienna's social media accounts… contact her friends?"

"The police are already doing that."

"Maybe tomorrow I could hand out posters or something in Wokingham or Reading. It's a long shot, I know, but someone must have seen her… She must be devastated to run off like this." I was babbling, but it was better than slowing down so my brain could dwell on the various things that could have happened to Sienna. The best case scenario, as far as I was concerned, was that Sienna had heard about her mother's death, and unable to cope emotionally, she'd run away. The alternative was much worse. Sienna hadn't run away… Something or someone had prevented her from returning home.

Steve made an odd sound, a cross between a laugh and a sob as he walked closer to me. He had a smudge of charcoal on his left cheek. "Thanks for caring, Abbie. But Sienna will come back eventually."

"You don't think Sienna…"

"I don't mean to be rude, Abbie, but I'm not up to talking about Sienna yet."

I stared at him. Not up to talking about Sienna? His stepdaughter was *missing*. His wife had been murdered, and I would have thought he'd be desperate to know whether Sienna was safe.

I swallowed, trying really hard to understand his behaviour. People reacted to grief in strange ways. The last thing Steve needed from me was judgement.

"Okay, Steve. Just let me know how I can help."

Maybe I could have been more sympathetic. I could have said I understood, but the truth was, I didn't. I couldn't understand why he wasn't more worried about Sienna.

"That's just it. There's nothing you can do to help. Nicole is dead." His features tightened as he said those words. "I know you want to help, but no one can."

He moved past me, walking quickly back towards the house, leaving me staring at the flickering flames of the bonfire.

I felt like I'd been talking at cross purposes with Steve. Of course, nothing I could do would bring Nicole back or make him feel better, but there were practical things I could do to help. For a start, I could look for Sienna. I could help with the funeral arrangements and contact Nicole's friends to let them know what had happened.

I took a step back as the bonfire crackled, hissed and released a plume of smoke. I turned to look back at Yew Tree House.

Would the funeral be delayed? The fact Nicole had been murdered must make it difficult to arrange things. I didn't know when the police would release Nicole's body or whether they'd already done so.

I wanted to help him because he was Nicole's husband and Sienna's stepfather, but Steve and I had never been close, and I couldn't blame him for not wanting to confide in me now. I walked away from the crackling bonfire and back into the house. It was time for me to leave. I'd offer again to help Steve in a day or two but understood why he wanted to be alone now.

As I stepped into the kitchen, I heard a low whining sound.

It was coming from the utility room, the small room off the kitchen that stored the washing machine, tumble dryer and large chest freezer. I opened the door and saw Charlie lying on the floor. His basket was beside him, but he'd chosen to lie on the flagstones. It was a warm night so perhaps that was his way of cooling down.

"Hey, Charlie, how are you doing, boy?" I asked and knelt down beside him.

He looked up at me with big, sad, intelligent eyes, and I wondered how much he understood. He'd obviously picked up on the atmosphere in the house and had to be missing Nicole. It must have been very confusing for him.

I wasn't sure why he'd been shut in the utility room. Was that Angie's doing? Or Steve's? Charlie normally had the run of the house. He was a gentle, well-behaved dog and was usually happy to greet visitors with a wagging tail. Perhaps a dog with a more exuberant personality would have to be shut away when the house was full of strangers, but Charlie had always reacted well to new people. I stroked him and muttered reassuring words. I doubt it helped a great deal, but maybe some human interaction would make him feel less lonely.

His water bowl was nearly empty, so I filled it at the small sink in the utility room and put it back beside him on the floor. He had a full bowl of food that he hadn't touched. That was definitely a sign he was upset. Nicole was always joking any food they dropped on the floor was hoovered up within a fraction of a second by Charlie.

I had an overwhelming urge to take Charlie with me. But that was ridiculous. The hotel wouldn't allow dogs, and besides, Charlie belonged here with Steve and Sienna.

"I'd better go now, Charlie, but I'll see you soon."

Charlie raised his head when I reached the door, and when I opened it, he rested his head back on the floor and gave another soft whine. I reluctantly closed the door behind me.

There was no sign of Steve downstairs, so I said goodbye to the family liaison officer and headed for my hire car. My feet crunched over the gravel, and halfway across the driveway, I turned and stared back at the house.

I felt an odd sensation someone was watching me, but there was no one there when I looked. I unlocked the car and got in. As I started the engine, I noticed my hands were trembling.

I needed a place to stay and wanted to be as close to Yew Tree House as possible in case Sienna returned. The DeVere Hotel in Eversley was the nearest place to stay. I hoped they'd have a vacant room. I wouldn't be staying there for long, though. It wasn't cheap.

* * *

IN LESS THAN FIVE MINUTES, I PULLED ONTO THE LONG ROAD LEADING to Warbrook House. The large mansion had been built in the eighteenth century and recently converted to a hotel and conference centre. I'd grown up in the area and knew of Warbrook House, but I'd never stayed there before. It felt odd coming back here and having to stay in a hotel. Despite being less than a five-minute drive from Nicole's house, the hotel was actually in the neighbouring county of Hampshire rather than Berkshire.

I parked, grabbed my luggage from the boot and headed to the entrance. The reception area had been modernised, and the lobby was relatively quiet. A receptionist sat behind a high desk, I wasn't sure whether she was very short or her chair was too small, but she could barely see over the top of the counter.

I asked for a room and gave the receptionist my details. My luck was in. They didn't have any single occupancy rooms, but she offered me a deal on a standard double room, including breakfast. The price made me wince, but I was too tired to look for anywhere else.

She got to her feet, gave me a tentative smile and started the check-in process. She kept shooting me nervous glances, and I wondered whether I'd seen her before at some point. I tried to organise the jumble of thoughts in my head as I filled out the paperwork, but it was no good, I couldn't place her.

"Thank you, Miss Morris," she said quietly. "You're in room thirty-two. That's just up the stairs to your right. Breakfast will be served between seven thirty and nine thirty tomorrow morning."

I thanked her, leaned down to grab my bag, and headed for the stairs.

My legs ached as I climbed the stairs. Travelling had drained my energy, and I was looking forward to getting some sleep. I walked down the corridor glancing at the room numbers until I finally reached room thirty-two. Using the key card, I opened the door and held it open with my hip as I put the card in the slot beside the light switch.

The lights flickered on, but it didn't make much difference. I always found hotel rooms too dark. It was almost as though they didn't want you to see into the corners of the room.

The door was heavy, a fire precaution presumably. I gave it an extra hard shove as I made my way into the room. Unfortunately, as it swung closed again, it caught the edge of my bag, and I groaned knowing that it had probably hit my laptop.

Inside, I put my holdall on the luggage rack and headed to the bathroom to wash my hands and face. The bathroom mirror gave me a clue as to why the receptionist had regarded me so strangely. I had a black smear of dirt on one cheek. I rubbed the mark with a finger and it came away easily. I must have somehow got some charcoal on me from the bonfire.

My hair was a mess, the result of hours of travelling, and my eyes were wide. I looked wired, like someone on the edge. No wonder the receptionist had been a little wary of me.

I washed up. I really wanted to take a shower, but first I needed a drink.

I took a miniature gin and small can of tonic water from the minibar and fixed myself a G&T. Relieved to see my hands had stopped shaking, I swallowed down the drink in three gulps.

I'd needed that.

I couldn't shake the feeling there was something strange about this situation. The tragedy of Nicole's death alone was enough to turn my world upside down, but the fact no one knew where Sienna was had me on the edge of panic.

The atmosphere at Yew Tree House had been odd, too. I'd expected sadness, grief and tears, but it was almost as though everyone had been waiting for the other penny to drop, preparing themselves for more bad news.

I couldn't allow myself to think that way. There was no reason to believe any harm had come to Sienna. The most logical explanation was that she was distraught after her mother's death and needed some time alone.

I put the empty glass on the desk and walked back to the bathroom.

I took a quick shower, fiddling with the impossibly small bottles of shampoo and shower gel the hotel provided. It seemed to take an age to get enough shampoo out of the bottle to create a lather. But letting the hot water wash away the grime of travelling felt good.

Wrapped in a towelling robe, I grabbed my laptop and put it on charge. There wasn't much I could do to find Sienna tonight. My search would have to begin in earnest tomorrow, but I could at least send her a message so she knew I was here for her if she wanted to talk.

I sat at the desk, even though I longed to lie down on the bed and put my feet up after such a long day, because the battery on the laptop was nearly empty, and I wanted to send Sienna a message before it got too late.

It should have been easy to type a quick message to let Sienna know I was thinking of her, but it was harder than I'd expected.

I started off typing: *Sienna, I'm so sorry…*

Chewing on a thumbnail, I paused to think over why I was sorry. I was sorry for so many things. I was sorry that Nicole's death had left Sienna motherless at only fifteen, but I regretted letting Sienna drift away from me over the past few years.

I took a deep breath, put my fingers back on the keyboard and continued with the message.

I flew back to the UK as soon as I heard the news. Please come back home. If you need me, I'm staying at the DeVere hotel in Eversley. I'd love to hear from you if only to know that you are safe. As I'm still using my Indian mobile, calls will probably be expensive, but you can contact me through messenger if that's easier.

I added my mobile number at the bottom of the text and stared at the message on the screen for a few seconds and then hit send. I waited, hoping that she had messenger on her phone and would see the message straight away. There was a small tick mark by my message, indicating it had been sent. That should change to read once Sienna had seen it.

When Sienna had been younger, I emailed her a few times a week. She loved to get emails in the same way I'd loved to get letters when I was a little girl, but slowly, I'd drifted out of the habit of sending the emails.

I looked at Sienna's Facebook profile. There was nothing new of note. Just a few more messages from her friends offering their condolences, still no responses from Sienna at all.

I clicked over to my own profile page, opening up the photographs. I had quite a few with Nicole. I hadn't had a Facebook account when I'd been at college studying nursing — thank God! Facebook hadn't existed then. That was definitely a good thing in my opinion. I was glad my drunken exploits wouldn't be visible to the world for the rest of my life.

But Nicole had scanned and uploaded some of our old photographs from our last year at university in Southampton. We looked so young! I clicked on one of the images, enlarging it. Both Nicole and I smiled widely at the camera, drinks in hand. I didn't remember the occasion but we both looked happy. We were sitting on the grass, probably outside the uni bar. Nicole looked so vibrant and happy. I studied her face as though I could commit every last detail to memory. I focused on her curly hair, pale skin and expressive, big, blue eyes. She had been so beautiful.

I clicked on to the next photograph. It was also taken in our third year, and I remembered it had been taken shortly after an awards ceremony. I was wearing a black T-shirt and jeans and beaming at the camera, or whoever was taking the photograph, like a mad person, holding up my bottle of Corona. My eyes were slightly unfocused. It hadn't been my first bottle that night.

Nicole stood beside me, wearing a purple jersey dress and thick black tights. We were surrounded by friends. Tom, a medical student, who looked even more drunk than me, gave the camera a goofy smile. Sammy had an arm around Tom's shoulder and her mouth was open as though she'd been in the middle of a sentence when the photo was taken.

Nicole stood on my left, but she was the only one not looking directly at the camera. Instead, she looked off to her right. Her face was pensive and tense. It was hard to see what she was looking at.

The photograph had been taken in the student union bar, I remembered that night well. Nearly all the students from our course were there as well as some of the professors. After a tense week preparing our final presentations, everyone was letting off steam. For our degree course, we were required to give a presentation about a clinical subject of our choice, and afterwards the top three were given an award.

After overcoming my fear of speaking in public, I'd been allocated third place overall. I'd been thrilled and determined to celebrate into the early hours. Perhaps that's why I hadn't noticed Nicole wasn't relaxed and happy like the rest of us.

She was looking towards a group of teaching assistants and professors. The majority of them had their backs to the camera, and it was hard to tell who was who. It didn't help that over fifteen years had passed since that night. I recognised Professor Elaine Johnson from her closely cropped hairstyle and her shoulder pads. Her jackets were like something straight out of the eighties. Beside her stood Professor Eric Ross, who'd taken our biochemistry classes. I recognised him from his signature tweed jacket. A couple of others looked familiar, but I couldn't place them after all this time.

I shut the laptop, climbed into bed and sighed. The photograph was a moment frozen in time. A passing expression on Nicole's face had been captured, but it didn't tell the whole story.

I closed my eyes and leaned back against the pillows. I was reading too much into an old photograph because I was on edge. The picture must have been taken around the time Nicole discovered she was pregnant with Sienna.

Of course, that was it. No wonder Nicole was looking tense. Being pregnant during her last year and final exams hadn't been easy, and her mother's reaction hadn't helped. She'd been a mixture of disappointment, fury and panic rolled into one.

Nicole had spent days crying and fretting over what she should do. It would be nice to travel back in time and tell Nicole what a wonderful mother she'd be. She'd manage to pass her exams *and* build a career. Nicole had been an excellent nurse, and more importantly, she'd been a wonderful mother. Sienna was the sweetest baby and happiest toddler I'd ever known. She'd always been giggling.

With a sigh, I rolled over, pulling up the duvet. Tomorrow I would start a full scale effort to find Sienna. I couldn't change what had happened to Nicole, but I could try to help her daughter.

The police would be ringing around and talking to her friends, but if Sienna was scared and upset, she wouldn't want to talk to the police. If I spoke to her friends, I was sure it would be different. She'd know I'd have her best interests at heart.

CHAPTER NINE

I WOKE at two a.m. with my heart pounding and my skin clammy with sweat.

Disorientated, I shivered beneath the bed covers. I'd dreamt of Sienna and Nicole. They'd both been standing on the footbridge over the dark water of the ford in New Mill Lane. It didn't start out as a bad dream. I'd spotted them from some distance away and called out. They both waved at me and smiled as I walked towards them. The air was warm and birds were singing when suddenly gunshots cracked through the air. Nicole was hit, and I watched a deep red stain creep across her white blouse, before she tipped forward and tumbled into the ford.

I'd called out to Sienna, telling her to get off the bridge, to run to me, but she didn't. She leaned over the edge of the bridge, reaching out for her mother, teetering there for a moment before she too tumbled down into the dark waters of the River Blackwater.

I stayed still, rigid in the bed, willing my heart rate to slow down.

It was just a dream, I told myself. A nightmare. I tried to reason with my panicking mind and think logically. There was no reason to believe Sienna was with her mother when she was shot. The police would have checked the area around the ford on the River Blackwater.

I knew I wouldn't be able to get back to sleep for some time, so I threw back the bedsheets and switched on the lamp on the nightstand. I pulled out the tea tray from a deep drawer in the desk. The hotel had provided a selection of herbal, black and green teas along with small plastic sachets of milk. I filled the tiny kettle with mineral water and set about making myself a cup of chamomile tea.

While I waited for the tea to cool a little, I opened up my laptop and clicked on the messages icon in Facebook. There was nothing new. The small circle was still at the bottom of my message to Sienna, indicating that it hadn't been read.

I closed the lid of the laptop and rested my hand on the cool surface before walking to the window. Pulling open the curtains, I looked out towards the woods behind the hotel. Everything looked ominous in the dark. Something evil lurking in every shadow.

I shook my head. There was nothing to be scared of here in England. There were no big cats lurking in the woods. No snakes hiding in the grass. So why was it that I felt more scared here tonight than I ever had in India?

I picked up my tea and carried it back over to the window. I breathed in the warm, steamy chamomile scent before taking a sip.

A movement in the darkness caught my eye. A small fallow deer appeared at the edge of the woods. It seemed to sense it was being watched and raised its head. I didn't move. Finally, sensing it was safe, the deer continued to carefully pick its way along the line of trees.

I watched it for a long time before it finally ducked beneath the cover of the woods again, and I was alone.

I stood at the window for an hour or more until, shivering, I closed the curtain and made my way back to bed.

* * *

I DIDN'T WAKE AGAIN UNTIL EIGHT A.M. AND BLINKED IN SURPRISE AT the time when I checked my mobile phone. After the nightmare, I'd slept well, better than I had in a long time. There were no night crickets chirping and no snores coming through the thin wall from Rich in the next room.

I felt guilty for sleeping so soundly. After I used the bathroom, I checked my laptop for a message from Sienna, but I had no new messages. She still hadn't even read the message yet. My stomach churned. Sienna was a teenager, and didn't all teenagers exist with their phones permanently attached to their hands?

Trying not to think the worst, I closed the laptop again and began to get dressed.

By the time I reached the dining hall for breakfast, it was almost empty. The smell of fried bacon and coffee made my stomach rumble in anticipation. A fresh-faced, brunette waitress smiled at me and directed me to a table beside an elderly couple working their way through full English breakfasts. They looked up at me curiously as I sat down, and I smiled politely at them and muttered, "Good morning."

The waitress handed me a card menu and asked me whether I'd like tea or coffee. I asked for coffee and she left me to read the menu.

I'd barely started reading the first few lines when a booming voice called my name. I froze and looked up.

"Abbie Morris! It *is* you, isn't it?" Nigel Clark got up from a table in the corner and began walking towards me.

I wanted to curl up into a ball. I'd managed to avoid this sort of confrontation for the past five years, and surely I should be desensitised to it by now. Nigel, had been in my year at secondary school, and was a close friend of my ex-fiancé, Rob.

"Nige, nice to see you again," I said, trying to sound relaxed and natural although I really wanted to bolt for my room.

"It's Nigel now, actually. It sounds a bit more mature, don't you think?"

The years hadn't been kind to Nigel. He was losing his hair. He'd always had a big build and had put on more weight since I'd seen him last. He wore a pair of navy trousers and a pale blue shirt that was miles too tight.

He stood there staring at me, expecting me to continue the conversation.

I wished he would just go away. "Are you here for a meeting?"

Nigel was one of those people who never moved far from their hometown, and I couldn't imagine anything would have persuaded him to move away from Wokingham. The hotel was also a conference centre, so I suspected that was why he was here.

"I'm staying here on business," he said putting his thumbs in his belt loops and looking speculatively at the empty chair at my table.

There was no way I was going to invite him to sit down and join me. That was the last thing I wanted.

"You're staying here? But don't you still live in Wokingham? It's only a few miles away."

He broke out in a broad grin and winked at me. "Don't tell anyone, but sometimes I need to get away from the house for a bit of peace and quiet. It's hard when you have to work all day and then get home and have to look after a house full of kids."

Nigel had married Julia shortly before my own failed wedding. As far as I knew, Nigel only had two children. It wouldn't have surprised me to learn he expected his wife to do all the childcare and housework. Using social media made it easy to keep up with the lives of acquaintances without actually communicating with them.

"I just want to say I think the way Rob treated you was terrible. It must have been horrible for you. The least he could have done was to tell you before the day of the wedding."

I slipped down low in my seat, cringing. "It wasn't the best day of my life."

The waitress arrived with my pot of coffee and I thanked her.

"I'm sure I would have done the same thing if I were you," Nigel said. "I don't blame you for hiding away in Africa."

"India, actually."

"Yeah, yeah, I knew you'd gone somewhere like that. I was surprised to see you back here actually."

He hadn't mentioned Nicole's murder and I could only guess that was because he hadn't yet heard. I should tell him, I thought, break the news to him gently. He'd known Nicole, too. But I was reluctant to share anything about Nicole's memory with this man. He would be full of fake sympathies just like he'd been after Rob dumped me. Nicole's death felt too important to mention in a casual conversation only to have Nigel spread the word about her death like it was an item of gossip.

It had been all over the local as well as the national news so it was surprising Nigel hadn't read about it. Hardworking businessman or not, most people our age these days checked Facebook at least once a day.

Before I could choose the right words to tell him about Nicole, we both heard a high-pitched female voice coming from the other side of the room.

"Nigel!"

We'd both turned and watched a tall woman sashaying towards us as though she was on a catwalk or the red carpet. I don't think I'd ever seen somebody sashay in real-life before, but this woman was certainly working it. Swaying her hips, she made her way towards us, balancing on a pair of impossibly high heels. The heels were the first thing I noticed — silver and sparkly, definitely more suited for evening wear, but they were pretty!

I'd never been a follower of fashion, hence the fact I was happy to wear Crocs back in India just because they were practical, but even I had to admire those sparkly shoes. Though, I'm pretty sure I wouldn't have been able to wear them without falling on my face.

When my gaze left her feet and travelled up to her face, I realised she seemed vaguely familiar. I knew her from somewhere, but she most certainly wasn't Nigel's wife, Julia.

I could smell her heavy floral perfume when she was a few feet away.

If I was a kinder person, I could have given Nigel the benefit of the doubt and put her down as one of his business colleagues, but deep down I knew that wasn't true. The possessive way she looked at him and the bright red stain on Nigel's cheeks told me this woman was his bit on the side.

He hadn't expected to get caught out.

"I thought you said you didn't have time for breakfast this morning," Nigel stammered.

"I changed my mind, sweetie." She pouted and shot me a cold look as though weighing me up and deciding it was just as well she'd changed her mind about breakfast.

Of course, in her eyes, I was clearly a man-eater unable to resist snapping up this delicious hunk of man that stood between us. I rolled my eyes and turned my attention back to the menu.

In a sulk over getting caught, Nigel said, "I've finished my breakfast. I'm just about to leave."

"Suit yourself," the woman said and stuck her nose in the air before making her way towards a freshly-laid table.

Nigel cleared his throat nervously. "Um, Abbie, I don't suppose you'd keep this to yourself if you see Julia. It's really not what it looks like."

I hadn't seen Julia for over five years and it was unlikely I'd run into her on this trip back, but I felt a pang of compassion for the woman and was sorely tempted to visit her today to let her know what a scumbag her husband was.

"No, Nigel. I don't owe you any loyalty, and I don't want to be involved in your sordid little secrets. Now, if you don't mind, I'd like to eat my breakfast in peace."

The elderly couple at the next table smothered their laughter as Nigel stalked out of the dining room.

"Good for you," the white-haired lady said and raised her cup of tea in my direction.

CHAPTER TEN

I MANAGED to eat my breakfast without any further interruptions and quickly polished off my toast and marmalade. I needed a plan for today. Looking for Sienna wasn't going to be easy. The obvious first step was to talk to her friends, but they didn't know me, and it was likely they'd close ranks against an outsider. I also didn't want to step on anyone's toes and thought it was best if I told Sienna's grandmother what I was planning to do.

I telephoned Marilyn after breakfast from the lobby area of the conference centre, where the call charges were cheaper than from my room or my mobile. I sat beside a large window and punched in the familiar number. It felt strange. Marilyn still lived in the house where Nicole had grown up. We'd been friends before the invention of mobile phones, but that hadn't stopped us spending hours chatting away to each other. We'd get home from school and immediately ask to phone each other on the landline. My parents would insist I waited until after six p.m. when it was off-peak. "Why on earth do you need to call her now when you've spent all day at school with her?" my exasperated mother would ask.

The phone was answered on the third ring, but to my surprise it wasn't Marilyn who answered. It was Janet.

"It's Abbie," I said. "I'm sorry to bother you. I hoped I could talk to your mum."

Janet huffed. "She's pretty upset at the moment, Abbie. Is it important?"

The last thing I wanted to do was intrude and make things harder for Marilyn. If it had been anybody else, I would have said I'd call back, but Janet had always been prickly, and I sensed her reluctance to put Marilyn on the line was more because she disliked me.

"Yes, it is important."

There was a silence on the other end of the line. Janet was probably deciding whether or not to hang up. Finally she said, "All right. I'll see if she wants to talk to you."

I soon heard Marilyn's voice in the background. "Of course, I want to talk to her." Then, "Abbie, is everything okay?"

"Yes, have you heard anything from Sienna?"

"No, there's been nothing. The police aren't getting anywhere either. I'm starting to think…" She trailed off and then inhaled a harsh breath. "Well, I'm starting to get very worried."

"I know the police have spoken to her friends, but I thought I might talk to them myself. They might be more willing to open up to me."

"Maybe they will. If anyone knows where she is, it will be Zach. Sienna told her mother they were just friends, but she and Zach are joined at the hip."

"What's Zach's last name?"

"Ryan."

Zach Ryan. He would be my first port of call.

"Thanks, Marilyn. I'll try Zach first and let you know if I find out anything."

We said goodbye and I hung up.

I decided to contact Zach via Facebook and went back to my room to use the laptop. It was so dark in there it made me feel claustrophobic. I pushed open the curtains wide and then sat at the desk.

Zach Ryan was one of Sienna's friends on Facebook, so he was easy enough to find. His profile picture told me he had black hair and extremely pale skin. His hair was cut in a jagged style with a long fringe falling down one side of his face. He looked delicate and the idea that he was Sienna's boyfriend surprised me. Some of Sienna's friends had reached out publicly to Zach, posting how sorry they were on his wall. But Zach, like Sienna, hadn't replied.

That didn't give me much hope. If he wasn't replying to his friends, would he really take the time to reply to me?

Still, I had to try.

I typed out a quick message, introducing myself and asking him to contact me. After pressing send, I stared at the laptop. There wasn't much I could do now but wait. I jotted down a few names from Sienna's friends list, thinking I would contact them next if I got nothing from Zach.

The top bar on the screen of the laptop told me it was nearly 10 a.m.

My life would be a lot easier if I had a UK based phone or at least a sim card. I was pretty sure you could pick up a pay-as-you-go sim from any supermarket. Maybe that should be my first port of call.

The laptop made a pinging noise, notifying me of an incoming message.

Holding my breath, I clicked on the message icon. It wasn't from

Sienna, but it was the next best thing. Zach had replied to my message.

I know who you are. Sienna told me about you. What do you want to know?

I stared at the message for a moment. *Sienna told me about you.* Was that a good thing? The message was emotionless and hard to interpret. It almost felt as though he were accusing me of something, but maybe that was my guilt talking.

I typed a reply:

I just want to talk. Could we meet? I could come to you.

Waiting for his reply, was frustrating.

Okay. We could meet in town.

Zach lived in Wokingham so I assumed that was where he meant.

Great. Meet you in Costa Coffee? I can be there in half an hour.

Okay.

It didn't take me long to gather my things together and leave the hotel. The drive to Wokingham from Eversley would take less than fifteen minutes at this time of day, but I would need to park and wanted to be at the coffee shop before Zach arrived.

If I got there late, it could give him a reason to change his mind.

Wokingham is a market town with an abundance of coffee shops and chain restaurants like Zizi's and Nando's. When I'd lived there, the selection of shops and restaurants had been far more limited. Things had certainly changed.

I parked in Waitrose car park and walked through Old Row Court to Rose Street. After stopping at NatWest to get some cash, I headed along the marketplace to Costa Coffee. It was a warm day and the town was busy. Renovation work was underway and there were signs and placards up everywhere.

I ducked out of the way of a fast moving mobility scooter, driven by a determined pensioner, and entered Costa. Compared to the bright sunshine outside, inside it was dark. I joined the end of the queue and looked around for Zach. There were a few tables taken, many by teenagers, but that wasn't much of a surprise considering it was the school holidays.

There was no sign of Zach yet.

It was noisy as the baristas operated multiple machines, including a smoothie maker. Small children belonging to the woman in front of me in the queue, squealed and tried to chase each other around the tables. I felt for the woman who clearly needed a caffeine fix. Hopefully she'd take the children to burn off some of their energy in the park after her coffee.

A female barista who had pink hair and wore a nose ring asked me what I wanted, and I ordered a latte. She turned away and began to ring up my order on the till, and the coffee shop door opened.

It was Zach.

In real life, he looked even more delicate than he had in the picture on Facebook. A gust of strong wind could blow him over. His hair was too dark to be natural, almost blue-black, and he had dark shadows under his brown eyes. His eyes locked on to me.

Smiling, I asked, "Zach?"

He nodded but didn't return my smile.

"What would you like to drink?"

He asked for a hot chocolate, and I added it to my order. After I'd paid, I let him lead me to a table at the back of the coffee shop.

I placed the tray on the table and slid into the seat opposite him. I'd bought some miniature muffins along with our drinks and pushed them towards him, hoping they didn't look like a bribe.

He shook his head almost imperceptibly and cupped his hands around his mug of hot chocolate.

They'd put marshmallows and whipped cream in it. Such a colourful, fun, childlike drink made an odd contrast to the serious young man sitting opposite me.

"I'm worried about Sienna," I said, not bothering with any preamble. I wanted to see how he would reply. If he didn't know where she was, he would be worried too.

His long, thin fingers tapped the edge of his mug. "Do they know who was responsible for the shooting?"

I shook my head. "Not yet. I spoke to a police officer yesterday, a family liaison officer, who was at the house, and they are still investigating."

Zach shifted back and his heavy fringe fell across his eyes. He flicked the strands off his face with one hand. "I thought they'd have found out something by now."

"I suppose these sorts of things take time." It was a weak comment, but I didn't know how else to answer.

He shrugged.

"Have the police spoken to you?" I asked.

"Yes, they've been speaking to all of Sienna's friends. It's really freaked everyone out."

I wondered whether he meant they were freaked out by the police or by the fact Sienna was missing.

"Do you know where she is, Zach?"

He didn't reply, so I pressed on, "Everyone is really worried."

"Who is everyone?"

He sounded angry. I didn't want to rile him, but I did want answers.

"Her grandmother, her stepfather... *Me*."

He raised an eyebrow and looked at me in such a cold, calculating way it was easy to forget he was just a teenage boy.

"Sienna said she hasn't seen you in years."

I took a moment before answering and sipped my latte. His words made me feel guilty and defensive. But what did he know about it?

"That's true. I've been working abroad so haven't had much time to get back to the UK."

He looked at his hot chocolate rather than me and gave the impression I was boring him.

"If you know where she is, and don't want to tell me, then just please tell me that she is safe."

His features tightened. "I didn't say I knew where she was. I didn't say anything."

"I'm not trying to catch you out, Zach. I'm scared."

That got his attention and he looked directly at me. "Scared?"

"Of course. I heard what happened to Nicole and got the first flight back. When I turned up at the house, and they told me Sienna was missing… I didn't know what to think. I'm scared something has happened to her."

Zach chewed on his lower lip and looked at me through his thick, angled fringe.

He quickly looked back down at the table. He didn't trust me, and why should he? Maybe I'd be better off gaining his trust before I launched into an interrogation.

"So, how long have you and Sienna been dating?"

From the look of horror on his face, I realised I'd said the wrong thing. For one thing, I'd asked another question. I was still in interrogation mode. Why was this so hard?

"Dating?" he repeated, his voice hoarse.

"Yes." Was that not the term teenagers used these days? "You know, going out… Boyfriend and girlfriend?"

Zach swallowed hard and shook his head. "It isn't like that."

He spoke in almost a whisper, and it was hard to hear him over the din of the coffee shop. Cups crashing together, the coffee machine roaring into life and the chatter of people around us made it hard to have a conversation with this softly-spoken young man who'd made it clear he was not comfortable talking to me.

His skin was so pale it was almost translucent. A thin blue vein was visible at his temple. I thought desperately for some way to connect with him. It would have been easier if I'd spoken to Sienna about her friends. I should have made more of an effort to keep up-to-date with her life.

A group of kids walked into the coffee shop. There were only five of them, and they looked unthreatening to me. One boy and four girls. But Zach obviously knew something I didn't, he sank down low in his chair.

"Do you know them?" I asked, wondering if he didn't want to be seen talking to me.

Zach shrugged.

The girls wore typical summer clothes that could only be carried off by teenagers, shorts that were cut so high on the leg they couldn't have been comfortable to wear and skin tight T-shirts that didn't quite meet the waistband of their shorts, displaying strips of white skin.

The boy wore a surfer-style T-shirt and a pair of long blue shorts that finished just below his knee, together with a set of bright green flip-flops. He wore his light brown hair long, so long, I imagined he got into trouble over the length at school.

They were determined to dress to make the most of the few hot days an English summer provided. But here in the coffee shop with the air conditioning blasting out frigid air, they shivered, goose bumps appearing on their skin.

"Oh look," one of the girls said. "It's sad sack Zach." She pointed at Zach and giggled.

"Cheer up, Zach. It might never happen." That came from the only male in the group and made all the girls laugh.

Zach stonily ignored them but the faint flush of his cheeks showed their words affected him.

One of the other girls stepped forward, grinning. "Are you out with your mummy today, Zach?"

These kids weren't physical bullies, but they knew their words were hurting the boy sitting in front of me, and they carried on regardless. They enjoyed humiliating him in front of everyone in the coffee shop, including me.

It wasn't my place to intervene. I didn't know the history between this group of kids and Zach, but I did know that Zach wasn't enjoying it. Any normal, decent person would stop.

I knew the type though. If confronted, these children would say, "It was just a bit of a laugh." "We were only messing about."

But were they completely oblivious to the harm they could do just by making Zach feel like an outsider?

I turned to the girl who had spoken and snapped, "Stop it."

The smile slid from her face, and she shot an uncertain look at her friends who looked equally shocked. Perhaps they hadn't expected an adult to respond to them, but to be honest, considering the mood I was in right now, they were lucky that was all I said.

Predictably, the girl raised her hands and shrugged. "Lighten up. It was just a joke. I didn't mean anything by it. I was just teasing him."

"No, you weren't. You were trying to embarrass him. Now go away. We've got more important things to talk about than you."

The girl's eyes narrowed, and she folded her arms over her chest, covering up her tight T-shirt.

A moment of silence followed, and I hoped they would just buy their drinks and move to another table, but the boy decided to try again.

"We've got more important things to do," he said in a high-pitched voice apparently meant to mimic my own. He pulled a silly face and waited for the others to laugh, but they didn't.

"Now you're putting on a high voice and repeating what I say? You're clearly a comic genius." I rolled my eyes and turned back to Zach. "Do you want to go somewhere else?"

The one girl in the group that hadn't spoken yet said, "Come on guys, let's just order our drinks."

There was something vaguely familiar about her. She had long wavy hair, very similar to Sienna's. But what struck me most about her was her large, green eyes. Where did I recognise her from? Was she one of Sienna's friends?

I didn't have much time to mull it over.

Zach straightened in his chair and pushed his hot chocolate away from him. "I need to go."

"Wait, I'll come with you."

Zach shook his head. "No."

What did he mean no? I was sure he must know something about Sienna's disappearance. His behaviour was just plain odd.

I reached out and grabbed his forearm. "Wait," I said more firmly this time. "I'm sure you know something, Zach. You need to tell me."

He shot a glance to the group of school kids, standing by the till and paying for their drinks. The smoothie maker roared into life.

I leaned closer to him. "Either you are a terrible friend and don't care about Sienna at all, or you know she's safe."

Zach's eyes grew guarded, and he pulled his arm away roughly. "I didn't say anything. I only came here because I knew you would be worried. Sienna said you were very close to her mum and you'd probably be freaking out."

"When did Sienna say that?"

I was hoping to trick him and get him to say last night, so I'd at least know Sienna was alive, safe somewhere, but Zach wasn't that stupid.

"I didn't tell you anything," he repeated again.

"Anything you tell me will be in confidence," I said as a desperate last resort because I knew he was about to walk away.

He shook his head. "I know you're worried, but I'm sorry. I can't say any more."

I clenched my fists as he walked away. He definitely knew something. I had to tell the police. They'd know how to get him to talk. And that's what we needed.

I watched Zach leave. His tall, thin frame hunched over as he crossed the traffic lights outside the coffee shop and walked past the town hall.

I'd blown it. Conversations with teenagers obviously weren't my strong suit. But at least I had something to tell the police. Despite what he said, Zach definitely knew something about Sienna's disappearance.

CHAPTER ELEVEN

I PUT our used cups back on the tray. I intended to take them back to the counter but it was surrounded by people. I left the tray on the table and exited the coffee shop.

Zach was long gone.

After the chilly air conditioning, the sun was warm on my skin, and I stood there for a few moments soaking it up and wondering what to do next. Should I try more of Sienna's friends or should I go straight to the family liaison officer and let the police know Zach was hiding something?

A sign in the window of the shop next door – Superdrug – was advertising phones, and although I didn't want to fork out for a brand new mobile, I guessed they would probably sell Sim cards that I could put into my small Nokia.

Superdrug was busy and smelled of perfume and body sprays. I picked up a small basket. Since I was there, I decided to pick up a few toiletries, so I wouldn't have to struggle with the tiny bottle of hotel shampoo every morning.

I grabbed a few essentials and when I was rounding the last aisle, heading towards the phone counter to ask for a Sim card, I had the sensation I was being watched.

I turned slowly and saw one of the girls from the coffee shop standing a few feet away, staring at me.

It was the girl that had urged the others to get on with buying their drinks and stop teasing Zach. Her wavy hair fell down past her shoulders. She continued to watch me. Her green eyes were bright and were accentuated by the thick, black eyeliner she'd applied above her upper lashes.

"Abbie," she said. "Do you have a minute?"

I realised then who she was. Jessica Richardson. She'd been Sienna's friend since the girls went to nursery. I wondered how close they were now.

"Jess? I didn't recognise you in the coffee shop." I put the wire shopping basket on the floor and moved closer to her.

"Is there any news about Sienna?" she asked.

Her eyes were hopeful, and she looked genuinely upset. She probably wouldn't be able to tell me where Sienna was. If she knew, she wouldn't be asking me for news.

"Not yet. Her grandmother is really worried. When did you last see her?"

Jess licked her lips. "About a week ago. We've been doing drama classes during the summer holidays. A bunch of us from school have been taking them."

"But you haven't spoken to her since her mother…died?"

I hesitated over my word choice. Died sounded less violent than *murdered*.

Jess shook her head. "No, and no one I know has spoken to her."

"That's why I was talking to Zach. I hoped he might be able to tell me something."

Jess pulled a face. "They've been close recently. Did he tell you anything?"

I shook my head and leaned down to pick up the basket. "Unfortunately not. It was nice to see you, Jess. Let me know if you hear from Sienna. I'm on Facebook."

I turned to walk away, but Jess stepped in front of me. "There's something else," she said.

"Yes?"

Her big eyes widened a little and she looked around us to make sure no one else was listening.

"Last week, Sienna had this big blowup in drama class. She was really upset about something."

"Why was she upset?"

Jess's face crumpled, and she looked as though she might cry. "I don't know really. Some people were talking and laughing when she was practising her part, and she screamed at them. She swore and called them all sorts of names. I mean, they *were* being annoying but it wasn't like her to overreact like that. I followed her outside and asked what was wrong but she wouldn't talk to me." Jess frowned. "We haven't been very close over the past few months."

"Why is that?"

"I'm not really sure. We used to do everything together, but now she hangs around with Zach Ryan." Jess pulled a face.

"The things your friends said in there to Zach weren't very nice, Jess."

"I know. But you don't know Zach. He asks for it most of the time."

Although I failed to see how Zach was asking to be bullied, I didn't want to derail the conversation. "So Sienna was upset about something last week, but you don't know what?"

I couldn't see how this was relevant to Nicole's murder or to getting Sienna back home, but I filed the information away just in case.

"Where do you go for these drama classes?" I asked, thinking I could perhaps talk to some of the other students or maybe even the teacher.

"They're in Finchampstead, in the Memorial Hall. We go three days a week. Monday, Wednesday and Friday. Ten 'til two. There are only twelve of us, and the class is taken by Mr Owens." She rolled her eyes. "There are only two boys in the class. Most of the girls are there because they fancy Mr Owens."

I raised an eyebrow. "Why are the classes held in Finchampstead and not Wokingham?"

Jess shrugged. "I don't know. I suppose a lot of the kids come from Finchampstead, and Mr Owens lives there, too, I think."

We both shuffled out of the way of a large metal trolley loaded with toiletries pushed by a shop assistant.

"I wondered if maybe Sienna had tried to find her real father," Jess said quietly.

My hand tightened around the handle of the shopping basket. That wouldn't have gone down too well with Nicole. She'd had a one-night stand at university and always insisted she couldn't remember the name of Sienna's father.

If Nicole had admitted that to Sienna, I could understand how she'd be upset.

"Did she tell you she wanted to look for her father?"

"She's wanted to look for him for ages. She used to talk about it all the time, but I don't think she ever did anything about it. It was just with her being so upset I wondered if she'd finally tried to track him down."

I looked into Jess's bright green eyes and was sure the girl was telling the truth.

Jess, once one of Sienna's closest friends, couldn't tell me where to find my missing goddaughter, and Zach was refusing to tell me what he knew.

I wasn't getting very far with this.

I thanked Jess for her help, bought a new Sim card for my phone. After I'd put my purchases on the back seat of the car, I inserted the new SIM card in my phone and called Janet. I still had her mobile number from two years ago when I was organising the delivery of a birthday present for Nicole.

Janet answered the phone with an impatient, "Yes."

"Janet, it's Abbie. This is my new UK number."

"Marvellous, thanks for letting me know. Bye."

"Wait! I need to talk to you."

"Now?"

"Yes, unless you're busy…"

A few seconds passed before she answered. "No, it's fine. What do you want?"

"I've spoken to Zach Ryan. I'm pretty sure he's hiding something."

I imagined Janet rolling her eyes on the other end of the line.

"Look, are you with your mum or at home? I'm in Wokingham now," I said. "I can be with you in five minutes."

"I can hardly wait. I'm at the flat."

She hung up. It would be kind of me to think this was just Janet's way of reacting to her sister's death, but truthfully this was how Janet acted normally. Her prickly exterior was generated from years of insecurity. It was better not to engage.

I left my car in the car park and walked back towards the High Street, heading for Janet's flat. She lived above the bookstore on Peach Street.

The door buzzed open as soon as I rang the bell, and after I climbed the narrow staircase, I saw her waiting at the top of the stairs.

"Come on then," she said. "Tell me how you managed to get information out of Zach Ryan when the police couldn't."

She spoke scornfully. She thought I was wasting my time. Perhaps I was. After I'd spoken to Zach, I'd been convinced he was hiding something, but now I needed to explain why I felt that way to Janet, I was a lot less sure of myself.

She led the way into her flat, and I followed her along the hallway into an open plan living area. The air smelled faintly of cigarettes and bleach.

She gestured towards a light grey sofa, and I sat down.

"Drink?" she asked.

The kitchen was at the far end of the living room. There were only two work surfaces, and I spotted a full jug of filter coffee on one of them.

"I'd love a coffee, thanks," I said.

I'd probably regret it later as I knew Janet made her coffee strong and I'd had a latte a short while ago.

As Janet poured us both a mug of coffee, I told her about my conversation with Zach.

"He didn't say he knew where Sienna was in so many words, but he wasn't worried. If he didn't know where she was, he'd be as worried as the rest of us. But when I pressed him on it, he insisted that he hadn't *told* me anything."

Janet looked at me blankly. "Is that it? That's your big discovery?"

She put the mugs of coffee down on the glass coffee table in front of me and then sat in the grey armchair opposite.

"Okay, I'm not saying he broke down and confessed Sienna was hiding in his house, but you have to admit he would be distraught if he didn't know where Sienna was. He's one of her closest friends."

Janet shrugged and blew over the top of her coffee mug. "People react differently to things, Abbie."

"True, but I'd appreciate it if you'd pass my message on to the family liaison officer. Perhaps if the police interviewed Zach again, he might open up to them."

Janet regarded me steadily. "All right. I'll let her know."

She pulled a packet of cigarettes out of her pocket, reached for the large, blue glass ashtray on the coffee table and balanced it on the arm of her chair.

It had been awhile since I'd been in Janet's flat. I'd seen it once years ago and only for a brief visit. It was nice and airy. The walls were painted in neutral colours, the floor was pale wood and hanging on the walls were a variety of abstract paintings. I wasn't keen on abstract art, finding it too noisy and messy, but the art Janet had chosen had muted colours and soft shapes. They gave the room a peaceful, relaxing feel.

"You've got some lovely artwork. Are they prints or originals?"

Janet made a scoffing noise. She really couldn't take a compliment.

"What? I'm being serious, Janet. They look nice."

I gave up trying to be nice to Janet. It was a losing battle. I took a large gulp of the coffee, wanting to finish it and get away before I managed to annoy her even more.

"You know they brought that lady in for questioning, don't you?" Janet said.

"What lady?"

"The one you said had an argument with Nicole over a school matter. She's fuming. You really should think before you speak.

It's very unlikely Nicole was shot because she had an argument over the PTA," she said sarcastically.

I shook my head. "I didn't say anything of the sort. The officer asked me if anything had been bothering Nicole. That was the only thing I could remember Nicole telling me."

Janet gave a tight smile. "She really didn't tell you very much, did she? And to think you two used to be inseparable."

I bit down on the inside of my mouth. I knew I shouldn't react. Janet liked to make barbed comments. It was her way of making people feel as insecure as she did. She'd just lost her sister so I let it slide and changed the subject.

"I also spoke to Jess Richardson," I said. "Do you remember her?"

Janet rolled her eyes and tutted with impatience. "Of course, she is one of Sienna's closest friends."

I was tempted to reply that actually they hadn't been close for several months just to show Janet she didn't know it all, but that would be mean and petty, so I held my tongue. "She mentioned Sienna may have started to look for her father."

I paused to see how Janet would react.

She took another sip of her coffee and then said, "Do *you* know who Sienna's father is?"

I shook my head. "Nicole told me it was a one-night stand. She didn't know his name."

Janet laughed. "Does that really sound like Nicole to you?"

I frowned. It didn't actually. I hadn't known Nicole to have a one-night stand before or since. Not that I judged people who did, but Nicole was a serial monogamist.

"Did she tell you?"

Janet gave me a sly smile. "If she did, I'm not going to tell you, Abbie. She obviously didn't want you to know."

We were going around in circles. Janet was a master manipulator. Her aim was to make me doubt my friendship with Nicole, to make me feel that I hadn't been important in her life. I'm not sure whether Janet's comments were driven by jealousy or just a need to make everybody as unhappy as she was.

But arguing with Janet was futile. We needed to focus on Sienna.

"Did Sienna ever ask you about her father?"

"This is a family matter, Abbie. I don't feel comfortable discussing it with you."

I took a deep breath, controlling my anger. "Fine. I just wanted to point out that if she is in contact with her father, she may have gone to him."

Janet nodded slowly and played with the packet of cigarettes on her lap and then said, "Perhaps."

"Well, if you do know who he is, you should tell the police so they can question him."

Janet nodded again but didn't reply.

"Well, thanks for the coffee," I said, putting my mug on the table. I needed to get out of Janet's flat before she made me scream.

"Where are you going now?" Janet asked, finally lighting her cigarette.

"I thought I'd go and talk to Angie Macgregor. Do you think she'll be at the house now?"

"Probably, but I don't think you should go there. Steve is grieving. He won't want you hanging around and neither do I for that matter. Are we done?"

CHAPTER TWELVE

JANET'S COMMENTS made me think long and hard about whether to contact Angie Macgregor. I didn't want to disturb Steve while he was grieving, but I had no other way of contacting Angie. Her phone call had been disturbing. Of course, a call to tell me my friend had died would be disturbing under any circumstances, but it was Angie's behaviour that made me think there was a reason she had called me.

As far as I knew, I was the only one of Nicole's friends Angie had called, and she hadn't told Nicole's family she was going to do so.

I drove back to Finchampstead slowly, considering my options. In the end, I decided to go to Yew Tree House and hope it was Angie or the family liaison officer who answered the door rather than Steve.

When I pulled into the driveway, I started to have second thoughts. Maybe there had been nothing ominous about Angie's phone call. Perhaps she had just called me because she thought that was what Nicole would want. I was upset and probably reading too much into things.

My tyres crunched over the gravel, and I was tempted to turn around and drive back to the hotel. I sat in the stationary car with the engine running, debating what to do. I could leave her a note with my new contact details. I grabbed my handbag and rummaged inside, looking for a pen and a scrap of paper.

But I had nothing suitable. I could hardly scrawl something on the back of a receipt and put that through the letterbox without an explanation.

There were two other cars parked in the driveway. I recognised Steve's silver Audi. Parked a few feet away was a blue Mini. I guessed that had to be Angie's.

I wrote my new phone number on the back of the Superdrug receipt and got out of the car. This wouldn't take long. I could just hand Angie my new number, and it would be up to her if she wanted to contact me again.

I turned off the engine, climbed out of the car and walked slowly to the front door. Luckily, it was Angie who answered.

Her eyes widened when she saw me, and after a brief hesitation, she stood back and opened the door wide for me to come in.

"I'm not stopping," I said and held out the scrap of paper with my new telephone number. "I just wanted to leave you this in case you wanted to talk to me."

Angie's face paled. "Not now."

"I'm sorry for turning up unannounced, but when you called me, I got the sense there was something else you wanted to say."

When I said the words aloud, I realised how ridiculous they sounded. I was looking for an extra meaning when there was none.

Angie waved her hands, gesturing for me to step backwards, and when I did so, she stepped out and pulled the door closed behind her.

She spoke in a low, raspy voice. "I can't talk to you here. Meet me in one hour at my house. Number sixty, Reading Road."

"But…"

Angie silenced me with a firm look and a shake of her head. "One hour."

Before I could gather my thoughts, she had stepped back into the house and shut the door behind her. For a moment, I stood on the doorstep, rooted to the spot. What was all that about? Was Angie afraid of us being overheard? Or was she afraid of getting into trouble for talking to me while she was supposed to be working? That didn't seem very likely.

I turned slowly and walked back to the car, wondering where Lizzie, the family liaison officer was. If she had answered the door, I could have mentioned Zach Ryan's strange behaviour to her and saved Janet the trouble.

I was travelling back along the gravel driveway to the main road when I was forced to slam on my brakes. A large forensic police van, followed by two marked police cars were heading towards me at quite a speed. I pulled over to the side of the driveway so they could get past.

I didn't leave straight away but watched the police in my rearview mirror. They handed Angie a piece of paper and shortly afterwards Steve appeared by Angie's side. Even from some distance away, I could see the look of horror on Steve's face.

I was so intent on watching what the police were doing I didn't spot the officer coming up to the side of my car. He rapped on the bodywork and made me jump. I lowered my window.

The uniformed officer had grey hair, pink cheeks and watery blue eyes.

"Can I have your name please, Madam?"

"Abbie Morris. I'm a friend of the family."

The police officer didn't smile.

"Can I ask what's going on?"

"I'm sorry but I'm going to have to ask you to move on," he said, looking over his shoulder back towards the house.

I glanced again in the rearview mirror and saw forensic officers dressed in white suits heading into the house. Nicole wasn't killed here, so what were they looking for? Sienna? Did they suspect something had happened to her?

"Is this about Sienna?" I twisted in my seat, turning to get a better look at the house. "She's my goddaughter," I added in an attempt to get him to tell me something.

"I'm sorry but you'll have to move along now."

I couldn't tear my eyes away from Yew Tree House. A tall officer was leading Steve out of the house towards one of the marked police cars.

"Are they *arresting* him?"

Had Steve killed Nicole? Is that why Sienna hadn't come home? Maybe she knew he was responsible and was terrified of her stepfather.

"Mr Carlson is helping us with our enquiries." He cleared his throat. "I really must insist you drive on."

Finally, in a state of shock, I did as he asked. I had so many questions. At least Angie would have some idea what was going on. If she still met me in an hour as arranged, she might be able to give me some answers.

I pulled out onto Fleet Hill and drove aimlessly. It wasn't until I was at the junction for New Mill Lane and Park Lane that I realised tears were streaming down my cheeks. Could Steve be a killer? Had Nicole been afraid of her own husband?

The beep of the horn from the car behind me, jogged me back to reality. I put my hand up to apologise and turned left into New Mill Lane.

There were no other cars on the lane, and I travelled slowly, taking everything in. There were houses on the left-hand side and only hedgerow and a meadow to the right. Blackbirds sang and swooped over the car as I steadily drove along the winding lane towards the ford.

This wasn't a good idea. Visiting the murder scene was a gruesome thing to do. It wouldn't give me any peace or any answers, but I was compelled to drive on.

As the ford came into view, I saw that it was still cordoned off, police tape blowing in the breeze. There was no sign of any police vehicles or officers, but it was clear they didn't want the public contaminating the scene.

I parked beside a grass verge. My hand was shaking as I opened the door. Stepping outside the car, I realised how peaceful it was. Birdsong, buzzing insects and the hypnotic sound of the sloshing water. The air smelled warm and grassy. Leaning against the car, I stared at the bridge. There was nothing ominous about the scene now.

When Nicole had stood on the bridge, had she realised her life was in danger? Or had it all been over in seconds?

The hot sun beat down against the back of my neck and my mouth grew dry. I stood there for some time, staring at the River Blackwater and wondering who could have shot my friend. I couldn't imagine Steve doing it himself. He didn't seem like the type of man to own a gun, so I wondered if he had paid someone to do it for him.

Had the shooter stood in the very spot where I was now? Or had they hidden themselves in the long grass of the meadow, creeping closer and closer until Nicole was in their sights?

I felt a trickle of sweat make its way down my spine and shivered.

This speculation wasn't helping at all. Back in the car, I turned on the air conditioning and drove away without looking back.

CHAPTER THIRTEEN

I PARKED up near the army barracks in Arborfield and called Nicole's mother, Marilyn. I hoped the police would have warned her about Steve's imminent arrest, but if they hadn't, I thought she should know. As it turned out, she had only just found out and was tearful and angry on the phone. She could only say a few words and kept repeating that she didn't understand what was happening. I didn't think she should be alone in such a state, but she promised me Janet was on her way.

After I hung up, I checked the clock on the dashboard. It was time for my meeting with Angie.

Angie Macgregor lived in a semi-detached house on Reading Road. It had a large open driveway with an oak tree on the right-hand side. There was no garage, and I breathed a sigh of relief when I saw the blue mini parked in front of the house. I had started to worry that after the unannounced police visit, Angie wouldn't be able to get away.

Reading Road was the main A327, and it was busy. I sat indicating and waiting to turn for at least a minute before there was a gap in the oncoming traffic and I could pull onto Angie's drive. I yanked on the hand brake and climbed out of the car in a rush. I pressed the doorbell and waited impatiently.

When she opened the door, I had a hundred questions on the tip of my tongue but couldn't decide which one to ask first.

"Come in," she said in her raspy voice.

She led me through the long front room into a much smaller kitchen at the back. The kitchen had a view of the large back garden, and a man I guessed was her husband was at work in the garden. He was using a pair of crutches but that didn't seem to hinder him. He was tackling weeds with an upright hoe.

It was cool in the kitchen, and I was glad to escape the heat.

"Kettle's just boiled," Angie said. "Tea?"

I nodded. My throat felt parched. "They arrested Steve?"

"Yes, they did. It's a terrible business." Angie poured hot water into a brown teapot and then turned to face me.

I'd guessed she was close to retirement age. Her hair was streaked with grey but she had unusually smooth, good skin. She was at least six inches shorter than me and looked up with watchful, brown eyes.

"Is that why you couldn't talk at the house? You were worried about Steve overhearing?"

Angie cocked her head to one side. "I just feel it's better to talk in private."

"You sounded very worried on the phone when you called me. You said I needed to come back."

Angie crossed the kitchen to the fridge and pulled out a carton of milk. "Well, of course. You were a close friend of Nicole's. I thought you'd want to come back."

Was that all it was? I leaned my hip against the kitchen counter. The hum of the fridge was the only noise in the kitchen.

"I saw the police cars as I left. There were officers in white suits. Do you know what they were looking for?"

Angie said nothing as she carefully poured milk into a small jug and began to set the tea items on a tray.

"I'm really worried about Sienna. Do you think the police believe harm has come to her?"

You heard that sort of thing all the time on the news. The police dug up patios and found bodies buried in the garden. Had Sienna found out who killed her mother? Had Steve wanted to silence her? Had he killed her too?

"I've no idea. They didn't say much when they turned up." Angie poured the tea and turned to me. "Would you like to sit down?"

"I don't mind." I didn't want a seat. I wanted answers.

Angie carried the tea tray into the front room and set it down on a coffee table. She sat in an armchair next to the empty fireplace and I sat in the chair opposite.

"Angie, there's a good chance I'm going to sound crazy, but I was so sure there was something you wanted to tell me."

Angie picked up her cup, and it rattled against the saucer. She looked over her shoulder nervously. An odd thing to do in her own home. "I'm sorry, Abbie. I was upset. I shouldn't have called you like that, but I didn't know who else to trust."

I sat forward in the chair eager for her to continue.

"The trouble is, I don't have anything concrete to tell you. I talked it over with my husband, and he thinks I'm being ridiculous."

"You don't strike me as the ridiculous type," I said and meant it. Nicole had described Angie as a stern, no-nonsense woman with a heart of gold.

Angie smiled. "I think in times of stress it's easy to let your imagination run riot. She was such a good, kind woman."

I caught my breath as tears pricked my eyes. "She was."

Angie took a sip of her tea, and I reached out for mine. "Why did you feel there was no one you could trust?"

"Nicole had been acting strangely in the week leading up to her death," Angie said. "She was nervous. She didn't want to go walking with Charlie on her own and had started to let him run around the garden instead, playing fetch. It was very unlike her. When Steve was away, she was paranoid about making sure all the windows and doors were locked. She got very upset when I'd opened a downstairs window one morning." Angie shook her head and looked down at her lap. "But it was July and stifling."

"Have you told the police about this?"

Angie huffed and raised her eyes heavenward. "I have but I don't think they've done anything about it. I don't know why she was scared, so I suppose my telling the police about it wasn't really very helpful. When I mentioned it to Steve, he got very angry and said I was gossiping." Angie's face tightened. "I would never do that."

The sun was streaming in through the window behind me, and I could see tiny motes of dust floating in the air. The clock on the mantelpiece ticked steadily as I tried to work out what to say to Angie. "I expect Steve was just upset and lashing out."

Angie gave me a grim smile. "You're probably right, but it was hurtful, and because Nicole's mother was in such a state, I didn't feel like I could confide in her. And you know what Nicole's sister is like. I didn't think anyone would take me seriously, but I knew how close you'd been to Nicole. I thought if anyone would listen to me, you would. Of course, I'd managed to convince myself that whatever Nicole was so scared of may be behind Sienna's disappearance, too."

"I'm glad you called me. I think you're right. If the police discover why Nicole was so scared, they might find her killer faster."

I finished my tea and put the cup on the table. "When did Nicole's strange behaviour start?"

"A week ago."

We both looked up as we heard the back door open. Angie patted her hair and straightened in her seat self-consciously.

Through the open door, I could see Angie's husband in the hallway removing his boots. He had a shock of white hair and wore baggy denim dungarees and a white vest beneath. His shoulders were tinged pink from the sun.

He saw me, smiled and ambled into the living room on his crutches. "I didn't know we had a visitor!"

He reached out and I shook his hand.

"This is Abbie Morris," Angie said and licked her lips. "She was a friend of Nicole's."

The smile slid from the man's face, and he dropped my hand like a stone.

"We talked about this, Angie. You're making a mountain out of a molehill. I don't want you involved in this business."

"Don't make a scene, Jock," Angie said. "The young lady just stopped by for a cup of tea, that's all."

"Yes, thank you for the tea, Angie. I'd better get going." I stood up and then Angie led me to the front door.

Jock scowled after us.

"Don't worry about him," Angie said. "He worries about me, that's all."

I smiled and squeezed her hand. "Thank you for the tea. Talk soon."

I walked to my car and thought Jock was probably right to be worried. It was starting to look like Angie had been working for a killer.

CHAPTER FOURTEEN

I LEFT Angie's and headed straight back to the hotel. After taking a shower, I felt human again. The air had become progressively more humid through the morning, and I suspected a storm would hit later this afternoon.

I checked my messages only to find I had nothing from Sienna. I replied to an admin email telling me a temporary helper was being sent out to Rich Michaels. I'd completely forgotten about it. My job seemed to be another world away.

I spent half an hour on the phone trying to speak to an officer related to Nicole and Sienna's cases. All I wanted to do was make sure they were still putting pressure on Zach Ryan to talk. I was sure he knew more about Sienna's whereabouts than he was letting on. Although Janet had promised to let the family liaison officer know my suspicions, I didn't trust her. I knew she was scornful of my attempts to help. I couldn't really blame her for that. But I couldn't rest until I knew the police would focus again on Zach.

I was transferred to four different people before I finally reached somebody who made a note of Zack's name and promised to get back to me.

After that I went down to the hotel bar and ordered a prawn mayo sandwich. I picked at it as I thought over what Angie had told me. Why had Nicole been so scared? She hadn't mentioned it to me and I had spoken to her multiple times over the last few weeks. I tried to think back. Had I noticed anything? The awful truth was I had been too wrapped up in my own issues to be a good friend.

I was tempted to order a gin and tonic to go with my sandwich but knew I'd regret it if I needed to drive somewhere later. I couldn't stay in the hotel all afternoon and evening. It would drive me crazy.

After lunch, I decided to go to Finchampstead. I thought I'd check out the Memorial Hall and the drama classes that were being held there. They weren't running today, but I might find someone willing to talk to me. There was usually something going on at the Memorial Hall, and if that failed, there was the local garage opposite. The petrol station had a small shop and an MOT garage, and the people that owned it had worked there for years. They might know something. At the very least, they might be able to tell me where Jason Owens, Sienna's teacher, lived.

It didn't take me long to drive to Finchampstead. The Memorial Hall hadn't changed in the time I'd been away. Finchampstead was a typically English village and would have been the perfect setting for a murder mystery. The hall was constructed in the sixties, before I was born, and was next to a large park and a cricket club. It was hard to see how it could have been any more English.

I parked at the front of the hall and then walked across to the entrance to investigate. I could hear children playing in the park, their shouts and laughter carrying all the way across the field.

The sky was getting darker now but it was still so hot. Wasps flew in drunken loops over the bonnet of my car, scavenging the splattered insects. They made my skin crawl.

Inside the hall it wasn't that much cooler. There was a meeting going on, a mums and toddlers group. People were just packing up to leave as I entered. I looked at the noticeboard beside the door, and the poster advertising the drama class caught my eye. It was printed in brightly coloured ink. I shuffled out of the way as a group of mums leading excitable two- and three-year-olds started to leave the hall.

One of the mums, a short plump woman with frizzy hair, smiled at me. "Sorry, you're a bit too old for that class." She winked at me and pointed at the notice. "That Mr Owens is enough to make me wish I was back at school, though." She gave a throaty chuckle and tried to herd the two young children in front of her.

"Do you know him?" I asked.

She turned back to me, seemingly surprised at my question. "Oh, are you looking for him?"

One of the children tugged at her hand. "Swings, Mummy."

"Yes," I said, but didn't elaborate further. I didn't want to go into details here.

She stepped to the side to let others go past. "He lives at number ten. The thatched cottage, opposite the school."

"Great, thanks."

She followed me out. "His great aunt left him the house. It must be worth a fortune. There's no way he could afford it on a teacher's salary."

She continued to chat about house prices as we walked through the car park and finally gave me a wave as she and the children headed off towards the park.

I had a dilemma. Could I just turn up on Jason Owens's doorstep? Or would that be a bit strange?

I ran a hand through my hair, which felt limp and damp from the heat. Crossing over to the petrol station, I bought myself a bottle of water and decided to leave the car at the Memorial Hall car park and walk towards the primary school.

Finchampstead was a pretty village. Coming back now, I could view it with fresh eyes. I'd taken it for granted growing up. I walked past the perfectly cut green playing fields and the cricket ground at the back of the park and walked towards the school.

The size of the school made me smile. It looked so tiny now. It had seemed huge and scary when I was there. Directly opposite the school, was a large thatched cottage. As children we used to whisper that it was haunted, and it was easy to see why. The large, heavy thatch hung down low, creating mysterious shadows. Its windows were small and looked like they were dark eyes staring at me.

I shivered at my fanciful thoughts and kept walking. The front garden was beautiful. A colourful array of flowers blossomed in every corner. Impressive this late in the summer. There were delphiniums, lupins and hollyhocks — a perfect country garden. From a few feet away, I smelled the warm, sweet scent of roses mingled with pungent lavender.

I was almost at the gate when a movement in the garden made me pause. A tall dark-haired man, wearing a navy blue polo shirt and dark jeans was deadheading the roses. It had to be Jason Owens. He hadn't yet spotted me so I took the opportunity to study him unobserved. He had smooth, tanned skin and a strong jaw, a perfect example of tall, dark and handsome. He was extremely good-looking in a clean, preppy kind of way.

As though he felt my eyes on him, he stopped, his hands fell to his sides, and he raised his head and smiled. The kind of smile I imagined could melt dozens of teenage hearts.

I half lifted my hand in a greeting. "Hello, Mr Owens?"

"That's right." He put the secateurs in the back pocket of his jeans and walked towards me, brushing his hands together.

"I'm sorry to disturb your gardening. My name is Abbie Morris, and I hoped you might have time for a chat."

He gave me another winning smile. "Of course, how can I help?"

"I'm Sienna James's godmother." I hesitated wondering how to phrase my question.

"Oh, the poor kid," he said. "Is there any news? Have they found her?"

I shook my head. "Not yet."

"Where are my manners? Come inside. We can chat out of this heat."

I followed him along the garden path and into the house. My eyes blinked into the gloom. The ceiling was low with dark beams, and the small windows were leaded and didn't let in much light.

"Have a seat," he said pointing to a floral, overstuffed armchair. It wasn't the kind of furniture I imagined a single, thirty-something man would buy himself, so I guessed he'd inherited the furniture from his great aunt along with the house.

"I'll get some drinks. Something cold?"

"That would be great."

"I've got Coke, bottled water or ice tea."

"I'd love a Coke."

He left me sitting in the living room. Every surface seemed to be covered by ornaments. Every wall covered by small paintings and photographs. There was a large fireplace, surrounded by brass horseshoes. Above it, an antique rifle was hung on the wall. As my eyes slowly took in the circuit of the room, they stopped and widened at the object sitting opposite me. A craggy-looking, stuffed fox glared at me. I was still staring at it when Jason Owens walked back in the room and handed me my Coke.

"Yes, that was my great uncle's idea of interior decorating. Things were different back then, I suppose. He'd been fond of it and so my aunt never wanted to get rid of it. Now she's gone, I keep meaning to…" he said and trailed off.

He turned the fox around, so its glass eyes were no longer staring at us reproachfully.

He tugged at the ring pull on the coke, and it gave a small hiss as it opened. After taking a long drink he sighed and said, "That's better. Now, how can I help?"

I felt all fingers and thumbs as I tried to open the can. "As you know, Sienna's been missing since her mother's murder. I really wanted to ask you if you had any idea where she could be."

He sat down in the chair opposite me and took another mouthful of coke. "I've spoken to the police already. But I'm afraid I have no idea where she might be. She is one of my brightest students... I can't imagine what she's going through."

"You take her drama classes, don't you?"

"I'm actually an English teacher. The drama classes are something I volunteered to do over the summer. It gives the kids something to do, stops them getting into mischief. At least, that is the idea. Drama is popular. They all want to be famous these days." He smiled again.

I finally managed to open the Coke and took a sip. "I spoke to one of her friends who told me there was an argument during one of the drama classes. Apparently Sienna was very upset."

A frown creased his brow. "Really? I don't remember that."

"Yes, she got upset with some of the other students and ran off."

"Oh, I know what you mean. I don't think it was anything serious. Sienna is just a little temperamental. You know these drama types. And she did have a point. They were talking over her performance."

Sienna, temperamental? That struck me as odd. She'd always been a quiet and shy child. Even a few months ago, Nicole had been puzzling over ways to try and get her to come out of her shell.

"I've spoken to Zach Ryan. He's one of her friends, but is there anyone else I should speak to?"

He gave a small shrug. "I can't think of anyone. To be honest, I've found Sienna prefers her own company. She is not really in with the popular crowd." He put up a hand. "Not that I'm suggesting she is unpopular. She isn't."

The coke was cool and refreshing, and I drank it quickly. "I'm pretty sure Zach knows something he's not letting on."

Jason leaned forward in his seat, resting his elbows on his knees. "I wouldn't be surprised. He's probably her closest friend. What did he say?"

"It wasn't really what he said, more what he didn't say. I got the sense he knew something but didn't want to tell me." As I said the words aloud, I realised how foolish I sounded. I shrugged. "It's just a hunch."

"Well, I wish I could be more help. I did think it might be a good idea to start a search for her, focusing on the local area, but the police were set against it."

"They were?" That didn't sound good. I couldn't think of a logical reason for the police to be against a search for Sienna unless they had reason to believe we weren't going to find her... I didn't want to consider that possibility.

I wanted to ask him how well he knew Nicole and Steve or whether he'd heard that Steve had been arrested, but that felt too much like gossip.

"Thanks very much for the drink," I said. "I'm sorry to have bothered you."

"Not at all," he said, getting to his feet. "Please keep me updated. Do you have a card? I can give you mine."

I didn't but told him my new mobile number and he jotted it down on a pad beside the telephone. He gave me a cream card with his contact details.

"My brother works at a printers. He gave them to me as a gift."
He smiled sheepishly. "As a teacher, I don't often have an opportunity to use them. When Sienna turns up, tell her I'm always
here if she needs someone to talk to."

I was grateful he'd said *when* she turns up, not *if*.

He took my hand in his. He had large, warm hands, but as they
lingered on mine, I felt slightly uneasy. "It was nice to meet you,
Abbie. I'm sorry it wasn't under more pleasant circumstances."

He placed his other hand over mine and squeezed gently.

CHAPTER FIFTEEN

I LEFT Jason Owens's house feeling disappointed. I shouldn't have got my hopes up, thinking he'd be able to tell me something he hadn't already told the police was a long shot. I opened the garden gate and prepared to turn right and go back to the Memorial Hall to pick up my car. Before I stepped out onto the pavement, I glanced left, just for a moment, but long enough to spot Zach Ryan.

He was carrying a Tesco's bag for life, swinging it in his right hand.

I stood still for a moment and watched him. Then on the spur of the moment, I decided to follow.

I'm not sure why I thought that would be a good idea. But after my earlier phone call to the police, I felt talking to Zach again probably wasn't their number one priority. And I was sure he was hiding something. If I could just get him to talk to me and open up, he might be able to tell me where Sienna was, or at least tell me why she was afraid to come home.

At the back of my mind was a niggling doubt, a fear that perhaps

Zach knew nothing and I was on a fool's errand. Perhaps he just didn't show his emotions well and I was reading him all wrong.

I followed him until he turned into Church Lane. There was no pavement and the lane went up a winding, steep incline.

I hadn't been this way often. At the top of the hill, I knew there was St James's Church and the Queen's Head pub, but I couldn't guess why Zach would be going to either of those. There were a few houses scattered along the lane. Maybe he was going to one of those?

By the time I reached the top of the hill, I was hot and sweaty, and my calves were burning. Zach travelled up the hill like a whippet. He was certainly fitter than me. He turned left when he reached a quaint white cottage. He didn't go in through the front door, but instead, walked around the side of the house. I stood at the edge of the lane beside a lilac tree, wondering what to do. I could hardly follow him around the side of the house. I was starting to feel incredibly stupid.

I thought about turning around, going back to the car and enjoying the air conditioning. Looking up, I saw grey clouds gathering, and I was sure a storm couldn't be far away.

My T-shirt was sticking to my skin, and I tugged at it uncomfortably. Despite the coke I'd had with Jason Owens, I was thirsty again.

After coming all this way, I didn't want to turn around and go back to the car. I could always say I was here to give Zach another opportunity to open up. It wasn't unreasonable. But I did draw the line at following him around the side of the house. Instead, I walked up to the white, wooden front door. There was no doorbell so I used the old-fashioned brass knocker.

I was starting to think nobody was home when the door finally opened, and a tall old lady with a heavily lined face smiled at me. She was leaning heavily on a walker.

"Hello, dear, can I help you?"

"I was looking for Zach."

"Oh, my grandson! He's in the garden now. He's been helping me all summer. Such a lovely boy. I really can't get about as well as I used to. He's such a help to me."

"Is it all right if I have a quick word with him? My name is Abbie. I spoke to him earlier today but there was something I forgot to say."

"Of course, dear. Just go around the side of the house and that will lead you into the garden. You'll find him there hard at work."

I thanked her and skirted around the flowerbed, following the narrow concrete path to the garden. It was a long garden, thin and narrow, and I could see why the old woman needed help to maintain it. I stayed close to the house and scanned the garden for Zach. I'd expected to see him busying himself over some plants, but I spotted him at the end of the garden beside an old wooden shed.

He still had the Tesco bag looped over one hand as he opened the door.

I walked towards him. I wasn't trying to be quiet, but the grass muffled my steps. A wasp flew straight at my face, and I batted it out of the way. Still Zach hadn't heard my approach. He'd entered the shed now, and I could hear him moving around inside.

There was a small, dirty window on one side of the shed that had been propped open. It was lined with cobwebs, and I couldn't see inside. Before I reached the door, Zach stepped out, looking furious.

"What are you doing here?"

I smiled, trying to defuse his anger. I hadn't meant to creep up on him but could understand it looked that way.

"Your grandmother told me it was okay to come and talk to you."

He narrowed his eyes. "What do you want?"

"Just to talk. I don't think you were entirely honest with me earlier, and I thought you might appreciate another opportunity to talk."

He made a scoffing sound and sneered at me. "Well, I don't appreciate it. So you can leave."

He had started to sweat. A lot. It was incredibly warm today but surely it wasn't that hot. A bead of sweat dropped off the tip of his nose. He hadn't had a chance to do enough gardening to build up a sweat like that. And he'd marched up the hill effortlessly, leaving me panting for breath as I followed him. His gaze flickered quickly to the shed and back to me again, and then he stepped to the side so he stood in front of the entrance.

He was blocking my view of the shed. Why?

"There's no need to be like that, Zach. We are both upset about Sienna. I want to help."

He shook his head rapidly from side to side. "You can't."

I put my hands on my hips and peered over his shoulder. "Why are you trying to stop me looking into the shed?"

His body went rigid. "I'm not."

I raised an eyebrow. "I'm not stupid." I pointed to the carrier bag in his hand. "What's in the bag?"

"None of your business."

"Let me look inside the shed. If there is nothing there, I'll leave you in peace." I was absolutely convinced he was hiding something from me. Part of me hoped Sienna would be sheltering in there. That was a long shot, though. Perhaps he was just storing food and blankets for her to use. Either way, I wasn't going to leave without looking inside.

"No! You have to leave now. You're trespassing." Zack's voice was full of strangled panic.

A soft voice behind him said, "It's okay, Zach."

Then Sienna stepped through the doorway.

CHAPTER SIXTEEN

I COULDN'T BELIEVE my eyes.

Relief coursed through my body, quickly followed by frustration. Had Sienna been hiding there all this time? Did she not care about the people who'd been frantically looking for her?

Not to mention the stupidity of being inside a shed like that in this weather. Her cheeks were flushed, and her skin was coated in a light sheen of sweat.

"Abbie must have followed me!" Zach growled the words with anger. Spittle gathered in the corner of his mouth, and his eyes blazed as he glared furiously at me.

"It's not your fault," Sienna said.

She didn't smile or react emotionally in any way. Her voice was a dull monotone.

"Are you okay?" I asked her, scanning her up and down, looking for injuries. "You're not hurt, are you? You know everyone has been looking for you."

Her copper-coloured, wavy hair fell in tangles about her face. Her skin was pale, and her blue T-shirt and jeans were grubby.

She didn't answer my questions, but she didn't look injured in any way. She looked like she'd been sleeping rough.

"Is that where you've been staying?" I stepped past her and looked into the shed. There was a screwed up sleeping bag, empty crisp wrappers and fizzy cans of drink on the floor.

She nodded.

"We'll have to let your grandmother and aunt know you're safe, and then I'll tell the police to call off the search."

"I don't want to talk to them." Sienna sounded defiant and angry.

"Who? Your family or the police?"

"The police."

"You don't have to do anything you don't want to," Zach said, putting an arm around Sienna's shoulders.

I wasn't about to contradict him. But she most certainly would have to talk to the police. She'd been a missing person since her mother's murder. The police would want to find out anything she knew about the day her mother died. I'd seen enough *Crimewatch* episodes to know that even small details could provide the police with big clues.

Still, I wasn't about to push the matter now.

"I just don't feel ready to talk to them," she said.

She looked terrified. I reached out and put a hand gently on her shoulder. She flinched. I wanted to envelop her in a hug and tell her that everything would be all right.

But when my gaze met hers, I thought I saw anger in her eyes. Was she angry at *me*? What could I have done to upset her?

"They want to help, Sienna. They want to find out who did this to your mum."

She shook her head and looked down at her dusty converse trainers. "You don't understand."

"Then tell me what you're afraid of."

She said nothing but bit down on her lower lip and continued to stare at the floor.

"I know this is the worst thing you've ever been through, and I can't imagine how bad you must feel at the moment. I want her back too," I said.

Sienna's face crumpled, and her shoulders lifted as she started to cry. She let me pull her in for a hug, but she didn't hug me back or cling on to me. Her body felt rigid.

I didn't have a tissue to give her, but when her sobbing stopped, I brushed the hair back from her face and then put a hand on her cheek and said, "I'm going to call your Aunt Janet and your grandmother now, if that's okay? They are going to be so relieved to know that you're safe."

Sienna sniffed and then bobbed her head. I took that as agreement.

I pulled out my mobile, and despite the patchy signal, I managed to give Janet the good news. She was full of questions, and I didn't have any answers, but I promised to bring Sienna straight to her flat. Janet said she would call Marilyn and then inform the police.

I gave Sienna a sideways glance as I spoke on the phone. She was on edge, and I was scared she might bolt at any moment. But I couldn't allow police resources to be wasted looking for her.

"Are you coming with us, Zach?" I asked after I hung up and put my mobile in my pocket.

He pushed his long, layered fringe back from his face and nodded.

"Then you'd better let your grandmother know. You can catch us up as we walk down the hill."

As Zach strode off towards the house, Sienna retrieved her duffel bag from behind the door of the shed.

"Ready?" I smiled at her.

She swallowed hard and didn't reply but she followed me towards the cottage. We followed the path around the side of the cottage and crossed the front garden to the lane. I wondered how much Zach had told his grandmother about Sienna. I'd bet the old woman had no idea she'd had a teenage runaway camping out in her shed.

I wanted to ask Sienna so many questions about the day Nicole went missing, and I wanted to know why she ran off. But as we walked down the hill, she put her headphones on, leaving me to listen to the tinny music that escaped her earbuds.

I felt a flash of irritation. Was she sorry for making everybody worry about her? It seemed especially cruel to allow her grand-mother to fear the worst after what had happened to Nicole. But a tragic event could affect people strangely. Sienna was still so young and probably hadn't considered how her actions would affect other people.

I should have been thankful for the earphones. They saved me having a very awkward conversation about Steve. How should I tell Sienna her stepfather had been taken to the police station?

She had to find out at some point, but it certainly wasn't a conver-sation I was looking forward to.

The wind started to pick up as we walked down the hill. Sienna didn't turn her head to look at me but folded her arms across her chest and walked quickly down the hill. I could have reached out and removed her earphones and begged her to talk to me, but I wasn't sure how to comfort her. She must be hurting desperately.

It was probably the cowards way out, but I thought I'd let Janet and Marilyn tell her about Steve.

Rain started to fall in big, fat drops. At first, they made dark spots on our T-shirts and jeans, but within a minute, our clothes and hair were saturated. Thunder rumbled ominously, and by the time Zach caught up to us, my skin was slick with rainwater.

He put up a hand to shelter his face, which wasn't very effective. The driving rain hit my skin like needles.

We walked quickly, only pausing to climb on the grass verge when a Range Rover passed us on the lane. It sloshed through the puddles, sending up a sheet of water that drenched the bottom of my trousers. Not that it mattered. They were already soaked through.

At the bottom of the lane, we walked quickly, heading towards the village. As we got closer to the school, I suggested sheltering at Jason Owens's cottage until the rain let up.

Sienna looked up at me sharply, and Zach said, "No. Let's just keep going to the car."

His hair was plastered against his scalp, and rain dripped off the strands of his hair and trickled down his face and neck.

When we finally reached the Memorial Hall and got to my car, the rain was starting to ease off. I gave Sienna the dry cardigan from the boot. It was the only dry item of clothing I had on me.

"You okay, Zach?" I asked.

He was shivering. "I'm fine."

"I can drop you at home if you'd like before I take Sienna to Janet's flat."

Zach frowned. "I thought I was coming with you."

I got behind the wheel and shook my head. "That's not a good idea. Sienna's family will want to speak to her alone."

"But I really think I should be there," Zach protested, sliding into the back seat as Sienna got into the passenger seat beside me.

"It's okay, Zach. I'll see you later," Sienna said, looking straight ahead.

Zach flopped back into the seat in a sulk, but I ignored him. This wasn't about what Zach wanted or needed.

I dropped him off at his parents' house on Barkham Road on the way to Wokingham.

There was no parking at Janet's flat, so I parked in the pay-as-you-go car park just off Rose Street. I paid for a ticket at the one machine that wasn't out of order, thankful that the rain had finally stopped and the sun had come out. The grey clouds still remained, but a vivid rainbow shone in the sky above us.

I hoped that was a good sign.

CHAPTER SEVENTEEN

"ARE YOU READY?" I asked Sienna after I'd paid for the parking ticket and put it on the dashboard.

She climbed out of the car slowly. She was definitely reluctant, but I didn't know why. We walked side-by-side across the car park and out onto Rose Street before turning left and heading for the main High Street.

Just before we reached the entrance to Janet's flat, I put my hand on Sienna's arm. "If there's something worrying you, you can tell me, you know that, don't you?"

She looked at me with glassy eyes, her face blank. After we stood there in silence for another moment or two, I became resigned to the fact she wasn't going to confide in me.

We walked on, and I pressed the buzzer at the entrance door beside the bookshop. Janet must have been waiting by the intercom. She buzzed us in straight away.

I let Sienna walk in front of me. I'd expected her to show some enthusiasm at seeing her aunt, but her footfalls were slow and heavy as she climbed the steps.

Janet obviously couldn't wait. She met us at the halfway point on the stairs.

"Sienna!" Janet was glowing with happiness. I don't think I'd ever seen her so joyful. It was certainly a contrast to the prickly side she showed me.

She wrapped her arms around Sienna, but the girl didn't reciprocate or return the affection.

After a moment, Janet put her arm around Sienna's shoulders and led her upstairs. I followed, feeling a bit like a third wheel. I didn't want to get in the way, but I was desperate for some answers.

Inside the flat, Janet fussed over Sienna and glared at me as though I were personally responsible for the thunderstorm.

"She's soaked through!" she said accusingly.

"I know," I said. "So am I."

Janet went to get some towels. She brought fresh clothes for Sienna to change into, a long, lemon-coloured T-shirt and white leggings. "You'll feel better after a nice hot shower."

She turned to me, and I thought she was going to offer me a nice pink fluffy towel to wrap around my shoulders, but instead, she used it to cover the armchair. "So you don't get the furniture wet," she said pointedly.

She turned back to Sienna. "Grandma will be here soon, sweetheart. Then you can get straight in the shower. I've spoken to Lizzie—she's the family liaison officer. She'll be here shortly, too. But I'm sure she won't mind waiting to talk to you until after you've had a shower and changed your clothes."

Sienna blinked tearfully. "But I don't want to talk to the police. They can't make me."

Janet looked taken aback, and for the first time in history, I think she was lost for words. She looked at me but all I could do was shrug.

The intercom sounded, and Janet hurried to unlock the door for her mother.

Marilyn was overjoyed to see Sienna. Tears ran freely down her plump cheeks as she hugged her granddaughter.

They sat down on the sofa, and Marilyn wouldn't let go of Sienna's hands. "You put us through hell, young lady," she said hoarsely. "We were ever so worried. You must promise never to do that again."

To give them a little privacy, I left my towel-covered armchair and went into the kitchen area. "Should I make some tea?"

Janet looked like she was about to snap at me, but Marilyn got in first and said, "That would be lovely, Abbie."

While Marilyn was fussing over Sienna, Janet walked over to me and leaned on the kitchen counter. "Where did you find her?"

"I told you. Zach Ryan's grandmother's place. She was hiding out in the garden shed."

"But why?" Janet asked, her face screwing up in confusion.

I shrugged. "I have no idea. She wasn't in a very talkative mood."

I put the mugs of tea on the table, and Sienna headed off to take a shower.

"She's only a child," Marilyn said and took a sip of her tea. "Surely she doesn't have to talk to the police straight away."

"The thing is, she might know something that could help the police find out who killed Nicole," Janet said. "So I don't blame the police for wanting to talk to her as soon as possible."

"What could she possibly know? She is a child," Marilyn insisted. She looked over her shoulder, making sure Sienna really had got in the shower and wasn't eavesdropping. "Has anyone mentioned Steve?"

I shook my head. "No, I wasn't really sure what to tell her. Has he been charged?"

"I don't know," Marilyn said. "Lizzie promised to keep us updated, but I've not heard anything. If she's coming here now to talk to Sienna maybe she'll give us all an update."

"Do you think he did it?" I blurted out.

Janet and Marilyn both looked horrified at my blunt question.

"I really don't know what to think," Marilyn said eventually. "The police found out there was a gun cabinet in the house and that Steve owned a shotgun, so they're running some tests on the gun."

I swallowed and felt slightly queasy. It was horrible to think that while we were all sitting around in that house yesterday, the murder weapon was close by.

"Wouldn't it be a very obvious mistake to use his own gun?" I asked.

"Maybe he acted on the spur of the moment?" Janet suggested, pulling her cigarettes from her cardigan pocket.

"Oh, please don't smoke now, dear," Marilyn said, dabbing her eyes with an embroidered handkerchief.

"Sorry," Janet muttered, stuffing the packet back in her pocket. "It's a habit. I wasn't thinking."

When Sienna emerged from the shower room, she was wearing Janet's clothes, which hung loosely on her frame. The T-shirt was oversized, and the leggings looked more like narrow trousers covering her thin legs. She'd wrapped her long hair in a towel.

"Feeling better, darling?" her grandmother asked and patted the seat beside her on the sofa.

Sienna sat down beside her grandmother. She looked so fragile and vulnerable. I wanted to hug her and tell her everything was going to be all right.

I was glad it was only the family liaison officer coming to Janet's flat. Lizzie was relatively young, and I thought Sienna might be able to relate to her. Talking to one female officer would be less threatening than talking to older male detectives. A one-on-one situation would make it easier for Sienna to relax.

The intercom made a sharp buzzing sound, and Janet asked me to answer it.

I pressed the button on the small, cream-coloured intercom in the hallway and saw Lizzie's face on the screen. "Come on up," I said and pressed the door release button.

"It's Lizzie," I called to the others and then walked to the front door and waited for her to climb the stairs.

I opened the door, and to my surprise, I noticed it wasn't just Lizzie walking up the stairs. She was followed by two other people. A tall, thin man and a plump, short woman. I wondered if they were visiting another flat and then remembered that Janet's was the only flat above the bookshop.

A sinking feeling settled in my gut. They were all here for Sienna.

As Lizzie reached the final steps, she said, "Abbie, I'd like you to meet Detective Inspector Tom Green and Detective Sergeant Carly Dawson."

They gathered in the stairwell and held out their hands. I shook them in turn and then led them inside.

So much for Sienna only having to deal with Lizzie.

Everyone looked shocked when I led the detectives into the living area. Sienna most of all. She appeared terrified and sunk down into the sofa cushions.

The detectives tried to be friendly, but it was no good, Sienna was so scared she could only provide monosyllabic answers.

Janet asked the detectives if they'd like some tea as they settled down to start the questioning. DI Green sat on the last remaining armchair. DS Dawson stood beside him, and Janet wheeled in a computer chair she had taken out of one of the bedrooms for Lizzie.

"Would you be willing to come to the station, Sienna?" DS Carly Dawson asked.

Sienna looked aghast. She opened her mouth but shut it abruptly without uttering a sound.

"I don't think that's a good idea, at all," Janet said. "I think Sienna needs to be somewhere she feels safe. She's incredibly fragile at the moment."

Janet's voice had an underlying steely quality, and despite our differences, I mentally cheered for her. The family obviously wanted to help the police as much as they could to find out who was behind Nicole's death, but not at the expense of Sienna's mental health.

I helped Janet finish the tea and then brought the cups over to the coffee table.

Lizzie began to talk about Steve's questioning, and Marilyn used exaggerated facial expressions to try and convey that Sienna didn't yet know her stepfather had been questioned over her mother's murder.

But either Lizzie missed the frantic looks Marilyn was sending her way or the police had decided they didn't think it was a good idea to keep Sienna in the dark because she didn't let the matter drop.

DI Tom Green leaned forward, resting his elbows on his knees and looking directly at Sienna. "Your father was questioned this afternoon."

"Her *stepfather*," Janet put in.

DI Tom Green made a nod of acknowledgement. "Yes, I have to stress that he was helping us with our enquiries, nothing more."

What on earth did that mean? Did the police have any reason to suspect he was involved in Nicole's death? How could they leave us hanging like this? How were we supposed to act towards

Steve now? Was he a suspect or merely providing background information for their investigation?

"But do you think he did it?" Janet asked, pushing a cup of tea towards the detective inspector. "We can hardly let Sienna go home if you think Steve was responsible, can we?"

Marilyn was beside herself, and I think if she could have put her hands over Sienna's ears to block out this conversation, she would have.

Sienna was getting quieter and quieter and was no longer making eye contact. She was turning in on herself and blanking everyone else out.

But despite Janet's direct question, the detectives wouldn't be drawn on whether or not they believed Steve was responsible for Nicole's death. All they would say was that he wasn't being charged with any crime.

"He will be back home later today," Lizzie said.

"But is he *dangerous*?" Marilyn asked, looking horrified. "I really think if you have any reason to suspect Steve, you should share it with us now."

"Like we said, Steve has been helping us with our enquiries."

"But do you have any evidence against him?" Marilyn asked. "At least you could tell us that."

DI Green shook his head. "I'm afraid there are certain aspects of the case we can't discuss."

Marilyn was outraged and gave the detectives a piece of her mind. I could understand where she was coming from, but I could also see the police's point of view. They couldn't release all the information they had in case it compromised their case. But Marilyn's priority was Sienna's safety, and there was no way she wanted Steve anywhere near her granddaughter if the police had evidence he was involved in Nicole's murder.

The police continued to insist that Steve was only helping them with their enquiries. "We felt it was better to question him at the station, and he agreed."

"So you're not charging him for anything, and he'll be back home at some point today?" Marilyn's face was creased with frustration.

"That's right."

That still wasn't good enough for Marilyn, and I expected the conversation to run and run. I could see now why the police were keen to question Sienna at the station. That way she would still have a responsible adult or guardian with her, but it would be the police asking the questions.

Janet's small flat was getting overcrowded with the police officers as well as Janet, Marilyn and Sienna in the small living area. I was in the way.

I said my goodbyes and promised Sienna I would call her later. Her gaze flickered up to me briefly, but she didn't smile or respond in any way.

After Janet reluctantly agreed to call me later and tell me how things went, I left them to it.

CHAPTER EIGHTEEN

I DROVE BACK to the hotel, looking forward to a nice shower and finally stripping off my wet clothes. My T-shirt was now dry in patches, but my jeans were still cold and damp.

I strode through the lobby in a world of my own, wondering how Sienna was getting along with the police. Would she be able to tell them anything useful? I hoped she was bearing up okay.

I was lost in my thoughts and didn't notice that Steve was sitting in the lobby until I was almost on top of him.

He'd been sitting on one of the long, grey sofas and stood up when I approached.

I'd been rummaging around in my handbag, looking for my hotel key card. When I saw him, I stopped dead.

He walked towards me looking like an ordinary businessman who wasn't quite comfortable in his casual clothes. He wore a white shirt and dark jeans. He looked tired, and there were shadows under his eyes.

Could this man have gunned down my friend in cold blood?

He cleared his throat. "Abbie…" He hesitated, no doubt unsure how I would react to him.

I slowly took my hand out of my bag and readjusted the straps on my shoulder. "Steve."

"I heard you found Sienna." He gave me a half smile that looked sincere. "It's such a relief."

I said nothing. I wasn't sure how much I wanted this man to know about Sienna's whereabouts. The last time I'd spoken to him, he'd seemed unable to deal with Sienna's disappearance on top of his wife's death. I'd found his behaviour odd, and just because he was here looking relieved and thankful, it didn't mean I could trust him.

"I was wondering if you had time for a chat?" Steve asked.

I considered his request. We were in a public hotel. There was minimal risk so I agreed. What could go wrong?

The hotel had a small room off the bar that was open during the day and served afternoon tea. I suggested we talk in there.

We sat at a small table, looking awkwardly at each other. I didn't know where to start. When the waitress arrived to take our order, I studied his face. Was this the face of a killer?

I requested Earl Grey tea, and he asked for a pot of English Breakfast. The young waitress left us and then there was nothing to stop us talking.

But I still didn't know where to begin.

Steve ran a hand through his hair. He looked thoroughly worn out. He hadn't asked me where Sienna had been hiding, so I presumed he'd heard everything from the police.

"What happened Steve?"

That was a big question, encompassing a lot of smaller questions. I could have been asking any number of things. What happened today with the police? What happened on the day Nicole died?

And what had happened to make Sienna afraid to come home to her stepfather?

He sighed heavily. "Do you suppose they serve real drinks here during the day?"

He didn't wait for me to answer and beckoned the waitress over again. His voice sounded gravelly as he ordered a whiskey on the rocks.

When the waitress left us again, Steve took a deep breath and then looked me steadily in the eye. "Someone told the police I had a shotgun at home, and they said they'd seen me on New Mill Lane the day Nicole died."

I held my breath as panic fluttered in my chest.

Steve went on, "It wasn't true, of course. It didn't take the police long to realise their anonymous tipster was lying."

"So you weren't near New Mill Lane the day Nicole died?"

Steve shook his head. "No, I was working in London. I'd already told the police that. They checked and found plenty of CCTV footage to prove it. Luckily for me, we live in a Big Brother world."

"Then who would say such a thing?"

Steve shook his head. "They wouldn't tell me. Said it was an anonymous caller. Somebody clearly has an axe to grind."

The waitress arrived, carrying two teas and a small crystal tumbler containing Steve's whiskey on a tray. Crumbly, short-bread rounds were balanced on the side of the saucers.

The waitress put the items on the table carefully. "Will that be all?"

"Yes, thank you," I said.

Steve waited until the waitress was out of earshot and then said, "Look, I'm sorry I wasn't particularly pleasant to you when you arrived. I was feeling overwhelmed. There were so many people in the house. I just wanted to be alone."

I nodded slowly. That was understandable, but what I didn't understand was why Sienna hadn't been at the top of his priorities.

I figured as he was being honest with me, I may as well come straight out and ask him about his relationship with Sienna. "Is there a problem between you and Sienna?"

Steve looked surprised. "Not really. The teenage years have been a bit difficult, I suppose. There have been lots of arguments. And on occasion she caused disagreements between me and Nicole. I did resent her a bit for that." He looked at me sheepishly. "I know it's pathetic. She's only a kid. I just thought Nicole should be a bit tougher on her sometimes."

I wondered what would happen now. Would he want Sienna to come back and live with him, or would she be better off living with Janet or her grandmother?

As her godmother, I wanted to do everything in my power to make sure she was safe and happy.

"Have the police cleared you completely now?" I asked as I poured the tea.

"Well, I doubt they'll ever say that, but I don't see how they could possibly still think I'm involved. They are running forensic tests on my shotgun, but when the tests come back negative, hopefully they'll start to look for the real killer."

"I didn't know you owned a gun."

He shrugged. "Hardly ever used it. Bought it when I was taking some clients on a shooting trip with Toby. It was his idea. A silly whim. We only went shooting once."

"What will you do now?"

Steve took a deep breath and exhaled. "I don't know. Take one day at a time, I suppose. I still have a funeral to organise, and I hope Sienna will want to come home eventually."

We talked for a little while longer, and I tried to get a better sense of the man. Despite the years he'd been married to Nicole, I really didn't know much about him. It was hard to think of Steve as a killer, though. He looked so ordinary, and as he said, his alibi had been checked out by the police. But then again, a wealthy man like Steve wouldn't necessarily do the deed himself. And if he didn't kill Nicole, then who did?

I promised to keep in touch with Steve and gave him my number in case he needed to contact me in the future. I watched him leave the tearoom. His shoulders were slumped, and he looked like he had the weight of the world on his shoulders.

I glanced at my watch. Sienna's interview with the detectives would end soon, and Janet would call me. I was desperate to find out if Sienna knew anything that could unravel this mystery.

CHAPTER NINETEEN

I WENT up to my hotel room and stripped off my damp clothes. I felt like I was getting a chill. My cheeks looked flushed, but I couldn't stop shivering.

I took a shower with the bathroom door open, not wanting to miss a call from Janet. After wrapping myself in a towel, I checked my mobile to make sure I hadn't accidentally put it on silent. I hadn't.

I didn't understand why it was taking her so long to call me. Or Sienna was still talking to the detectives?

I took my time getting dressed, blow-dried my hair, put on some make-up, and waited for her call.

I felt like I was in limbo. What should I do now?

I pulled a chair over to the window and sat down, looking out at the hotel grounds. There was no sign of the deer today.

I sat there for ages, just staring at the tree branches swaying gently in the breeze and the pink-streaked sky, thinking about Nicole and what she would want me to do.

It was at least an hour later when Janet finally called. I fought against the urge to moan and ask why she had taken so long.

Instead, I said, "Thanks for calling. I really appreciate it."

"Well, I said I would. Look, do you want to come to Wokingham and maybe get something to eat? Sienna has gone home with Mum for the night. She seems settled, but I'm starving."

"Sure, I haven't eaten yet," I said.

I wanted to demand answers over the phone but knew irritating Janet wasn't the best idea.

We arranged to meet at Côte Brasserie at Janet's suggestion. I had to Google it as I didn't recognise the name of the restaurant. The drive seemed to take ages, not because there was much traffic on the road, but because I was impatient to hear what Janet had to say.

I finally arrived in the town centre and again parked in the small car park off Rose Street. I made my way to the Côte Brasserie, checking my phone to make sure I was heading in the right direction. When I arrived, I was surprised to see they'd converted the old Lloyds bank building into the restaurant.

It was a nice evening now that the thunderstorm had cleared the air. The slight pinkish tinge on the wispy clouds made me wonder if we'd have better weather tomorrow. "Red sky at night, shepherd's delight."

On the other side of the road was another restaurant, which had tables and chairs crowded with people drinking wine, laughing and chatting outside.

I headed inside where the air was warm and smelled distinctly of garlic and red wine. I gave Janet's name to the chap at the door as she had made the booking, and he led me to a table. After ordering a bottle of still mineral water, I lingered over the single page menu and waited for Janet to arrive.

I didn't have to wait long.

As she sat down, I was engulfed by her Chanel No.5 perfume and the faint smell of cigarette smoke.

She'd put on fresh lipstick but hadn't bothered to retouch the rest of her make-up. Her skin looked red and shiny, and she appeared tired and stressed, which was hardly surprising.

"So, what happened?" I asked as she looped the strap of her handbag over the back of the chair.

She sat down. "At least give me the chance to order a drink first!"

She waved at a waiter, who took her order for a glass of red wine. I shook my head at the offer of another drink. I needed to keep a clear head and was determined to stick to water tonight, plus I had to drive back to the hotel.

"It didn't go particularly well," Janet said after the waiter had left us.

"What do you mean?" I pictured Sienna having a breakdown and running off somewhere.

"I think it was just a bit overwhelming for Sienna. She didn't really tell the police anything."

"So, she doesn't know anything?"

"I didn't say that," Janet said as the waiter smoothly positioned a glass of red wine on the table.

"Are you ladies ready to order?" he enquired in a heavy accent.

I ordered the butternut squash risotto and garlic bread, and Janet opted for the sea bream. He gathered up our menus and left us to talk.

"To tell you the truth, Abbie, I think something besides her mother's death has put the fear of God into Sienna. Obviously, I'd expect her to be emotionally distraught but... I'm sure she's scared of something."

"Steve?" I wondered aloud.

Janet shook her head. "That was my first thought, too, but apparently not. She said she's happy to go back to Yew Tree House with Steve. Mum thought that was a bit much tonight so she's taken Sienna back to her place."

I had to agree with Marilyn. Even though I'd spoken to Steve earlier and he'd seemed rational and calm, I would have felt uncomfortable knowing Sienna was there with him on her own with no one to protect her.

"Did the police give you any other information? Do they know why Nicole was targeted?"

"Not really. Though they did say they think she was the intended victim. They are working on the assumption that it wasn't a random attack. I'd assumed it was some sort of robbery gone wrong when I'd heard she'd been shot, but it seems that's not the case. None of her personal belongings were taken. She still had cash in her purse and her rings were still on her fingers."

"Did Sienna tell the police why she ran off?"

"She just said she was scared."

"Did she tell them how she heard about Nicole's death? I mean, nobody in the family saw her after Nicole was shot. She just disappeared."

Janet tensed. She picked up her wine and took a sip. "That's a good point. I don't know how she found out. The police want to talk to her again tomorrow. We've agreed that she can be questioned at the station, so I'm going to go with her."

I didn't object. It wasn't my place and besides, whatever I thought of Janet personally, I truly believed she wanted the best for Sienna and wouldn't let her be railroaded in an interview.

I leaned forward and in a quiet voice said, "I saw Steve earlier."

Janet, who was just taking another sip of her wine, spluttered. "What?"

"He was waiting for me in the lobby of my hotel when I got

back," I said quickly so she didn't think I was sticking my nose in where it wasn't wanted. "He came to see me."

"What did he want?"

I shrugged. "Just to talk apparently. He thanked me for finding Sienna and apologised for his behaviour when I turned up at the house."

"Did he seem...?" Janet looked at the ceiling as she searched for the right words. "Did he seem guilty to you?"

I wasn't sure what guilt looked like. I'd watched his body language, looking for tell-tale signs that he was hiding something. But I was no expert.

"I don't think so. He said somebody had tipped off the police and told them he was in New Mill Lane the day Nicole was shot, but the police checked out his alibi and proved he was in London. Somebody was just trying to make trouble, I suppose."

Janet looked surprised. "I didn't know that. I knew they'd taken the shotgun away, so I thought the gun was the reason they'd taken him in for questioning. I wonder who would have said something like that?"

I shook my head. "Steve said it was an anonymous tipoff."

Janet's eyes narrowed. "Some mean, busybody with nothing better to do. People like that should be charged with wasting police time."

"I couldn't agree more."

When our meals arrived, we paused our conversation.

"What will Sienna do now? Will she stay with your mother indefinitely?"

Janet speared a piece of salad with a fork. "I'm not sure. But we'll decide what's best."

"What if Sienna decides she wants to go home to Yew Tree House?"

Janet looked up sharply. "To Steve?"

I nodded.

"She's just a child." Janet scowled. "She doesn't know what's best for her."

I raised my eyebrows but said nothing.

Janet narrowed her eyes. "We are her family. And we'll decide what's best for her."

Again, I didn't respond. I didn't want to argue with Janet and have this end up in a fight, but my refusal to engage only seemed to infuriate her further.

"I just want to see Sienna settled," I said, eager to pour oil over troubled waters. I didn't say I wanted to see Sienna happy because I thought it would be a long time before she would feel happy again. After what had happened, it was going to take time for her to come to terms with her loss.

Janet dropped her fork onto her plate and pointed at me with her index finger. "Don't even think about it. You are not taking Sienna off to India or God knows where."

I hadn't even considered that. Not seriously anyway.

"I'd never take Sienna away from her family, Janet."

"You wouldn't be able to even if you wanted to. No court would allow it."

"Calm down, Janet," I said. "We are on the same side here. We both want what's best for Sienna. I want to help you."

Janet looked at me scornfully and pushed her plate away. She drained her wine glass and said, "I seem to have lost my appetite."

With a sinking heart, I watched Janet throw her napkin on the table, set a twenty pound note beside her plate and send me one last wounded look before she got up and stalked out of the restaurant.

I shouldn't have been surprised. I hadn't had many conversations with Janet that hadn't ended in an argument or disagreement. Usually Nicole had borne the brunt of Janet's moods.

The worst part was, I was sure that Janet really did love Sienna and wanted to help her. But for some reason, she saw me as a threat.

CHAPTER TWENTY

THE NEXT FEW days passed slowly. I guessed Janet must have said something to the other members of the family because I was suddenly persona non grata. I'd left messages for Marilyn and Steve, offering to help with the funeral. But Nicole's mother had sent me a curt text message back refusing and Steve hadn't responded.

I sent Sienna a few messages on Facebook and she was quick to respond, but when I suggested meeting up, she sent back a message explaining her grandmother wanted her to stay at home with the family until after the funeral. She signed off the message with an eye-roll emoji.

I'd had to phone the London office of the Trela Health Foundation and explain I was going to be absent a little longer. I'd originally expected to return to India after the funeral, but everything was still up in the air. Nicole's murder was still unsolved, and I felt very out of the loop. At one point, I'd been tempted to phone Lizzie, the family liaison officer, and see if she'd give me an update. But then I changed my mind. If there had been a big development, surely even Janet wouldn't be so cruel as to leave me in the dark.

I'd spoken to Rich and was pleased to hear he was getting on well with my replacement. My direct boss on the other hand, wasn't happy with my extended leave. In the end, she said if there were any further delays in my plans, she'd offer a full-time position to my replacement, and when I was ready to go back to work, they'd have to see where they could fit me in.

I'd hoped the charity would be more sympathetic. It was a charity after all. But it seemed my boss had decided I'd spent a little bit too long on compassionate leave since I wasn't directly related to Nicole. She didn't have an answer when I pointed out I was using my own annual leave for this trip back to the UK.

The hotel I was staying in wasn't exactly cheap, and if I had to stay in the UK much longer, I was in danger of losing my job. That meant I needed to move somewhere cheaper.

* * *

THE DAY OF THE FUNERAL CAME AROUND QUICKLY. THE SKY WAS A cloudless blue, and the air was warm and scented with cut grass as I walked across the hotel car park to get into my hire car.

That was another expense I was going to have to cut back on. The car was stiflingly hot, and I groaned as I got behind the wheel. I'd parked under the shade of a large oak tree but that didn't seem to have helped at all.

Yesterday, I'd had to buy a black dress from a small boutique in Wokingham as I hadn't brought anything suitable for a funeral with me. I was already regretting my choice. The outfit had looked smart and appropriately somber when I tried it on in the changing rooms, but today the dress felt too tight around my stomach and the man-made material was itchy.

I turned on the engine and pressed the air conditioning button, which sent jets of tepid air from the vents. I was very early so I waited for a couple of minutes for the car to cool down.

My head ached and my throat hurt with the effort of not crying, and I hadn't even arrived at the church yet. I closed my eyes and took a deep breath as I fastened my seatbelt.

The funeral was held at St James's Church, close to Zack Ryan's grandmother's cottage. I parked just off Church Lane, slotting my car in between two other vehicles.

I fought the urge to run away and turned off the engine. The sadness of today was overwhelming. I got out of the car and squinted towards the church, shading my eyes from the sun. There were lots of people here and the mourners had gathered outside near the entrance. I walked slowly along the lane and then up the small path to join them. There was no sign of Nicole's family yet, just groups of people I didn't know. I stood awkwardly beside the entrance of the church, wishing my headache would go away.

I hadn't been standing there long when I felt a hand on my shoulder. Turning, I saw Nigel. He was standing beside his wife, Julia, and there was no sign of the woman he'd been with at the hotel.

He wore a sheepish expression and gave me a goofy smile. "Hello, Abbie, we haven't seen you in yonks," he said, his eyes beseeching me to go along with his little charade.

I tried to summon a smile but I really didn't feel like it today.

I greeted them both solemnly. "Nigel, Julia, how are you?"

Julia dabbed the corner of her eye with a tissue. "Finding it a bit tough to be honest. She was so young and it was such a brutal way to die."

I swallowed the lump in my throat. "Yes, it's horrible."

"You were so close. I can't imagine how bad it must be for you." Julia reached out and squeezed my arm.

I felt tears prick the corner of my eyes and quickly changed the subject. "How are the kids?"

"Oh, not bad. They've been playing me up recently, the little monkeys. Kids will be kids, I suppose."

I tried to think of something else to say, to fill the awkward silence with mundane small talk, but I couldn't. A moment ago, I'd been hoping for some company, so I didn't look so conspicuous standing alone, but now I found myself wishing I was alone again. I didn't want to make polite conversation today.

A long black car pulled up beside the church and a hush ran through the crowd of mourners. It wasn't the hearse delivering Nicole's body yet, though. It was the car for her family.

Steve got out, followed by Janet, Sienna and Marilyn. They must have overcome their fear of Steve being dangerous. Did they now believe Steve had nothing to do with Nicole's murder?

There were whispers all around me. And I was sure I heard somebody say, *"Isn't it always the husband?"*

I turned sharply, and the people behind me broke eye contact and looked guiltily at the ground.

"Excuse me," I said to Nigel and Julia then headed down the path to meet Steve and Sienna. I kissed Steve once on the cheek and squeezed his hand.

His face was tense, his features set in a stoic expression, but his eyes were glassy with unshed tears.

I moved past him to Sienna. She'd tied her tangle of coppery hair back from her pale face. She looked even more scared than the last time I'd seen her.

I pulled her in for a hug and felt her cling to me tightly for a moment. "Are you doing okay?" I whispered.

She managed a slight nod, and I kept my arm around her shoulders as I said hello to Marilyn and Janet who greeted me frostily.

Inside the church, I sat a couple of rows back from the family. It didn't matter where I sat. I still got to say goodbye to Nicole and that was really all that counted.

No matter what Janet might think, I didn't want to make this day any harder on her or her mother. So I gave them the privacy they needed to grieve on their own.

My heart was close to breaking through most of the service. Tears rolled down my cheeks when I heard Sienna sobbing in the front row as the pallbearers carried Nicole's coffin into the church.

I tried to find comfort in the rector's words, but it wasn't easy.

After the funeral, people lingered at the church. The wake was being held at Yew Tree House, but I wasn't sure I'd be welcome. I walked towards my car, intending to duck away early but Steve called out to me.

He apologised to the two women he'd been talking to and walked over to me, "Abbie, are you coming back to the house? Do you need a lift?"

"I have my car," I said. "In fact, if there's anyone who needs a ride, they can come with me."

"Thank you. Could you give Mrs Partridge a lift? She hasn't been able to drive since her stroke."

"Sure. I'll go and find her now."

I headed off in search of Mrs Partridge. She used to be a teaching assistant at Finchampstead C of E school and was an integral part of the village. Everyone knew Mrs Partridge.

I didn't see her immediately. It seemed nobody was in a hurry to get away from the church, which made it hard to spot people in the crowds.

I walked away from the church and down Church Lane, thinking perhaps she was chatting to someone she knew, when a familiar figure caught my eye.

Rob. And not just him, but Rob *and* his new wife.

I was tempted to blank him but that would be childish. Nicole's death had put things in perspective. No one here was watching me or Rob. No one cared. Gossip had died down over the years. I tried to conjure up a friendly smile and hoped he'd just let me go past without striking up a conversation, but no such luck.

"Abbie! It's good to see you. I'm sorry it's under such tragic circumstances."

"So how have you been?" I asked, determined to show I was past the emotional upset.

Rob smiled. "Pretty good. Business is going well." Before he could say any more his new wife cut in. Her arm was looped around his waist possessively. "Yes," she said. "Things are brilliant. We are so happy, aren't we?"

I was about to comment that people who had to boast about how happy they were to others, were rarely truly content. But I imagined Nicole's voice telling me to cool it. It almost felt as though she was standing next to me.

"Deep breaths, Abbie. Just let it wash over you. She isn't worth the waste of breath. You've got more important things on your plate."

My imaginary Nicole was right.

Over Rob's shoulder, I could see Sienna talking to Jason Owens. As Rob's wife began to witter on about the renovations on their new house, I tuned her out and studied the interaction between Sienna and Jason.

He was her teacher so it made sense that he'd offer condolences at her mother's funeral, but there was something about their body language that struck me as odd.

Jason leaned forward, lowering his head, attempting to look Sienna directly in the eye, but Sienna stubbornly stared down at the floor.

It was probably just her way of dealing with the stress of today. But I couldn't help feeling she wasn't comfortable talking to Jason.

"What do you think?" Rob's wife asked.

Damn. I had no idea why she'd asked me a question. What had she been talking about? I'd been too busy watching Sienna to pay any attention.

A flash of impatience passed over her face. "Rob always wanted a hot tub, but you didn't like them. You really should try the new top of the range one we've just installed in our garden. It's amazing, isn't it darling?"

Rob had the decency to look embarrassed.

I didn't remember ever talking about hot tubs with Rob. He shot me an apologetic glance.

"Perhaps I misremembered," he said and I guessed what had happened.

I'd wager Rob was the one who didn't want the hot tub. He'd probably tried to persuade his wife not to get one and my name must have come up somewhere in his argument. I couldn't help thinking, if he'd been better at expressing his feelings, I wouldn't have been left standing at the altar. We'd have split long before that happened.

"Excuse me, Abbie, could I have a quick word?"

I turned to see Toby Walsh, Steve's business partner smiling apologetically at Rob and his wife as he put his hand on my elbow.

I cringed inwardly. Every time I saw Toby I couldn't help thinking about Nicole's terrible matchmaking attempt.

"Of course," I said, letting him lead me away from Rob. "Is there something wrong?"

Toby smiled. His teeth looked unnaturally white against his tan. "I'm doing you a favour."

I frowned in confusion. "A favour?"

He raised an eyebrow and leaned closer. "I was trying to rescue you from your ex."

"Oh, was it that obvious?"

"Well, you were smiling through gritted teeth and clenching your fists. That was a dead giveaway." He winked.

Finally, I smiled. "Well, thank you. It was a bit awkward. How did you know he was my ex?"

"Oh, Nicole gave me all the details on your love life when she was trying to fit us up."

My skin was already flushed from the heat, but my cheeks burned at the memory of Nicole's clumsy matchmaking. "I should have guessed."

"Her heart was in the right place," he said and shrugged. His hazel eyes fixed on mine. "I'd broken up with someone, too. It wasn't the right time."

I put my hand on his arm. "Toby, it was embarrassing enough at the time. Please don't remind me of our blind date."

Toby's eyes widened and then he grinned. "Was it really *that* bad?"

"It was the definition of awkward."

People were filing past us, making their way back to the cars parked along the lane. Everyone was wearing traditional black for the funeral, the very worst colour to wear in this heat.

"I've got room in my car if you need a lift to the house," Toby offered.

"Thanks, but I've brought my own car."

"Okay. I'll see you there." He pulled his keys out of his pocket and then gave me one last smile before walking off.

I looked around the churchyard. The gathering had thinned, and Sienna should have been easy to spot but she was nowhere to be seen. She wasn't talking to Jason anymore. He was standing to my right, chatting to a woman I didn't recognise.

Perhaps Janet and Marilyn had already taken Sienna back to Yew Tree House.

There was still no sign of Mrs Partridge so I started to walk back towards the church, stepping over the tufts of dry, tough grass and noticing the wilted flowers left at the graves.

A robin perched on the gravestone in front of me, and I paused to watch it for a moment. When I was a girl, my grandmother told me robins and white feathers were signs from departed loved ones. But I'd recently read an article which said historically robins were considered harbingers of death. I shivered. The small, red-breasted bird cocked its head and appeared to look directly at me.

"Hello there," a voice said from my left. It was Jason Owens.

I turned and shaded my eyes from the sun. "Hello, are you going back to Yew Tree House?"

He ran a hand through his thick hair. "Yes, although I didn't drive to the church. What a mistake! It's sweltering."

"I can give you a lift to the house, if you'd like?"

Jason delivered a charming smile. "That would be very kind, thank you. I shouldn't have walked. I knew it was going to be a hot day, but there's something about walking that helps clear your thoughts sometimes, don't you think?"

"I suppose." I wasn't really invested in the conversation. I was too busy trying to work out how to broach the subject of his conversation with Sienna earlier. It seemed rude to just come out and ask him what they were talking about. After all, he was probably only telling her how sorry he was.

"I'm giving Mrs Partridge a lift as well," I said, finally spotting the stout lady, standing in the middle of the lane waving at me.

I waved back and so did Jason.

Even though we were standing amongst the gravestones, I could still smell the funeral flowers. The scent of lilies was strongest of all.

My new black court shoes were pinching the backs of my heels as I walked, and I wished I'd had the foresight to put some plasters in my clutch bag.

"I saw you talking to Sienna earlier," I said, as we walked side-by-side. "It's such a difficult time for her at the moment."

Jason nodded sombrely. "Yes, it's very sad." But he didn't offer any further information.

I was about to try again when I realised this was how paranoia took hold. Jason hadn't done anything to earn my suspicion. I gave him a sideways glance, taking in his handsome face. He had fine lines around his eyes, which became more pronounced as he squinted at the sun.

Jason Owens seemed like a nice guy. He was just one of many people who cared about Sienna. There wasn't anything menacing or threatening about him, I told myself. There was nothing to worry about. Nothing at all.

CHAPTER TWENTY-ONE

I'd NEVER SEEN Nicole and Steve's huge driveway so crowded. Cars were jammed into every available space. I only managed to park by blocking in a black Lexus. Jason assured me he knew the owner of the car and it wouldn't be a problem.

As soon as we entered Yew Tree House, two women greeted Jason enthusiastically, and after nodding hello, I left his side and went in search of Sienna.

Once I'd made sure she was okay, I would be free to leave. My cool reception from Marilyn and Janet at the funeral made me think they wouldn't appreciate my commiserations today. But I owed it to Nicole to find out how Sienna was doing.

People gathered in small groups in every room downstairs, and I was surprised to realise just how few of Nicole's friends I knew. There was a time when we moved in the same circles. But I saw no one from our time at university here. I wondered if everyone had been told?

I'd offered to reach out to our mutual friends, but Janet and Marilyn had made it quite clear they were in charge of funeral arrangements and didn't need my help.

I walked slowly through the downstairs rooms. The large dining room table had been moved into the living room and was filled with glasses of wine and fruit juice on the right side and home-made fruit cake on the left. The platters of sandwiches had been demolished. Only two small triangles of ham on white remained.

I caught sight of Angie Macgregor scurrying into the room, carrying another tray of sandwiches. Her cheeks were flushed, and she was so intent on winding her way through the groups of people in her way that she didn't notice me.

I looked through the window into the back garden. There were a few people outside chatting, but Sienna wasn't among them.

There was no sign of Sienna downstairs. She couldn't have simply disappeared. I wondered if she'd gone up to her room. Should I ask permission before going upstairs to look for her? Steve was busy accepting condolences from a long line of people, and I didn't want to ask Janet or Marilyn.

I couldn't leave without checking on Sienna. It would only take a minute. Apologising, I ducked around a large group of people who had gathered in the centre of the room then headed for the stairs.

At the top, there was a large gallery landing, which gave me a good view of the whole of the hallway and most of the sitting room. No one had noticed me coming upstairs so I continued towards Sienna's bedroom.

I knocked softly on the second door along the hallway and paused. There was no answer and I couldn't hear anyone inside. I knocked again and then pushed the door open.

The bed was made, the dressing table was scattered with various make-up products and there was a black dress hanging on the wardrobe door, but Sienna wasn't there.

I closed the door behind me, preparing to go back downstairs. But as I did so, I turned and saw Sienna standing in a doorway a little further along the hall, holding a black cardigan.

She stood still, her hair fell in messy waves past her shoulders. As I got closer, I saw her eyes were red.

"I came to see if you are okay," I said, walking towards her. "I thought maybe you could do with some company."

Sienna shrugged. She lifted the black cardigan in her hands and brought it close to her face before pressing it to her cheek. "I wanted to borrow Mum's cardigan," she said. "I thought it would smell of her, but it doesn't. It smells of fabric conditioner."

She handed it to me, but I wasn't quite sure what to do with it. Did she expect me to smell it and confirm? I hung it over my arm and put a hand on her shoulder. "Probably a bit too hot this afternoon to wear a cardigan anyway."

She pointed at Nicole and Steve's bedroom. "Do you want to come in? There's a photo of you, me and Mum on the dresser. I thought you might want it."

I swallowed the lump in my throat. "I'd better not. Steve might not want me in his room."

Sienna frowned. "It's not *his* room, it's Mum's."

"They had separate bedrooms?"

She shrugged and walked into the bedroom. "Yes. Steve works late a lot, so it made sense for him to have another bedroom."

I followed her into the room, my eyes drinking in everything that reminded me of my friend. Beside the dressing table was the new Dyson hairdryer she'd been raving about just a couple of weeks ago. The top of the dressing table was littered with things as though she'd be coming back to them at any moment.

Her Guerlain bronzer with the huge brush. She'd used that brand of bronzer for years. A Rimmel lipstick lay beside it with the lid removed, as though she'd had to rush away before she'd finished with it.

My hand trembled as I reached out to pick up the small, thick bottle of Lady Dior perfume. Nicole's favourite. I sprayed a little on the cardigan and held it out to Sienna.

She took it and lifted it to her face, breathing in deeply. "It smells like Mum."

The scent triggered so many memories. Nights out in Southampton, a boozy night at Jesters, the day Nicole told me she was having Sienna, our graduation day…

Sienna looped her arm through mine, bringing me back to the present. "Did Mum ever tell you anything about my father?"

The question came out of the blue and I wasn't quite sure how to handle it. Of course, getting flustered and hesitating wasn't the best idea because Sienna immediately assumed I was hiding something from her.

She tilted her head and looked at me through narrowed eyes. "You do know something, don't you?"

I shook my head. "I'm sorry, but I only know what your mum told me… She said she'd had a fling and fell pregnant while she was in the last year of our University course."

I could tell by the look in her eyes that she didn't believe me. Maybe she was right. Why hadn't I pushed Nicole on it at the time? We were friends. She could trust me with everything else. But I'd believed her when she said it was a one-night stand.

Sienna turned away and began to walk back towards the galleried landing. She was angry with me, but I couldn't tell her any more about her father. I didn't *know* anything.

I followed but instead of walking downstairs, she leaned on the light wood banisters, looking down at the marble floor in the hallway below.

"Do you think if someone fell from here they'd die?"

I frowned. "Probably, or be seriously hurt. It's a long way down."

"It wouldn't be so bad if it was over quickly." She must have seen the look of confusion mingled with horror on my face because she quickly added, "I'm not about to jump."

Before I could think up a response, I spotted Janet in the hall. She was staring up at us with a strange expression on her face. She marched towards the stairs, and I braced myself for a confrontation.

"What are you two talking about?" she asked before she'd even reached the top step.

The familiar scent of Chanel No.5 and cigarette smoke engulfed me as Janet walked briskly towards us.

"I just came upstairs to see if Sienna was okay," I said.

I really did feel sorry for Janet after losing her sister and didn't want to upset her. Janet pursed her lips and folded her arms across her chest.

I turned to Sienna. "You've got my phone number. If you need anything, anything at all, you can ring me."

Sienna tucked a lock of hair behind her ear. "How long are you staying in the UK?"

"A little while longer. I contacted head office and told them I'd need more time here before I return to India."

The expression on Sienna's face didn't change and I was left wondering whether I'd said the wrong thing. Did she want me to say I wasn't going back? Did she need me here? Or did she just not care? It was hard to tell.

Janet linked her arm through Sienna's and then patted the girl's hand. "Let's go back downstairs."

I followed them slowly, wondering how Janet felt about Sienna moving back here with Steve. I didn't think he could have hurt Nicole, not really, but even so, Sienna living at Yew Tree House with Steve after the police had taken him in for questioning was disconcerting. No matter how strong his alibi was, there was always a niggling doubt in the back of my mind asking what if…?

I was about to leave and head back to the hotel when Jason Owens spotted me. He smiled warmly.

"Abbie, come with me. There are some people I think you'd like to meet."

I gave a tight smile and followed his lead into the sitting room. My shoes were still pinching and it felt like the blasted things were rubbing my ankles raw. I was very tempted to take them off. If it had just been me and Nicole here, I would have. We'd have kicked off our shoes, lounged on the massive sofa and downed a bottle of wine or two.

I sighed. Why hadn't I visited more often?

I smiled politely as Jason introduced me to three school governors. It wasn't easy to pay attention because after commenting on the tragedy of Nicole's death they began a heated debate about parents taking children out of school for holidays during term time.

Behind our group, Toby Walsh stood by the refreshment table. He caught me watching him and pulled a funny face. He looked like a cheeky schoolboy, which was completely at odds with his expensive tailored suit, and perfectly cut hair. It was so unexpected and out of place for a sombre gathering, I giggled.

That earned me some surprised stares from the school governors, and Jason Owens leaned down to whisper in my ear.

"Are you all right, Abbie? Do you need some fresh air?" He smelled of sandalwood and soap, and his voice was gentle and concerned.

"I'm fine. Sorry. Ignore me."

He squeezed my hand. "Just tell me when you want to leave. I could walk back to get my car and give you a lift, if you'd like a drink?"

He kept hold of my hand, and to my surprise, I didn't have an urge to pull away. "Thanks, but I'm fine to drive. Alcohol can make me sad at the best of times. I don't need any more sadness today."

When I was sure I wouldn't laugh again, I risked a glance back over to Toby. He was now talking earnestly to Steve about something. Now, he looked perfectly respectable.

The conversation between Jason and the governors had moved on to the special needs provisions in the county and I was asked a question. After giving a noncommittal reply, I looked for Toby and Steve but the two business partners had disappeared.

I pressed my fingertips to my temple and rubbed. I was getting a headache and the talk about school boards wasn't helping.

I put a hand on Jason's arm and excused myself. "I'm just going to see how Angie is coping in the kitchen."

As I walked away, I could feel Jason's eyes on me. I'd probably freaked him out with my inappropriate giggling. He'd be watching me closely for signs of hysteria from now on.

As expected, I found Angie in the kitchen. She was making a pot of tea, and her cheeks were still flushed.

She turned to me. "Can you believe people are actually asking for tea in this heat?"

I gave her a sympathetic smile. We didn't have hot days often in the UK, and we Brits do love our tea. "Is there anything I can do to help?"

I'd assumed Steve would use a catering company. There were a lot of people here and it created a lot of work for one woman.

Angie shot me a glance before pouring boiling water into the teapot. "Yes, Steve originally planned to bring someone in from outside, but I wanted to do it. It probably sounds silly to you, but it's my way of showing how much Nicole meant to me."

"It doesn't sound silly, at all. But I can see you need some help, so just tell me what you want me to do."

Angie hesitated and then smiled. "Aye, well, if you don't mind, you could make up some more sandwiches. There's plenty of bread left." She pointed to the loaves of white and brown bread stacked around the bread bin. "I've run out of ham, but there's chicken and tuna mayo in the fridge."

Glad to feel useful, I washed my hands and then got to work as Angie left the kitchen with the tea. From where I stood making the sandwiches at the kitchen counter I could see into the utility room. Even though the door was open, Charlie lay forlornly on the floor. Poor thing. He had to be so confused. And with his thick fur he must be suffering from the heat. The cool tiled floor of the utility room was probably the coolest place for him.

The butter had been left out of the fridge and was very soft and easy to spread. By the time Angie came back into the kitchen, I'd already made a few rounds, and she grabbed a serving platter and began to load the sandwiches on it.

"I've never known people to eat so much. It's like a horde of locusts has descended out there."

After Angie's comment, we worked side-by-side in a comfortable silence. It felt good to be doing something useful. I didn't know how to make Sienna feel better, but even I knew how to prepare a sandwich. I was nearly at the end of the white loaf when Jason entered the kitchen.

"Sorry to interrupt," he said smiling at Angie. "Brian has offered me a lift home. I didn't want to leave without making sure you were okay."

Somehow I'd managed to cover my fingers with tuna mayo. "I'm fine."

He continued to watch me, a frown on his handsome face.

"*Really*. You don't have to worry. I was just laughing. I'm not hysterical, I promise."

He smiled. "All right. Before I go, I wanted to ask if you fancy meeting for a drink later this week."

My mind went blank. "Oh, um." Why was he asking me out for a drink? Was it some kind of date? Did he want to talk to me about Sienna? He stood there waiting for an answer. Finally, I said, "Yes, that would be nice."

His smile widened. "Great, I've got your number so I'll give you a call and we'll set something up."

"Okay, lovely," I said, trying to sound enthusiastic.

After he turned and left, I wondered why I took so long to agree. I was going to be in the UK for at least another week, and now that Marilyn and Janet had frozen me out, I wouldn't be seeing much of them. I'd only be sitting in the hotel bar on my own evening after evening. It would be nice to have some company.

I noticed Angie had let the sandwiches pileup on the breadboard, and when I turned, I saw her watching me quizzically.

"What's wrong?" I asked, wondering if I'd managed to get tuna mayo on my cheek.

Her forehead crinkled in a frown and she said, "Watch out for that one."

"Why?"

Angie gave a little shrug, and at first, I thought she wasn't going to respond. Then she announced, "His eyes are too close together."

"His eyes?" A smile tugged at the corner of my lips. I imagined Nicole giggling at that, but Angie looked completely serious so I didn't laugh.

"It's just a drink," I said. "It's not a big deal."

"Maybe so. Just be careful."

I turned my attention back to the sandwiches as an uneasy feeling coiled in my stomach.

Charlie's tail wagged and thudded against the floor of the utility room. The chatter of people in the sitting room drifted through to the kitchen, but it was just background noise.

The kitchen was a sanctuary of peace. It was hot, but at least it was calm. And right now, calm was exactly what I needed.

CHAPTER TWENTY-TWO

THE FOLLOWING MONDAY, I woke at eleven a.m. with a splitting headache. I hated to admit it, but I'd been holding a one person pity party since the funeral. I'd tried to call Sienna twice but she hadn't picked up or returned my calls. I couldn't help feeling hurt, and worse, feeling like I'd let Nicole down.

Janet was still ignoring me. That wasn't surprising. She'd always been exceptionally good at holding grudges, but I was surprised at Marilyn. Nicole's mother had always been kind to me in the past.

Jason Owens hadn't called me either, and even though I wasn't that keen on going for a drink with him after Angie's ominous warning, I found myself wondering why I'd been snubbed.

Last night, feeling thoroughly fed up, I'd sat alone at the hotel bar and drunk one too many gin and tonics.

My stomach churned as I got out of bed. I padded across the hotel room to the bathroom and winced as I caught sight of my reflection. I looked a state.

I'd called the Health Foundation again yesterday and arranged to have at least another fortnight off. It meant I was edging into unpaid leave territory and I'd need to find a cheaper hotel. This one was far too expensive for my meagre finances.

After a shower and a strong coffee, I felt a little more human. Paracetamol had taken the edge off the headache, but it wouldn't go away completely, which was no more than I deserved. I thought some fresh air might help and was getting ready to go for a walk when my mobile rang.

It was Sienna.

I smiled as I answered, pleased she was finally getting in touch. "Hi, sweetheart. I'm so glad you rang."

"Abbie..."

Even though Sienna had only said one word, I could tell by her tone there was something wrong.

"What is it?"

"There's somebody following me." Her voice wavered as she spoke.

"Now? Where are you?"

"I don't know if he's still there. I'm downstairs in your hotel."

"In the lobby?"

"Yes."

"Stay right where you are. I'm coming down."

I kept her on the phone as I ran out of my hotel room, forgetting to take the swipe key card with me. My shoes clattered against the steps as I raced down the stairs. My heart was pounding. Who was following Sienna? Was it the person who'd killed her mother? Was Sienna's life in danger?

I burst out of the stairwell and saw Sienna immediately. She was standing in the centre of the lobby. Her arms were wrapped around her body and she looked terrified.

Her eyes widened as I walked towards her.

"Sienna…" I wrapped my arms around her and hugged her tightly, noticing she was trembling. "It's okay. You're safe now. Let's go and sit down and you can tell me what happened."

We went to sit in the small lounge area where they served afternoon tea. It was too early for that, but I asked one of the staff if they'd bring us a pot of tea. Then we sat down side-by-side on a small sofa.

Sienna still hadn't eased her grip on my arm.

"It's okay," I said again. "Tell me what happened."

"I went to see some friends in Yateley. They wanted to get KFC for lunch, but I didn't fancy it, so I left them there and decided to walk home."

I squeezed her hand encouragingly. KFC was quite a distance from Sienna's house. I guessed it had to be over two miles.

Sienna closed her eyes and let out a shaky breath. "I just got the sense someone was watching me. When I looked over my shoulder, I saw a man… He was tall and he was staring at me. I went into the next cul-de-sac. I thought I'd know for sure he was following me if he trailed me around the cul-de-sac back onto the main road."

"And he followed you around the cul-de-sac?"

Sienna nodded. "Yes, he kept following me all along the main Reading Road. I was getting so scared because there were fewer houses around at that point and I didn't know what to do."

"Did you call the police?"

A fat teardrop rolled down Sienna's cheek. She shook her head. "No."

"Do you remember what he looked like? We can tell Lizzie, your family liaison officer, about this. I'm sure she'd want to know."

"Maybe. I'm not sure how well I can describe him. He was quite tall and looked middle-aged. I don't know how old exactly."

"What was he wearing?"

"Light-coloured trousers and a brown coat. He was tall and thin and that's all I can remember. I didn't get a good look at his face. He was never that close. I just walked as fast as I could. I was planning to walk home but then I remembered you were staying at this hotel..." She broke off and shook her head. "I was scared."

I put my arm around her shoulder. "I know. You'll be okay now. We'll let Lizzie know straight away just in case he's still hanging around."

Sienna's lower lip wobbled as she stared at me. "You believe me?"

"Of course. Why wouldn't I?"

Sienna opened and closed her mouth without saying anything. Then she shrugged. "I told Aunt Janet and Grandma when it happened last time. They said I was stressed and imagining things."

My stomach flipped over. "You mean this has happened *before*? Someone's *followed* you?"

Sienna's face crumpled. "The other time it happened... I didn't really see anyone. I just had this feeling. You know sometimes how you have that prickling sensation at the back of your neck and you just know that someone is watching you."

She gripped onto my arm, her fingernails digging into my skin. I nodded.

"That's what it was like, but because I couldn't give a description, they thought I was going mad."

"Nobody thinks that. Did you tell Steve about this?"

Sienna shook her head. "No, he's taken Mum's death really hard, and I don't want make things worse for him."

"You don't have to handle this on your own, Sienna. We're going to talk to Steve and the family liaison officer. We have to tell them."

Sienna's face crumpled but she didn't cry.

"Is Steve home now?"

Sienna shook her head again. "He had to go in to work to sort a few things out today. But he did say he wouldn't be too late."

"Right, I'm going to phone the police station and let them know what's happened. Then I'm going to drive you back home, okay?"

Sienna blinked at me. "You're not gonna leave me there alone, are you?"

I shook my head. "No, I'll stay with you until Steve's home. I promise."

I poured us both a cup of tea and then watched Sienna pick up the cup with shaky hands as I called the police station. Fortunately, Lizzie was at her desk and they transferred my call to her straight away.

After I'd filled Lizzie in, she promised to come to the hotel and she said she'd send a couple of units to scout the area to see if they could find anyone matching Sienna's description of the man who'd been stalking her.

By the time we finished our tea, Lizzie arrived in the lobby. She was kind and sympathetic to Sienna who repeated everything she'd told me to Lizzie.

After Lizzie left, I paid the bill for our tea and drove Sienna back home.

It was the first time I'd been back to Yew Tree house since the funeral and it seemed too big, too quiet and empty.

The first thing Sienna did as I shut the front door behind us was to go round and make sure all the windows and doors were locked. I couldn't blame her.

Charlie came out to greet us and I kneeled down to stroke him.

"Hi boy, are you feeling a bit better today?"

He wagged his tail enthusiastically so I took that as a yes.

A red light was blinking on the answer machine on the telephone table in the hall. When Sienna saw it, she put it on speaker phone and pressed the playback button.

It was a message from a local health club, informing Nicole she'd left some items in one of the lockers for over a week, which was against the rules. Lockers could only be used for one week at a time, apparently.

Sienna rolled her eyes and pressed delete.

"I could pick up your mum's stuff from the health club tomorrow, if you like?"

"Thanks," Sienna said. "It's probably only her gym stuff."

I'd clear it with Steve first, of course, but I wanted to make life as easy as possible for them.

We sat in the sitting room and watched a romantic comedy on Netflix. It was just what we needed to take our minds off everything.

I was trying to put on a brave front for Sienna but deep down I was really concerned. Why had someone been following her? I couldn't help worrying this was something to do with Nicole's murder.

CHAPTER TWENTY-THREE

STEVE ARRIVED HOME LATER than I'd expected. The weather had turned and rain hammered down all afternoon and into early evening.

Sienna had drawn the curtains in the sitting room. I wasn't sure if that was to block out the miserable afternoon or to block prying eyes.

After we'd finished the film, we'd moved on to binge watch the first series of *Scandal*. We were on the third episode when Steve got home.

Beside me on the sofa, Sienna tensed at the sound of Steve's key in the lock.

I put a hand on her arm and smiled reassuringly, but her body didn't relax until Steve called out, "Hello."

We heard his footsteps in the hall before he appeared in the doorway.

He blinked in surprise at seeing me and then smiled. "Hi, Abbie. Are you staying for dinner?"

He put his laptop bag on one of the empty chairs and ran a hand through his hair. He looked worn out and I wondered why he'd felt the need to go back to work so soon. He was the boss, surely he could take some extra time off. But maybe it was helping him to keep busy.

"We should get a pizza," Sienna suggested, sounding more like her old self.

Steve yanked off his tie. "Sounds good to me. It's Angie's day off, and I don't feel like cooking. What do you say to pizza, Abbie?"

"Sounds great." I shuffled forward on the sofa. "Steve, something happened to Sienna today, and I think you should know."

The smile slipped from Steve's face and he frowned. "What happened?"

Sienna's mobile phone began to ring. She fished it out from under the sofa cushions. "It's Zach."

She kept her head bent low so her hair hid most of her face as she stood up. As she passed Steve and walked out of the room, she slid a finger over the front of her mobile to answer the call.

Steve crossed the room and sat down on the sofa beside me. "What happened?"

He looked concerned, fatherly even, and I was pleased and relieved to see he was worried. When I'd first come back I'd been shocked by his lack of panic over Sienna's disappearance.

But perhaps that was because things had overwhelmed him. He did seem to care about his stepdaughter, and Sienna had chosen to move back to Yew Tree House to live with him so that had to count for something.

"Sienna thinks she was followed today," I said and paused to wait for Steve's reaction.

His expression was guarded and he looked away. "I see."

I leaned forward, trying to see his face. "Has she mentioned being followed before?"

He exhaled a long breath and leaned back against the sofa cushions. "She keeps checking the doors and windows are locked and never wants to be alone, but she didn't tell me anyone was following her. What exactly happened? Did you see anything?"

I shook my head. "No, she phoned me and came to the hotel. She'd been out with friends, and they'd separated. Sienna decided to walk home that's when she saw a man following her."

"What did he look like?"

"She said he was tall and gave me a description of his clothes, but she didn't get a good look at his face. He was wearing light trousers and a brown jacket. I called Lizzie, the family liaison officer."

Steve scratched his chin and looked pensive. "Do you think she was really followed or is she just jumpy because of everything that's happened? She's been through a lot."

"I believe her, Steve. Instead of walking on the main road, she took a detour through a cul-de-sac. He followed taking the same route. There was no reason for that unless he *was* following her."

Steve looked taken aback and struggled to digest what I was saying. "Do you think she could be in danger? In that case, we shouldn't let her out of our sight." He exhaled heavily and held his head in his hands. "I was planning to stay in London tomorrow night, but I can't do that now."

"Do you really need to work so hard at the moment?" I asked. It was really none of my business but he looked so worn out.

He pinched the bridge of his nose between his thumb and forefinger. "I wish I didn't, believe me. But everything has gone wrong. It's the worst possible timing."

"Is there no one else who could handle things for you? What about Toby? He's your partner."

Steve shook his head. "Toby is the last person I want helping right now. Most of the screw up is down to him anyway."

"Oh, I see."

Only I didn't see, not really. The screw up had to be bad to make Steve want to work with everything else going on. Toby hadn't seemed stressed to me.

"I could stay here with Sienna during the day," I suggested. "I contacted the Health Foundation and let them know I'd be staying here for another couple of weeks. I don't have anything else to do, so I'd be happy to help."

"I'd appreciate it. It would make me feel better to know that Sienna is not alone." He paused for a breath and then turned to face me. "Abbie, do you think the man following Sienna had anything to do with what happened to Nicole?"

He'd asked the same question I'd been asking myself all afternoon.

"I really don't know. I can't see how it is related, but to be on the safe side, I think you're right about not leaving Sienna on her own for the next few days. At least until the police look into it. Has there been any news on the investigation?"

Steve stared at the television, which was displaying a freeze-frame of a woman screaming after we'd paused the show.

"No, they've given me a few meagre updates, but they don't have any concrete suspects as far as I know. Of course, they could still be focusing on me, wasting time." His words were bitter and I could understand how he felt.

"You know, you could always stay here if that makes things easier. It must be costing you a fortune to stay at the DeVere… unless the Health Foundation Charity are suddenly paying a fortune."

I smiled at that idea. "No, they're not. I had some money saved because there's not much to spend my money on where I've been staying in India. It's not like living in a city like Mumbai. Actually, I was going to start looking for a cheaper hotel."

"That settles it then. Move in here for a couple of weeks until you go back. You'd be doing me a massive favour. I'd know that Sienna was safe and she'd enjoy having some extra time with you."

"If you're sure… It would save me quite a bit of money, that's for sure."

"Absolutely. And it would mean I could stay in London tomorrow night if that's okay with you?" He raised an eyebrow. "It would just be you and Sienna here."

I nodded. "I'll check out tomorrow morning. Thanks, Steve."

"I should be the one thanking you. I know you must think I'm an awful stepfather. The truth is, we disagree about things but I really do think of Sienna as my daughter. I couldn't stand it if something happened to her too."

"I know it can't have been easy when you first got together with Nicole. But I think by coming back to Yew Tree House to live with you, Sienna has shown she thinks of you as her father."

Steve's eyes were a little glassy. He blinked a few times before slapping his hands together and standing up. "Right, I'd better order that pizza. Don't tell me you're a Hawaiian girl, too?"

I grinned. "Afraid so. It's my favourite."

He rolled his eyes. "Just like Nicole and Sienna."

CHAPTER TWENTY-FOUR

WE POLISHED off a large Hawaiian and a spicy pepperoni between the three of us. Despite the stress of the day, I relaxed and began to believe things would get better. The police would bring Nicole's killer to justice, and Sienna and Steve would help each other through their grief.

I was worried about her reaction, but Sienna seemed pleased when Steve told her I'd be staying with them for a while. The evening produced some sad moments as we reminisced and remembered Nicole, but it was nice to share memories. Most of all, I was relieved to see how well Sienna and Steve got along. When I'd first come back from India, I'd been shocked by Steve's reaction to the fact Sienna was missing and was worried she'd be left with an uncaring stepfather, but it seemed that couldn't be further from the truth. He might not be the perfect stepfather but Steve cared about her, and Sienna relaxed in his company.

After Sienna went to bed, I left Yew Tree House and drove back to the hotel along the dark country roads. When I was at the house with Steve and Sienna it was easier to focus on the present and the future, but alone in the car, driving beneath the thick tree canopy, I began to feel uneasy again. The police were apparently no closer to finding out who had killed Nicole. I hated the thought of the killer walking around scot-free, but my worries went deeper than that. If someone was following Sienna, it was not much of a stretch to think she could be in danger, too.

In the hotel car park, I chose a spot as close to the entrance as I could. It was dark and I was on edge. As I got out of the car, I had the unsettling sensation that someone was watching me. Glancing over my shoulder, I called out, "Who's there?"

There was no answer but I spun around when I heard the crunch of gravel. Was someone lurking in the shadows?

I didn't wait to find out. I sprinted to the hotel, not slowing until I was safely inside. My heart was thudding in my chest as I turned to look at the car park through the glass doors. There was no one there. The bright lights in the lobby eased my panic and made me feel stupid for overreacting.

I stopped at the reception desk to let them know I would be checking out tomorrow and asked for my bill to be ready. Rather than heading straight up to my room, I stopped in the hotel bar for a nightcap.

It was relatively quiet. Two young men in suits, nursing pints perched on stools at the bar. Another man sat alone in the corner. He was wearing light-coloured chinos and a checked shirt, and beside him a brown jacket hung over the back of a chair.

She'd described him as middle-aged. I'd guess the man in the corner was in his mid-thirties, but perhaps to Sienna that was middle-aged?

I watched him warily. Lots of people wore brown jackets and chinos, I told myself. How likely was it the man who'd been following Sienna would now be sitting in my hotel bar? But I couldn't help stealing glances at him now and again as I drank my gin and tonic.

It wasn't long before he was joined by a woman with curly blonde hair, who sat down beside him and began to chatter away.

I shook my head. I was letting my imagination run riot. Was I really going to do a double take every time I saw a man in a brown jacket and light trousers?

I checked my phone for messages and was disappointed that Lizzie hadn't got back to me. The police were very busy with the investigation into Nicole's murder. Perhaps Lizzie didn't think we needed a follow up call. I supposed no news from Lizzie meant they hadn't found the man who'd been following Sienna.

I stood up, left a tip and walked out of the bar. I couldn't resist one last look at the man with the brown jacket. But he wasn't paying any attention to me. He was fully engrossed by the woman at his side.

See, Abbie, you're just paranoid.

* * *

THE FOLLOWING MORNING I GOT UP EARLY. I WANTED TO BE CHECKED out and at Yew Tree House before Steve left for work so Sienna wasn't left alone at any time. When I arrived, Sienna was still in bed, so Steve gave me a brief tour of the house, even though I knew where most things were.

He told me to make myself at home and glanced at his watch for the third time in a minute.

He was clearly stressed and in a rush to get away.

"I'll be fine," I assured him. "You should get to work. I know you've got a lot to do."

"Thanks, Abbie. I really appreciate this."

I waved him off and just as his car left the driveway, I spotted Angie's blue mini pulling in. I gave her a quick wave, left the door ajar and went to prepare a pot of coffee. The gleaming chrome machine looked complicated.

I grabbed the tin of ground coffee I'd seen Angie use yesterday. It smelled delicious. I was rummaging around for filters for the machine when I heard Sienna scream.

The spoon I'd been holding clattered to the worktop counter and I dashed out of the kitchen to see Sienna standing in her pyjamas with her back against the front door.

"What is it? What's wrong?"

"The door was open! Someone must be in the house."

"Oh, Sienna that was me. I'm sorry. When Steve left, Angie was just arriving, so I left the door open for her."

Her lower lip wobbled. "There is no one in the house?"

I shook my head. "No, I'd have heard if someone had come in, and Angie must be still outside. No one could have got past without her seeing them."

Sienna turned back to the door, and with shaking hands, she reached up to release the latch. She pulled the door open, and we both looked out onto the gravel driveway and saw Angie marching towards the house.

"I thought…" Sienna broke off.

"It's my fault. I shouldn't have left the door open. I'm sorry."

She gave an almost imperceptible nod and then drifted back towards the stairs.

"Do you want some breakfast? Coffee?"

She shook her head as she began to climb the steps. "No, thank you."

I could have kicked myself. What a stupid thing to do. If there was somebody prowling about I really had to be more careful. Angie would have spotted anybody walking into the house, but that wasn't the point.

Angie called out cheerfully as she came through the door. She actually smiled when I explained I'd be staying at Yew Tree

House for the next week or so. I was starting to realise her formidable exterior was a front.

I shut the door firmly this time and I walked back into the kitchen to finish making the coffee.

I poured a mug for Angie and handed it to her.

"Well, how kind. It's nice to be waited on for a change." She gave me another smile.

"Steve needed to go into London today. He won't be back until tomorrow. We thought it was a good idea for someone to stay with Sienna."

Angie nodded but didn't reply, so I continued, "I've taken another two weeks of leave from my job and thought it would be a good opportunity to spend some time with Sienna."

"That's kind of you," Angie said as she took bottles of cleaning products from under the sink and stacked them on the worktop.

"It's nice of Steve to let me stay here. To be honest, I was racking up quite a bill at the hotel."

Angie pulled a face. "I'll bet. It's not cheap."

I took my coffee into the sitting room and mulled things over as I sat on the huge sofa. The next two weeks weren't going to be easy. I didn't know what I'd do if they still hadn't solved Nicole's murder by the time my two weeks were up.

Could I really just abandon Sienna and go back to India? No. It was out of the question.

I sipped my coffee and looked out at the front garden. I didn't have to wonder what Nicole would want me to do. I knew. She would want me to stay until Sienna was on an even keel again. So that's what I would do.

CHAPTER TWENTY-FIVE

I TOOK a stroll around the garden while Sienna was upstairs and Angie was cleaning. Charlie kept me company. He seemed to be perking up a little. I found his ball on the lawn and threw it for him. He chased the ball eagerly and returned it.

"Good boy," I said, gently taking the ball from his mouth.

I threw it again towards the laurel bushes that encircled the back garden. As Charlie raced after the ball, I stared back at the house. The branches of the yew tree were just visible over the roof. Sienna's bedroom overlooked the garden but her curtains were still closed.

I spent half an hour playing with Charlie, which helped me relax and organise my thoughts. I'd made the decision I would stay in the UK for as long as Sienna needed me. But I couldn't stay at Yew Tree House indefinitely. I needed a plan.

Top of my list, was working out how long my savings would last. As a nurse, there was always the possibility I could get some agency work to tide me over.

I headed back into the house to ask Angie if I could have some paper to make a to-do list. The lists were something I'd learned from Nicole. In our first year at university, I'd poked fun at her constant list making, but she'd had the last laugh after our first set of exams, and in the end, she'd persuaded me to make lists for every subject, carefully highlighting the important points with fluorescent markers. Even now, I found making a list helped me focus.

Angie was cleaning Steve's office. I poked my head around the door and saw her dusting the windowsill. It was a large room with a bay window overlooking the front driveway. A huge desk dominated the room with a black, studded-leather chair behind it. The wall in front of me was lined with bookshelves, but it surprised me to see they were mostly empty. A couple of shelves were dotted with piles of paperwork and three black lever arch files. I guessed most of Steve's paperwork would be in the filing cabinet on the other side of the room.

"Sorry to bother you, Angie. I need some paper. Is there any in Steve's office I can use?"

Angie looked about the room before spotting a pile of paper on one of the bookshelves.

"Will this do?" she asked pointing to it.

"That would be great. I only need one sheet."

She plucked the first sheet from the pile and walked towards me, holding it out.

I took the thick, cream paper from her. It felt heavy and expensive. I was expecting to use a sheet of basic grade printer paper still, I doubted Steve would miss one sheet.

"Thanks."

"Is everything all right, Abbie?"

I looked up, surprised. "Yes, fine. Why do you ask?"

"I thought you'd picked up on it." Angie regarded me steadily.

"Picked up on what?"

She took half a step closer to me. "There's evil here. A malevolence surrounding this house. You've sensed it, too, haven't you?"

I shivered and wanted to deny it. But I couldn't. There was something unsettling me. "It's just sadness…only to be expected in a bereaved household," I said lightly.

A flicker of impatience flickered across Angie's face, before she frowned. "Yes, I suppose you're right."

I hadn't expected Angie to be so fanciful. She seemed so down to earth normally.

I smiled and turned away just before she said, "You be careful, Abbie. Don't let your guard down."

My mouth was dry as I swallowed. "I'll be careful."

I took the paper back into the sitting room with me, grabbed a pen from my bag, settled on the sofa, and put a copy of *Country Life* magazine on my lap to lean on, before using my pen to divide the paper in half. One column would be my income and the other would be my expenses.

I jotted down some figures, trying to ignore the sense of foreboding and jitters my conversation with Angie had given me. As expected, the expenses far outweighed my income column, even after taking my savings into account. Maths had never been my strong suit, but from my calculations, it seemed like I'd need to look for work by the end of the month.

Using my phone, I searched the Web for a couple of well-known agencies and then jotted down their telephone numbers. I didn't need to contact them today, but I would be needing them soon.

I was just scrawling down the last number when Sienna walked into the room. She looked fragile and vulnerable. There were smudges of purple beneath her eyes, obvious against her pale skin. I stood up, folded the paper in half and stuffed it into my bag.

"It's almost lunchtime. Do you fancy a trip to the pub? We could take Charlie for a walk."

I thought the fresh air and sunshine would be good for her. I didn't like the idea of her being holed up, scared to leave Yew Tree House. The weather wasn't as bad as yesterday. It was cloudy, but didn't look like rain.

She gave me a soft smile. "Okay. I'll get my phone."

Sienna went back upstairs and I went to look for Angie. I found her scrubbing out the sink in the utility room.

"We're going to get some lunch," I said. "Do you have time for lunch break?"

Angie looked up and used the back of her hand to push back a lock of hair that had escaped from her bun. "That's sweet of you, but I'd better stay here and keep on top of things."

"Well, if you're sure. I thought we'd take Charlie for a walk and get out of the house for a bit. We'll probably go to the Greyhound."

I felt it was a good idea to let someone know where we were going if there was someone stalking Sienna.

I had Charlie on his lead, my bag looped over my shoulder and was waiting by the front door by the time Sienna came back downstairs.

"Ready?"

"Yep," she said, and I opened the front door.

We walked along Fleet Hill, keeping close to the grass verge. I kept Charlie on a tight leash on my right-hand side, away from the traffic, but he was a very well-behaved dog and the passing vehicles didn't bother him. There wasn't a proper pavement until we reached the village, so Sienna and I walked in single file beneath the tall oak trees.

When we approached the petrol station, I glanced back at Sienna to make sure she was okay. Her hands were in the pockets of her jeans, and her shoulders were hunched.

"How are you doing?" I asked, expecting her to beg to be allowed to go home.

"All right, I suppose," she said, twisting a lock of hair around her fingers.

Her head jerked up and she took a step closer to me as a Range Rover pulled into the petrol station and stopped beside the pumps. She didn't relax until she saw a red-haired lady get out of the driver's side and walk towards the shop.

"Do you still fancy going to the pub for lunch?"

I thought some time away from the house would be good for her, but she looked incredibly tense and I didn't want to add to her stress levels. More pressure was the last thing she needed.

"Sure." Sienna reached down to pet Charlie, who lapped up the attention.

We walked on, passing the school and as we got close to Jason Owens's cottage, I turned to Sienna. Like most women, I wasn't fond of dwelling on my unsuccessful dating life. The fact he still hadn't called me to arrange that drink still niggled at me. But I thought talking about something frivolous would take Sienna's mind off things.

"We were supposed to be going for a drink," I said, glancing at the thatched cottage and wondering if he was home.

"You and *Mr Owens*?" Sienna looked shocked.

I grinned. "I'm not that ancient, you know. He's probably about my age."

"Oh, I didn't mean that. It's just…" She turned to look at me, pushing her coppery hair back from her face so I could see she was frowning. "I didn't think he'd be your type."

"I'm not sure I have a type."

"Don't you have someone back in India?"

I shook my head. "No. It's just me and an intern, a young American guy called Rich Michaels."

"Don't you get lonely?"

I thought about that for a moment. I was alone at lot but rarely felt lonely. "I'm used to it. I haven't been in a proper relationship since Rob."

Sienna's eyes widened and she tucked her hair behind her ears. "But that was *years* ago."

"Yes, it was. I suppose meeting someone new after Rob jilted me wasn't at the top of my priorities."

Sienna nodded knowledgeably and gave a huff. "Men!"

That made me smile. "What do you think I should do if Mr Owens does finally call me?"

Sienna looked down at the ground as we walked. "I don't know."

"Do you like him?"

"He's all right for a teacher, I guess."

"What about you and Zach?" I asked, wondering if I was pushing too far.

She didn't answer straight away. The sun broke through the clouds and felt warm on my back.

Sienna let her hair fall forward, covering her face. "We're just friends."

So she didn't trust me yet. At least, not enough to tell me about her relationship with Zach. I wasn't sure why she was hiding it when their relationship appeared to be common knowledge.

Lunch was nice, but we didn't stay at the Greyhound long. We'd had to leave Charlie outside and although the weather wasn't as hot as it had been, Charlie was sensitive to the heat and I didn't want to leave him for long. Although the pub didn't allow dogs inside, they did have a water bowl in the pub garden.

Sienna seemed to relax when we were in the pub's restaurant area. She was quiet and withdrawn but that was normal for a child who'd just lost a parent. The death of her mother was more than enough to cope with, and I couldn't stand the idea that the random weirdo following her on the street would make her more upset and reclusive.

Lying awake last night, I'd come to the conclusion that yesterday's incident couldn't be connected to Nicole's death. It was just a horrible coincidence. There was nothing to link the two events. Even so, I didn't want to let Sienna out of my sight for the next few days, just in case.

She did start and look up every time new customers came into the bar. I had to admit I'd scanned the pub myself to make sure there were no suspicious characters lurking in the restaurant.

I ordered a Caesar salad and Sienna had the chicken burger. She only managed to eat half of it but I was pleased to see her eating something.

When we'd finished eating, I paid the bill and then we went to collect Charlie from the pub garden. His tail wagged enthusiastically when he saw us.

The three of us walked back to Yew Tree House. Sienna wasn't talkative, and I didn't push the conversation on the journey back, but I was surprised and pleased when Sienna slipped her arm through mine as we walked past Jason's thatched cottage.

When we got home, Angie was vacuuming, but she switched it off and smiled at us broadly.

"Perfect timing. I was just about to make a cup of tea," she announced.

"Great," I said, leaning down to take the leash off Charlie's collar.

"None for me, thanks," Sienna said, heading towards the stairs. "I'm going to use the computer for a bit."

It wasn't until Angie and I had finished our tea that I remembered the phone call from the health club.

I put down my cup. "Do you know what time Narcissus Health Club closes today?"

Angie picked up my cup along with her own and took them to the sink. "Thinking of pampering yourself?"

"No, they left a message on the answering machine. Apparently, Nicole left some belongings in one of the lockers. I told Sienna I'd pick them up."

"That's kind of you. They don't close until nine p.m. most evenings." Angie sighed. "I found one of Nicole's lists earlier. She'd written down Steve's business trip dates for the next month. It's the little things that catch you off guard."

I agreed. "What time are you going home? I can go to the club now but don't want to leave Sienna alone today."

"I'm in no rush, lovey. I'll stay until you get back."

I thanked Angie and headed upstairs to find Sienna. She was sitting cross-legged on the floor, wearing earphones and didn't hear me knock. When I'd pushed the door open, she jumped and shoved something behind her.

There was something she didn't want me to see.

Of course, I wanted to know what she'd been looking at so intently. From the brief glance I'd had, it looked like she'd been staring at a collection of papers. That wasn't really so suspicious. She was a teenage girl, and they liked to keep secrets. Maybe she kept love letters or a diary. I'd been secretive too at her age, hiding my diary under my mattress.

She pulled one of the earbuds out of her ear and the tinny beat of music continued.

"Sorry to interrupt. I just remembered the phone call from the health club yesterday. I'm going to head there now to pick up your mum's things. You can come with me if you like, or Angie's going to be here, so you won't be alone."

Sienna's hand was still behind her back and she looked up at me guiltily. She wasn't very good at hiding her feelings, not that that was a bad thing.

"I think I'll stay here, thanks. Is Angie definitely going to be here until you get back?"

"Yes, she won't leave you alone, promise."

She bit her lower lip, a serious expression on her face. "Okay. Make sure you lock the door behind you."

"I will." Before I could say anything else, she popped the earbud back in her ear and looked away.

I left her to her music and her secrets. Under any other circumstances I would have found her behaviour amusing and cute. Maybe she had love letters from Zach or maybe she was offloading her grief into her diary.

But Nicole's death made me paranoid and scared for Sienna's safety, and I couldn't help wondering if the young girl's secrets had something to do with her mother's death.

CHAPTER TWENTY-SIX

As soon as I'd left Sienna's room, I dismissed the ridiculous idea she was hiding something related to her mother's death. Sienna had normal secrets just like any other teenage girl. Even so, I decided to give Lizzie a ring later to see if the police had had any luck tracing the man who'd been following Sienna.

It was a ten minute drive to Narcissus health club. The car park was almost full, and I had to park some distance from the entrance. The air was overcast and heavy, and I walked towards the health club, batting away persistent thunder flies. There'd probably be another storm this afternoon.

A man dressed in white shorts and a white polo shirt, carrying a squash racket, held the door open for me at the entrance.

I thanked him and stepped inside the reception area. It smelled faintly of chlorine and I guessed the pool was nearby.

There were a couple of other people waiting at the reception desk, so I took the time to look at my phone and check my emails. I thought Rich would have contacted me by now with some questions. No news was good news, but I couldn't help feeling a little put out that he seemed to be coping so well without me.

After the two women in front of me had been given timetables for the spinning class, I stepped up and leaned my forearms on the desk.

"How can I help?" the receptionist asked.

She was a young woman, who wore her hair neatly tied at the nape of her neck, and her lips were painted with a glossy, red lipstick.

"My name is Abbie Morris. I'm a friend of Nicole Carlson…"

As I said the words, I felt my throat close up. I was still talking in present tense.

"Yes?" the receptionist prompted, clearly not recognising Nicole's name from the news.

I cleared my throat and continued. "You phoned Nicole's house yesterday and left a message on the answer machine. At least, someone from the club did. I'm not sure if it was you… Apparently, she left some of her belongings here."

"Couldn't she come herself?" The receptionist looked at me in a disapproving manner.

I was speechless. The easiest thing would be to explain the situation and tell the receptionist that Nicole had died, but for some stupid reason, I didn't want to tell her. I didn't think I could stand to see the look of shock on the woman's face, knowing that she'd be gossiping and talking about it with friends later. She'd tell them in a thrilled, horrified voice how she'd known the poor, murdered woman from Finchampstead.

"No, she couldn't," I said more calmly than I felt.

"Well, I can't just give her belongings out to anyone, can I? So you'll have to ask Mrs Carlson to come in herself and pick them up."

I saw more people had joined the queue, and the receptionist's eyes flickered to them as though she were dismissing me.

I placed my hands flat on the desk. "Sorry, I wasn't making myself clear. Nicole is dead. Her fifteen-year-old daughter got your message, and I told her I'd come and pick up her mother's belongings."

The look of irritation faded from the woman's face and her mouth hung open. "I'm so sorry. I had no idea…" She paused and I imagined the synapses sparking in her brain.

"Was she the woman who was murdered?" She whispered the words.

Feeling uncomfortable and wishing I could get this over with as soon as possible, I nodded.

"Right. In that case, of course, I can give you her belongings. I'll need you to sign a receipt and provide some form of identification."

I agreed and heard whispering behind me in the queue. I was very glad Sienna hadn't decided to come with me.

"I'll need someone to cover the desk. I won't be a moment." She turned and rushed into the room behind the reception desk marked *staff only*.

It wasn't long before she was joined by one of her colleagues, a slightly taller woman with dark hair, who looked at me speculatively as the receptionist spoke to her in hushed whispers.

The receptionist left her dark-haired co-worker to cover the desk and beckoned me to follow her. She led me through a pair of double doors and along a corridor, and the smell of chlorine got stronger.

On entering the female changing rooms, we were immediately greeted by line upon line of cream-coloured lockers. A low, wooden bench was set in front of them, and it reminded me of the changing rooms we'd had when I was at school.

A woman strolled out from the main changing room, her wet hair hung around her shoulders and she was wrapped in a towel. She murmured hello and opened one of the lockers.

The receptionist reached into her pocket and pulled out what I guessed was a master key. "It's locker forty-five," she said, walking forward with the key raised. "I don't suppose you have Mrs Carlson's key, do you?"

I shook my head. "No, sorry. I'll return it if it turns up."

"You wouldn't believe the number of keys we've lost this year. People are forever *'forgetting'* to hand them back in after they finish in the gym. Technically they're not allowed to take them home, but many people do, especially if they're visiting the gym more than once a week. The manager is thinking of introducing a charge so people have to return the key to get their money back." She shot me a quick glance as she turned the key in the lock. "Sorry, I suppose you couldn't care less about our missing keys after what's happened to your friend."

She was babbling to fill the silence between us because she felt uncomfortable. That was largely my fault. I'd handled the situation badly. I should have explained everything to her as soon as I'd arrived.

"I'm sure Nicole didn't mean to take the key home," I said. "Maybe she just forgot."

"It's not a big deal in the scheme of things." She gave me an apologetic smile. "It could be empty, but some of our regulars have taken to storing their gym stuff for weeks at a time. They take home any kit that needs to be washed but leave their trainers and things here." She opened the locker. "Ah, she *did* leave something then."

She stood back to allow me to inspect the contents of the locker. Why had Nicole left her gym stuff here if they weren't supposed to keep their lockers? My mind started working overtime, wondering if this was some kind of clue to her death. But the contents looked pretty ordinary to me. It was empty, apart from a duck egg blue holdall at the bottom.

For a moment, I just stood there staring at it.

"I'll let you take out the contents," the receptionist prompted when I didn't move.

"Right, okay."

Finally I moved and plucked the bag from the locker and found it to be surprisingly light. I wanted to open it to see what was inside but decided to wait until I got the back to the car. Not that I really expected to find anything more menacing than some spare deodorant or a hairbrush. I looped the white straps over my arm and turned away from the locker, ready to leave and get back to Sienna. I didn't want to make Angie wait any longer than necessary.

A piercing double beep sounded, and the receptionist looked apologetically at me. "Sorry, I need to get this. I won't be long. Why don't you check there's everything you expected in the bag, and I'll get the paperwork for you to sign?"

She yanked her phone out of her pocket, pressed it to her ear and marched out of the changing rooms before I had a chance to reply.

I set the holdall down on the wooden bench and stared at it. Everything I expected? I didn't expect to find anything. How would I know there was something missing or not?

I tugged open the zip and peered inside. There was a L'Oreal moisturiser, a Denman hairbrush, a tube of lip balm and Fenjal body spray. I reached for the body spray and smiled. I'd used it when I was at university and expensive perfumes had been way over my budget.

"You don't want to pay any attention to her," a voice said behind me.

I turned to see the woman with wet hair grinning at me.

"Excuse me?"

"The receptionist. Her name is Rachel, and she's on a warpath at the moment. She's decided to crack down on people keeping personal lockers. Everyone does it. It saves lugging your kit here for every trip to the gym, and as you can see," she pointed to the lines of lockers. "There's hardly a shortage."

"Oh, so it's not unusual for members to leave things in lockers?"

She shook her head. "Not at all. Most of the long-term members do it. Thanks to Rachel's crackdown, I got a snooty voicemail on my phone the other day asking me to collect my belongings and return the key immediately. I ignored it." She winked at me.

She pushed her damp fringe back off her face. "I was very sorry to hear about Nicole. We weren't close friends, but I used to see her at the gym regularly."

"Yes, I still can't quite believe it."

"Do the police know what happened yet?"

I didn't really want to discuss Nicole's death with a woman I barely knew. She was being kind, but I felt protective of Nicole.

I was saved from answering her question by the receptionist marching back into the changing rooms, brandishing a form for me to sign. I filled in the paperwork as quickly as possible, eager to get back to Yew Tree House, but as I was about to leave the changing room, the woman with the wet hair called out.

"Just a minute. There's something else in there."

I turned back and saw she was right. I'd missed it when I'd taken the holdall out. A slip of paper was wedged between the metal join at the base of the locker.

I pulled out the sheet of cream-coloured paper and flipped it over.

There was only one line printed on it.

Keep your mouth shut.

The receptionist who'd read the note over my shoulder let out a gasp, and the woman with wet hair clamped her hand to her mouth, but all I could do was stare down at the note.

Keep your mouth shut.

That was a threat.

At that moment, I was sure that whoever had issued this threat was responsible for my friend's murder.

CHAPTER TWENTY-SEVEN

MY HEAD WAS SPINNING and my mouth was dry as I walked back to the car. I'd stuffed the note into the holdall and practically run away from the changing rooms. I needed space to think and I couldn't do that with those two women crowding round me.

With a trembling hand, I reached into my pocket for the car keys.

It wasn't until I was sitting in the driver seat with the blue holdall on the passenger seat beside me that I realised how stupid I'd been. The note would be covered with my fingerprints. Would the police be able to get any forensic evidence from it now?

My heart rate was just beginning to slow down. I took a deep steadying breath, and dialled the number I had stored in my phone for the Thames Valley police. I asked for the call to be put through to DC Lizzie Camden.

After a brief pause, the call connected and Lizzie answered.

"Abbie, I was going to call you today. I'm afraid we didn't have any luck tracking down the man Sienna saw following her."

"I wasn't calling about that," I said, my voice breathless as I spoke quickly. "I've just been at Narcissus Health Club. They called to say Nicole was still using one of their lockers. I went to pick up her belongings and in the locker there was a note. It said, *'Keep your mouth shut'*."

"Who was it from?"

I leaned back, resting my arm against the door, and saw a group health club staff in my rearview mirror. They'd gathered by the entrance and were watching me sitting in my car.

"It wasn't a *signed* note Lizzie," I said, unable to keep the sarcasm out of my voice. I was trying to sound calm but it wasn't working.

"Did it say anything else?"

"No, that's all it said."

"Did you touch the note?"

"Yes, I took it out to the car with me. I'm sorry, I wasn't thinking. There was a holdall in the locker too, and I put the note in there."

"Where are you now?"

"I'm sitting in my car, in the car park at the health club."

"Okay, here's what we going to do, I'm going to call the health club now and make sure no one else touches the locker until we get there. Who was the member of staff you dealt with?"

"I think her name's Rachel."

"Great." There was a pause, and I imagined Lizzie writing something down. "Now, where's the holdall and the note?"

"My passenger seat."

"Right, well, leave them there for now. I'm organising a team to attend the scene. I should be there in about ten minutes. Just sit tight and we'll be there soon."

I agreed and then hung up. Staring at my phone, I wondered if I should call Steve or Sienna to let them know what was going on, but decided against it. Right now, there wasn't much I could tell them. Maybe after the police got here they could explain what this note meant. Plus, I didn't want to tell Sienna over the phone.

I glanced again at the holdall that looked so innocuous sitting innocently on my passenger seat. The words on the note had been ominous and terrified me. Who was warning Nicole to keep her mouth shut and why? Had she stumbled across something? Something to do with Steve's business perhaps or... My train of thought evaporated when I suddenly remembered seeing the cream paper the note had been typed on before...

It was the same thick, cream, expensive paper Angie had given me from Steve's office.

The skin on the back of my neck prickled. It was Steve's paper... But why would he send his wife a note like that? It didn't make sense. Besides, if Steve had bought that paper, then anyone else could do the same. It didn't necessarily mean the note was from Steve. The more I thought about it, the more I realised Steve sending the note to Nicole was a ridiculous theory.

The wait seemed interminable. I wanted to look at the note again, just in case there was something I'd missed at first glance, but that would be a stupid thing to do. I shouldn't contaminate the evidence any more than I already had.

The minutes ticked past slowly and I leaned forward, cradling my head in my hands. Finally, there was a tap on my window. I turned to see Lizzie. I opened the door, climbed out of the car and leaned back against the bodywork. My legs still felt weak and shaky.

"Is that it?" Lizzie asked, glancing at the holdall.

"Yes, the note is in there."

"Did anyone touch the note apart from you?"

"I don't think so."

"Jeff, it's in here," Lizzie called over my shoulder, and I turned to see a man dressed in a white boiler suit approaching my car.

With gloved hands, he pulled out the holdall and carried it back to an unmarked van.

"What happens now?" I asked Lizzie.

She put her hand on my shoulder. "DS Dawson is going to go and speak to the staff, and we could have a forensic unit here to examine the locker. DI Green and DS Dawson will want to talk to you, but they can do it later. You look shaken up. Why don't you go home and I'll call you in an hour or so?"

"All right. I'm staying with Steve and Sienna at Yew Tree House."

Lizzie's eyes widened. "I see. Okay, we'll come by there later to have a chat."

I hesitated, wondering if I should mention the similarity between the paper in Steve's office and the paper the note had been typed on. But it felt disloyal. And there was no way Steve would have written that note to his wife, would he?

After giving me a brief smile, Lizzie turned and walked towards the health club and her colleagues.

Feeling wiped out, I slid back into the driver's seat and turned the engine on. Now came the part I was dreading. I was going to have to tell Sienna about the note.

* * *

I LET MYSELF INTO YEW TREE HOUSE QUIETLY AND SLIPPED OFF MY shoes. I flinched as I caught sight of my reflection in the hallway mirror. My eyes were wide my cheeks looked bloodless. Running my hands over my face, I turned away from the mirror. The air carried the faint scent of lemon from the cleaning products Angie had been using. She was humming in the kitchen and I padded across the hallway towards her.

She started when she saw me in the doorway. "Abbie, I didn't hear you get back."

I leaned against the doorjamb, trying to find the words to explain what I just found.

She narrowed her eyes and folded her arms. "Something's happened."

I managed to nod and pulled out one of the chairs at the kitchen table to sit down. "Yes, I need to talk to Sienna."

"I'll call her for you. She's still upstairs."

As Angie bustled away, I leaned heavily on the table and tried to organise my thoughts. I hadn't spoken to Steve yet, but I needed to focus on one thing at a time. First, I would explain what had happened to Sienna, then I would call Steve. He might want to come straight home. I knew that's what I would want to do.

Sienna tentatively entered the kitchen. "What's wrong? Angie said something had happened."

I nodded as Angie followed Sienna into the kitchen. They both sat down at the table opposite me.

"I found a note in your mum's locker. I've told the police and they are going to come here in a little while and talk to me about it."

Sienna's face crinkled. "A note?"

"Yes, it wasn't very nice. It said, '*Keep your mouth shut*'."

The last thing I wanted was to put Sienna through any more stress, but the police would be here soon and I couldn't hide this from her forever.

Sienna's face paled. "Keep your mouth shut...? Who was it from?"

I shook my head. "I don't know. And I don't know if your mum ever saw it."

"Oh my God," Sienna whispered, leaning back in her chair.

Angie put a hand on the girl's shoulder. "There, there. Don't upset yourself, sweetheart." The older woman met my gaze, and I saw my fear reflected in her eyes.

"Did somebody leave it in her locker for her to find or do you think Nicole put it there?" Angie asked, looking puzzled.

I frowned. I hadn't even considered that option. I'd assumed someone slid the sheet of paper through the gap around the locker door, but Angie was right, Nicole could have received the note and then put it in the locker herself.

"I really don't know."

"Where is it?" Sienna asked. "Can I see it?"

"I gave it to the police at the health club. They're going to run some tests."

"Will they find out who sent it?" Sienna trembled as she spoke.

"I hope so."

I wanted to reassure her, to try and make her feel safe and less confused, but there was nothing I could say. We sat in silence around the table, each of us baffled by what this could mean.

Even Charlie seemed to sense something was wrong. He left his basket in the utility room and made a circuit around the table, bumping his nose into each of our legs until we leaned down to stroke him.

"I don't feel very well," Sienna said suddenly and she did look very pale.

I got up and after putting my hand against her forehead, I said, "Why don't you go upstairs and have a lie down? The police won't be here for a little while yet."

She felt cool and clammy beneath my touch and I went upstairs with her, worried she might faint.

I sat beside her as she leaned back on her pink pillows and stroked her hair. She needed reassurance and comfort, and I was glad to have an excuse to stay by Sienna's side and put off having to telephone Steve and tell him what had happened.

She grabbed her teddy, a pink and white bear Marilyn had given her on her third birthday. As she hugged it tightly, she looked closer to five than fifteen.

After a few minutes, I told Sienna I needed to go downstairs and call Steve. Confusion and fear were clouding my judgement. Was I delaying telling Steve about the note because the note was typed on the same paper I'd found in his office? Or was it simply because I didn't want to hurt him when he was grieving?

Angie was still in the kitchen when I went downstairs and rather than phone Steve straight away, I went to his office. The paper was on the same shelf as before and I took a sheet, rubbing it between my fingers and turning it over, examining it closely. It *felt* the same. It *looked* the same. But what did that really mean? Only that Steve and whoever had sent the note had the same taste in expensive paper.

I'd been hoping to find a maker's mark or a name on the packaging, but there was nothing but a stack of paper on the shelf.

I slid the sheet back on top of the pile and went to get my phone from my bag.

The call went better than I expected. Steve was cool and calm when I told him, and more concerned with how Sienna was handling this development than anything else.

I told him she was lying down, and he said he would call her later. He made no mention of coming home, and I didn't press him on it.

Shortly after I'd finished with the call, the doorbell rang.

I wiped my sweaty palms on the sides of my jeans, feeling guilty. Logically, I knew I had to be completely honest with the police and that meant telling them Steve owned the same paper, but I didn't want to get him in trouble unnecessarily. He'd already been escorted to the police station for questioning, and I knew that he *couldn't* have killed Nicole. He had an alibi. If I mentioned the paper to the police, wouldn't that just cause more unnecessary upset?

I took a deep breath, ran my hands through my hair and opened the front door.

CHAPTER TWENTY-EIGHT

TWO DETECTIVES STOOD on the doorstep, the same ones who had come to Janet's flat after Sienna had been found. They introduced themselves again, possibly because they didn't recognise me or perhaps it was just procedure.

The man was tall and broad with a stern face that made me feel even more anxious.

"I'm DI Tom Green," he said and turned to his colleague. "This is DS Carly Dawson."

DS Dawson smiled at me as I opened the door wide for them and took a step back. "I'm Abbie Morris," I said. "I found the note in Nicole's locker."

Charlie was at my heels, and I almost stumbled over him when I took another step back. He was a good dog and was used to visitors. He didn't bark or jump up, but DS Dawson edged around him nervously. I leaned down, and asked Charlie to sit, which he did obediently.

"Shall we do this in the kitchen?" I asked and both detectives agreed.

I hadn't intended to call Sienna down from her room. Frankly, I didn't see the need to put her through any more strain, but she'd heard the detectives arrive and stood barefoot at the top of the stairs watching us. Her hair fell in waves past her shoulders. The skinny jeans she wore, emphasised the slimness of her legs and highlighted her fragility. She clutched the bannister as she came down the stairs.

I sensed she wanted to ask the detectives what they'd learned about the note, but she kept quiet, her eyes wide and watching, taking everything in, but not speaking. DS Dawson smiled at her, but Sienna looked away.

Wringing my hands together, I led them into the kitchen with Charlie walking beside me.

Angie was just shrugging on her lightweight rain jacket. She saw the detectives behind me and said, "I can stay if you'd like, lovey."

Her offer touched me, but I said, "No, you get off home. You've had to wait around long enough today. Jock will be wondering where you are."

Her husband didn't want her involved in this situation and was worried about her. Staying even later today, would only make life more difficult for Angie.

She gave me a firm nod and left the kitchen.

I offered to make tea, but the detectives shook their heads. They clearly wanted to get down to business. We all sat down around the kitchen table, and Charlie sat beside Sienna, as though he sensed she needed his support.

"Right, let's start at the beginning, shall we?" DI Green said, fixing his eyes on me.

I began by telling them about the message left on the voicemail service and explained how I'd found the note. As I spoke, I felt their eyes boring into me, weighing me up and judging me.

I told them everything, apart from the fact the same paper used for the note sat in Steve's office. I meant to tell them. I really did, but with Sienna sitting there trembling like a leaf, I didn't want to say anything else to upset her.

I was surprised by the depth of their questioning. They repeated themselves over and over, and I felt like they were trying to trip me up on some of the details. Paranoia gripped me. Did they think I planted the note myself? Though I hadn't felt that way at the time, I was now glad the receptionist and the woman with wet hair had both seen me find the note. At least I had two witnesses.

"So, who actually saw the note first?" DS Dawson asked.

"Um, the lady with the wet hair, I think. Sorry, I never asked for her name."

"Deidre Sadler," DS Dawson said.

"Have you spoken to her?" I asked. "She should be able to tell you what happened."

DS Dawson gave me a tight smile. "We have spoken to her, Abbie."

"Right, did she tell you the same thing? She saw the note at the back of the locker and then I went and picked it up."

I couldn't keep the impatient tone from my voice. They were only doing their jobs, and I was reacting badly because I was keeping something from them and the guilt was eating away at me.

"We have to talk to everybody, Abbie. I know that the questions can seem tedious, but it's routine."

"It's *too* routine if you ask me," I snapped. "You should be out there looking for the person who actually *sent* the note, not questioning the person who found it."

I was losing my cool, and the tension was rubbing off on Sienna. She looked chalk white and hadn't uttered a word since we'd sat down at the table.

DI Green and DS Dawson were unmoved by my outburst. They were probably used to it.

I exhaled a long breath. "I'm sorry. It's just finding that note scared me… Do you have any idea who sent it?"

DS Dawson put her pen back in her jacket pocket. "We're looking into it."

When Sienna spoke up, it was so unexpected we all turned to face her. Her voice trembled. "Do you think the person who sent the note killed my mother?"

DI Green leaned forward, resting his elbows on the table and lowering his head to look Sienna in the eye. "We don't know yet. It's certainly something we are looking into. Is there anything you can tell us about the note?"

"Me?" Sienna looked horrified.

"Can you think of any reason someone might be asking your mum to keep quiet?"

Sienna shook her head rapidly.

"We need to keep an open mind. It might have nothing to do with your mother," DS Dawson said. "The note could be unrelated."

I thought that was very unlikely. Normal, balanced people just didn't leave notes like that. Surely, whoever sent the note had killed Nicole because they didn't think she'd keep quiet. That was the only theory that made sense, but then who wanted her to keep her mouth shut…and keep her mouth shut about *what*?

The questioning continued, but the detectives focused on me rather than Sienna, who was monosyllabic. By the time they'd finished, I felt wrung out and hadn't learned anything new. Was that because the detectives were keeping their cards close to their chests, or did they simply have no idea who'd sent the note? I had to hope they were getting somewhere with the investigation. The idea that Nicole's killer would never be brought to justice was impossible to stomach.

After an hour, their questions finally dried up, and as I led them back to the front door, I realised time was running out. If I wanted to tell them about the paper in Steve's office, I had to do it now. I paused beside the doorway. There was no way I could do this without Sienna finding out.

"Actually, there's one more thing," I said. "It's in here." I pointed to Steve's office and when the detectives followed me inside, I closed the door behind us. "I think it's best if you wait out there, Sienna."

Neither detective spoke as I walked over to the bookshelf. "It's not a big deal," I said. "Sorry for the drama. I just didn't want Sienna to hear this." I pulled a sheet of paper from the pile and held it out to DI Green. "It's the same type of paper as the note."

DI Green ran his fingers over it and tilted his head to one side. "I see."

That was all he said, and it was maddening. What exactly *did* he see?

"I'm sure you can probably buy that paper in a lot of different places." I linked my fingers together to stop myself waving my hands about, something I always did when I was nervous.

"Thank you," he said and slid the piece of paper into a transparent plastic bag he'd taken from his jacket.

We stood there awkwardly for a moment until I realised they weren't going to say anything else. I led them back into the hall.

Sienna was still standing there, looking bewildered. I was sure as soon as we were alone she would have questions for me.

After the detectives left, I slumped on the sofa. "That was exhausting."

"I don't like the way they look at me," Sienna said, causing me to blink in surprise.

"What do you mean?"

She folded her arms over her chest and shivered. "They look at me like they want to see under my skin."

I had to admit they made me feel the same way. "I suppose that's their job. They need to find out who's hiding things from them so they can get to the truth."

Sienna nodded slowly. "I guess. What did you show them in Steve's office?"

I knew this question was coming, but still I cringed. "I wanted to show them some paper." I sighed as Sienna looked at me expectantly. "The paper in Steve's office is the same as the paper used for the note. Of course, that doesn't mean I suspected him of sending the note," I added quickly. "I'm sure lots of people have the same paper."

Sienna shrugged. "Sure, Steve would never have sent something like that."

"No, I agree… Are you happy living here with him?"

Sienna seemed surprised at the question. "Yes."

She'd answered quickly and honestly, without thinking, and I smiled with relief. "I'm glad."

She tilted her head to one side. "You know Steve would never have hurt Mum, don't you?"

I was taken aback but managed to say, "Of course."

"It's just you don't really know him that well, but I do. He would never have hurt her."

"You're right, I don't know him that well, and I'm worried about you. I just want to make things easier for you."

She sat beside me on the sofa and gazed up at me through waves of coppery hair. "I know and I'm glad you're here, Abbie."

"Do you want me to contact your grandmother or Janet? I'm sure they'd come straight here if I asked them."

Sienna shook her head thoughtfully. "No, they'd only worry and there's not much we can tell them, is there?"

I was impressed that she was putting their feelings before her own.

"Okay, well, I'm going to put the lasagne Angie made us in the oven. Do you want anything to drink?"

She shook her head. "I'm fine, thanks."

It took me a little while to figure out the controls on the oven, and as I leaned down to open the oven door, I saw Sienna out of the corner of my eye. She was checking the lock on the front door.

I straightened up to watch her as she made a circuit around the hallway then the sitting room, checking all the windows were shut and locked.

The poor kid. She was terrified of something. Was she scared of the unknown, or did she know more about Nicole's death than she'd been letting on?

CHAPTER TWENTY-NINE

I GRABBED some items from the fridge to make a salad to go with our lasagne and we ate early. Neither of us was very talkative. Steve called shortly before we ate to talk to Sienna. I was surprised he didn't change his plans and come home tonight, after all, he was Sienna's family now. When Sienna told me Steve would be staying in London, I tried to hide my consternation. It wasn't my place to interfere.

To be honest, I was in two minds over whether I wanted Steve to come home. On the one hand, there was strength in numbers, and I couldn't help feeling nervous being alone at Yew Tree House with Sienna. But on the other, my mind kept drifting back to the expensive, cream paper in Steve's office.

I didn't think he sent the note to Nicole. Not really. He had no reason. But still, I couldn't put it out of my head.

I took a mouthful of lasagne, and looked at Sienna, who sat at the kitchen table opposite me. She bowed her head over her plate, pushing the food around, barely eating. Angie was a good cook and the lasagne was very tasty, but neither of us had much of an appetite this evening.

Sienna pushed her plate away and I put my knife and fork together.

"I think I'll just listen to some music in my room this evening," she said.

I tried not to feel slighted. It was understandable for her to want some time alone. "Okay, I'll probably watch some TV and then have an early night." I began to clear the table.

Sienna helped me load the dishwasher and then went upstairs, leaving me alone in the kitchen with my thoughts. She was holding something back. That much was obvious, but I didn't know why.

Once the kitchen was clean, I sat down at the table, wishing I had something to drink. Steve had told me to make myself at home, but I didn't feel comfortable helping myself to his wine. He had a small, temperature-controlled room at the back of the house to store his wines. I remembered Nicole telling me he was a wine aficionado, and I guessed some of the bottles would be very expensive.

I wasn't a heavy drinker, but tonight a drink would really help ease some of the tension.

I crossed the room to the large American-style fridge freezer and opened the freezer section. Propped up on a shelf, nestled between a bag of frozen peas and a tub of Ben and Jerry's, was a bottle of vodka. I grinned. That would do nicely.

I poured a small measure into a glass and topped it up with orange juice. I didn't think I could stomach drinking it neat.

As I sipped my drink, I thought about Janet and Marilyn. They had a right to know about the note I'd found at the health club. They would find out eventually anyway from the police and would be hurt I hadn't told them. But then again, I didn't want an argument tonight, and for some reason, Janet saw me as the enemy. She'd never liked me. Did I really have enough energy to engage with her tonight?

By the time I was on my second vodka, I'd decided to call Janet. Yes, I was tired. And yes, it was in my nature to avoid confrontation, but Janet was Nicole's sister, and she had a right to know. She already believed I was trying to muscle my way into Sienna's life, and if I didn't tell Janet or Marilyn what had happened, it would only confirm Janet's suspicions.

I walked into the sitting room, grabbed my mobile phone and dialled Janet's number before I could change my mind. As expected, the call didn't go well. Rather than being glad I'd called to let her know what had happened, she was furious I hadn't called earlier.

I couldn't win. Pulling the phone away from my ear so I wasn't deafened by Janet shouting down the phone, I sighed and curled up on the sofa. Janet didn't pause for breath for a good five minutes, and when she'd finally finished telling me off, she didn't even say goodbye but simply hung up.

I was past caring. After putting my phone on the coffee table, I stretched out on the sofa and closed my eyes.

I must have drifted off because the next thing I knew there was a hammering at the front door. Waking up with a start, I sat up and pressed a hand against my chest. With my heart in my mouth, I rushed into the hall. Charlie made it to the door before me.

I heard movement upstairs and guessed Sienna had come to see who was at the door. I didn't know what the time was, but it was still light outside. Peering through the small spy hole, I saw a furious looking Janet standing on the doorstep.

My shoulders slumped. I should have guessed. Opening the door, I stood back out of the way as she stormed inside.

"Right, you'd better tell me all about this note from the beginning."

"You told her?" Sienna's voice sounded shrill, and as I shut the front door, I turned to see her standing on the galleried landing. "You asked me whether I wanted you to tell them and I said *no*.

What was the point of you asking me, Abbie, when you were going to do what you wanted anyway?"

Two red spots burned in her cheeks in her otherwise pale face as she glared down at me. Her outburst took me by surprise. It hadn't occurred to me that Sienna didn't want them to find out about the note. I thought she didn't want them to worry.

I opened my mouth to try and explain, but Janet got there first. "Of course, she should have told us. We are your *family*. You're just a child, and it's our job to protect you."

Sienna didn't look at her aunt. She was still glaring furiously at me.

"I didn't tell them to upset you," I said feebly. "I just thought they should know what happened. They want to support you, Sienna."

She scowled, turned on her heel and stalked off to her bedroom.

Great. Now I had Janet *and* Sienna angry with me. I only hoped Marilyn didn't turn up in the next five minutes. I wasn't sure I could deal with three against one.

"You'd better come in," I said to Janet as I walked towards the sitting room.

"How kind of you to invite me into *my sister's* house," Janet said with barely suppressed fury.

I let out a sigh and sat down on the sofa. "I'm sorry I didn't tell you earlier. You're quite right. I should have."

My apology took the wind out of Janet's sails and for a moment she was speechless. She sat down in the armchair opposite me and crossed her legs.

"I don't see what right you have to stay here," she said, finally finding her tongue. "It should be me and Mum looking after Sienna."

I shrugged. "Steve was doing me a favour. The hotel was using up all my savings, so he invited me to stay here."

"How convenient."

"Convenient?" My voice was raised but I couldn't contain my temper. "What are you talking about?"

"This was your plan all along, wasn't it? You think just because you were friends with my sister you can come in here and win Sienna over with your sad face and your pathetic '*I'm only here to help*' act."

I stared at her. She really thought badly of me.

She leaned forward, resting her elbows on her knees, warming to her theme. "Is it about money? Do you think you can replace Nicole, is that it?"

She was nuts. Full on crazy town.

"You're not making any sense, Janet. I'm here because I want to help, and I'm staying at Yew Tree House because Steve invited me. After all, it is *his* house."

She glared at me for a few seconds and then finally stood up. "Your meddling is going to get you into serious trouble."

She shot me one last venomous glare and stalked out of the room.

Dazed, I followed her, only to have the front door slammed in my face when I reached the end of the hallway.

* * *

AFTER JANET LEFT, I WAS SEETHING. PACING AROUND THE SITTING room, I came up with all kinds of intelligent comebacks I should have made, but wasn't that always the way. In hindsight it was easy to win arguments. Charlie watched me in bewilderment as I walked back and forth.

Janet was just upset and lashing out. Her sister had just been murdered and she was hurting. The logical side of me could see her point of view, but I was sick and tired of the way she treated me. Plus, her theory that I was trying to worm my way into Sienna's affections was laughable. My goddaughter wasn't talking to me right now either.

Only ten minutes later, the doorbell rang and I half expected it to be Janet returning for round two. But my anger hadn't affected my judgement. There was a chance Sienna's stalker could be hanging around, so I peered through the spy hole as Charlie banged into my legs and was surprised to see the visitor wasn't Janet.

It was Jason Owens.

I braced my hands against the front door and didn't open it immediately. Why was he here? To see Sienna? He didn't know I was staying at Yew Tree House so he couldn't be here to see me...

I peered through the spy hole again. Everything that had happened since Nicole's death made me suspicious, but he didn't look dangerous or threatening. Not long ago, I'd been contemplating going out for a drink with him. What had changed? Nothing. I was just paranoid.

I took a deep breath, plastered a smile on my face and opened the door.

"Hello, Abbie, sorry to come around unannounced."

He didn't look surprised to see me here.

"Hi, was it me you wanted to see?"

He nodded. "Yes, I did try to call your mobile, but I think I must have the wrong number."

Oh, so he *had* tried to contact me. I smiled. Although he could have left a message for me at the hotel while I was staying there if he'd been really keen.

"Do you want to come in?"

He gave me a charming smile and stepped into the hall.

I fixed us some drinks and then made sure he had my correct mobile number before we settled on the sofa. Sienna hadn't come downstairs, which surprised me. I thought she'd be curious when she heard someone else at the door.

We chatted for a while, and I told him I'd be staying in the UK for another couple of weeks at least.

"That is good news," he said smiling again, showing off his impossibly white teeth. "Is Sienna home?"

"Yes, did you want to talk to her?"

"I don't want to be a bother."

"I'll ask her to come downstairs." I put my drink on the coffee table. "Won't be long."

But no matter how much I cajoled and begged, Sienna refused to come down. She wouldn't even open her bedroom door. After a few minutes, I gave up. What did I know about looking after a teenage girl? Sure, I'd been one, but that was some time ago.

Sheepishly, I went back downstairs and admitted I couldn't coax Sienna out of her room. "It's not you," I said quickly. "She's angry with me for telling Janet something."

Jason's eyes lit up with interest. "What did you tell Janet?"

I'd been about to reply but began to feel uncomfortable sharing such information with Jason. He was Sienna's teacher, nothing more. Maybe he had good intentions, but there was a line between telling people what they needed to know and gossiping. Besides, for all I knew, the police could have wanted to keep the existence of the note secret.

"Oh, nothing important. I just wish I could persuade Sienna I'm on her side."

"I'm sure she knows that really."

I rolled my eyes and leaned back with a huff on the sofa.

"I'm serious. She's angry and confused. It's only natural, and as you're the only one on hand at the moment, you get the brunt of it, unfortunately."

I relaxed against the cushions. "I know you're right, but I can't help feeling I'm not doing enough."

"You're doing a great job with her. Hang in there."

I smiled. He really knew how to say the right things. I was starting to feel better.

When I reached for my drink, he said. "Are you free on Friday? I thought we could go and have that drink I promised you."

"Sounds good," I said and it did.

I'd have to make sure Steve was back and Sienna wasn't on her own, of course, but it would be nice to go out and chat and let off some steam.

"So how did you know I was staying here?" I asked him.

He blinked at me. "Oh, from Jess Richardson. She's in my summer drama class, and she found out from Zach."

"The next generation of the Finchampstead gossip network!"

He grinned. "Teenagers always know more than they let on. Sometimes it surprises me how much they know."

"You're braver than me. I couldn't work with teenagers."

"They're not so bad really. Though, they do sometimes give me sleepless nights. It's hard not to get caught up emotionally. One of the reasons I wanted to talk to Sienna was to encourage her to come back to drama classes — sort of a way to ease her into things before school starts again in September."

That was a good idea. Going back to school was going to be extremely difficult. Everyone would know what had happened to Nicole, and even if the children weren't intentionally cruel, they would be talking about the murder. Sienna would be centre of attention for all the wrong reasons. The drama class could make the transition easier.

"If she's talking to me tomorrow, I'll mention it."

Jason didn't stay long. After he left, I unloaded the dishwasher then set about making two cups of cocoa, intending to take one up to Sienna as a peace offering. I'd only just started heating the milk when the doorbell rang again.

Charlie scurried out of the kitchen, and I glanced at the clock on the microwave. It was nine p.m. — a bit late for a casual caller. I removed the saucepan from the heat and went to see who it was.

When I got to the front door, Charlie was sniffing the base. I heard a noise behind me and turned in time to see Sienna peek around the wall at the end of the galleried landing and then quickly duck out of sight.

I guessed she'd probably done that with Jason Owens as well. A quick look through the spy hole told me our visitor was Toby Walsh. What was he doing here at this time? Surely, he must have known Steve was away on business. To be honest, I'd expected Toby to be with him in London.

A deep frown furrowed his brow and he looked tense. My hand hesitated over the lock. I had an urge to pull back from the door and pretend there was no one home. Biting down on my lip, my fingers closed around the chrome door catch. It was Toby, Steve's business partner. The man who'd save me from a painful conversation with my ex and had always been kind to me.

He hunched his shoulders and kicked a pebble from the doorstep, then suddenly looked up and his piercing eyes appeared to look directly at me. I gasped and took a step back.

"What is it? Who's there?" Sienna called from upstairs.

I wiped my sweaty palms on my jeans and looked up at her. "Nothing to worry about," I said cheerfully. "It's just Toby."

She scowled at me and slunk off to her room. I exhaled and jumped as Toby rang the doorbell again. What was wrong with me? I was letting Angie and her ideas of evil get to me. I looked down into Charlie's expectant eyes.

Shaking my head, I opened the door.

CHAPTER THIRTY

"HI, Toby. Sorry to keep you waiting. I was just in the kitchen tidying up after dinner." It was a white lie. How could I say I'd been standing on the other side of the door debating whether to let him in?

He didn't return my smile. "Abbie, I didn't realise you were here. Is Steve home?"

Without waiting for an answer, he walked into the house.

I closed the door. "No, he's not been home all day. He's in London."

"Christ." Toby ran a hand through his hair. "I've been trying to get hold of him, but he's not answering his phone. You don't mind if I wait here for him, do you?"

I put my hands in my pockets and shrugged. "He's not coming back tonight."

Toby's eyebrows lifted. "Why not?"

"I don't know exactly. He told me he had business to do in London. Didn't he tell you about it? I thought he would have mentioned it. You are his business partner."

"It seems he's forgotten that," Toby muttered, stalking along the hall and then poking his head into Steve's study.

Did he think I was lying? Or suspect that Steve was hiding in his home office?

Why was he acting so strangely this evening? I looked up to see if Sienna was peeking out from behind the wall again, but there was no sign of her. Charlie sat by my feet and gave a low whine. I reached down to pet him.

Toby sighed, shook his head and then leaned against the wall. "So, you're staying here now?"

"For a week or so, yes. Just until I go back to India."

"Right. Do me a favour. If you see Steve, tell him I'd like to speak to him."

"Of course."

His piercing eyes met mine and held my gaze. His eyes had a magnetic quality I hadn't noticed before. I found it impossible to look away or break eye contact.

"All right then," he said eventually. "Sorry to interrupt your evening."

"It's fine. I hope you manage to track him down," I said as he walked towards the front door. "Is there a problem between you and Steve? Anything I could help with?"

"I think it's gone beyond that," he said. "I'll probably see you around before you go back, but if not, have a good trip."

"Thanks," I said and watched as he left the house, striding across the gravel driveway to his car.

When I shut the door, I leaned back against it, wondering what was going on between him and Steve, and as I did so, I happened to glance up and saw Sienna's pale, haunted face, followed by a flash of her coppery hair before she disappeared again.

So she *had* been watching and listening.

* * *

Sienna didn't come out of her room again that night. I'd intended to go to bed early, but after my three visitors, I couldn't settle.

The storm began just before midnight. I had the light on, but the lightning was so bright I saw the flash in the kitchen. A few seconds later, a crack of thunder made me jump. Charlie whimpered. I petted him and muttered reassuring words.

Normally, storms didn't bother me. I'd been through so many of them, working in India, but thanks to Angie's fanciful descriptions of each evil lurking around Yew Tree House, I was on edge, and the storm wasn't helping.

I decided to stay up until the storm retreated to take care of Charlie, who was trembling and trying to get under the table.

After another flash of lightning, I began to count. I didn't get far. Four seconds later, I heard an even louder clap of thunder. I could feel Charlie shaking as he pressed against my legs. I grabbed his basket from the utility room and shoved it beneath the table. If that was where he felt safe, at least he could be comfortable.

I walked through to the sitting room, pulled the curtains back and looked out at the front driveway.

The yew tree was swaying in the wind, and rain was falling in sheets. A flash of lightning illuminated the tree. Its branches swung dramatically, and it looked like an angry giant, towering over the house. Yew trees were associated with graveyards, superstition and death. Tonight, it was easy to see where it gained that creepy reputation. I shut the curtains and shivered.

Back in the kitchen, I checked on Charlie. He looked a little calmer now, and I wondered if that meant the storm was moving further away. Animals were more sensitive to those sorts of things.

"It's nearly over," I said, scratching behind his ears as I crouched beside the table.

I pulled out a chair and sat down, thinking about Toby's visit earlier. When he'd said Steve hadn't been answering his phone, it worried me. The man had just lost his wife and been dragged off to the police station for questioning. He was under a lot of stress and people could crack under that kind of pressure.

Unable to stop thinking he'd done something stupid, I called and was surprised when he answered.

I passed on Toby's message, and Steve shrugged it off, saying he'd get back to him tomorrow. I sensed he was trying to deflect my concerns. For whatever reason, Steve didn't want to confide in me.

It was more than likely, he'd had a disagreement with Toby over some business problem. Stress levels were running high at the moment, so it wasn't surprising. They spent a lot of time together and that could lead to frayed nerves.

A faint rumble of thunder told me the storm was retreating fast.

I ducked my head under the table. "See, it's nearly gone, Charlie. Nothing to worry about."

I swear I saw relief in his chocolate eyes, and he then rested his head on his paws.

Stretching and smothering a yawn, I walked back into the sitting room and looked at the family photographs on the wall above the fireplace. There was one of Steve and Nicole on their wedding day.

Nicole had worn a long, cream, bias-cut dress. I'd forgotten how beautiful she'd looked. Carefree and happy, she smiled at the photographer.

I rubbed my arms, feeling a chill. "Who sent you that note?" I whispered, staring at the photo. "Who was threatening you?"

I waited for some kind of divine inspiration, but of course, nothing happened.

With a sigh, I turned away from the photos and went to check on Charlie one last time before going to bed.

* * *

THE FOLLOWING MORNING, I WOKE LATE. I WAS MAKING SCRAMBLED eggs for breakfast when the doorbell rang. I took the frying pan off the hob and walked to the front door with Charlie trotting at my heels. I actually hoped it was a cold caller or someone selling something. *Anything but another confrontation with Janet, please.* I couldn't handle her spiky personality first thing in the morning.

But when I opened the door, I saw Zach. He pushed his dark fringe out of his eyes.

He looked different. I couldn't put my finger on it at first and then I realised he was smiling.

"Morning, Abbie."

"Morning, Zach. Do you want to come in? I think Sienna's awake. I heard her moving around upstairs."

"Yes." He held up his mobile as he stepped inside. "She knows I'm coming around. She answered my text."

I called up the stairs to Sienna to let her know her friend had arrived and then turned back to Zach. "Do you want some breakfast? Nothing fancy. I'm just making scrambled eggs on toast."

"No, thanks. I'm too excited to eat."

"Excited?"

He pulled some keys from his pocket. "I've just passed my driving test. I came straight here from the test centre."

"Congratulations. They must have started the test early."

"Eight a.m. I was the first one."

Still smiling, he followed me through to the kitchen and sat down at the table as I carried on cooking. I'd assumed Zach was the same age as Sienna and in the same year at school, but if he'd just passed his driving test, he had to be seventeen at least.

"So, you're in the year above Sienna at school?" I asked.

He nodded. "I'm in the sixth form. Studying for my A-levels."

"Coffee?" I offered, putting a cup beneath the chrome nozzle on the coffee machine.

"Thanks."

By the time Sienna came downstairs, I'd made the eggs and toast. She wasn't keen, but I persuaded her to sit down and have some breakfast before she went out with Zach for a drive.

She didn't seem as angry with me this morning, and I was grateful. I gave her just a small portion of scrambled eggs and one slice of toast but was pleased when she ate it all.

They kept me company while I ate. Zach leaned down to pet Charlie as they chatted about their plans for the day.

"Did you tell Zach about what happened the other day?" I asked, looking meaningfully at Sienna. I didn't want either of them to live in fear, but I did want them to be on their guard.

Sienna pushed her plate away. "Yes, he knows. I'll be fine. Zach will be with me all the time, right?"

She glanced at Zach, who bobbed his head obediently.

"Absolutely," he said and drained the last of his coffee.

"Good. You can call me if you need anything. I'll probably be here most of the day, although I'll take Charlie out for a walk this morning."

I felt nervous letting Sienna out of my sight, but I couldn't keep her wrapped in cotton wool at home. It wasn't fair.

As they prepared to leave, I started to feel worse. What if something happened? Was Zach really mature enough to handle it?

When he reached the door, Zach looked back and noticed how anxious I looked. "We won't go far, Abbie. We'll drive around the village and then go to the park and enjoy the sunshine."

I tried to relax and smile. "Have a nice time. I'll see you later."

Standing by the sitting room window, I watched them drive away. Charlie did too. He leaned his paws on the windowsill and pressed his nose against the window and gave a low whine.

"I don't think you're supposed to be doing that, Charlie. Come on," I said, and tapped my thigh to encourage him to follow me.

I measured out his breakfast and then set about clearing up the kitchen. Angie would be here this afternoon, and I was looking forward to seeing her. I had more questions. Maybe Angie wouldn't be able to give me the answers I needed, but I had to ask.

Once the kitchen was clean, I went to fetch Charlie's leash. He jumped up, as excitable as a puppy.

Charlie was a big dog who needed to be exercised regularly, and I decided to kill two birds with one stone and take him to the park. Dogs weren't allowed onto the pristine grass or near the playground, but walking there and back should give him more than enough exercise for the morning. I was hoping to see Zach and Sienna there. I wasn't checking up on them exactly... more just reassuring myself they were safe.

Worrying about them wasn't unreasonable, and if luck was on my side, I'd get there, spot them in the distance before returning home. They'd never know I'd been keeping tabs on them.

A twinge of guilt pricked my conscience, but I ignored it. So what if Sienna got angry with me for following them. I could deal with that. What I couldn't deal with was Sienna getting into trouble while I just sat at Yew Tree House, twiddling my thumbs.

It was a gorgeous day. The thunderstorm last night had cleared the air, and the sky was a cloudless blue. It wasn't yet noon, but it was already warm. Charlie and I strolled slowly along Fleet Hill, taking care to stick to the grass verge whenever we heard traffic.

The sunlight filtered through the tree canopy above us, and listening to the birds singing, with Charlie walking happily by my side, it was hard to remember the fear I'd felt last night. I'd let my imagination get the better of me. That plus Angie's influence had made me suspicious and scared of my own shadow. Today, with the warm sun on my back, my confidence had returned.

Soon, the police would arrest whoever was responsible for Nicole's murder and we could get on with our lives without living in fear and constantly looking over our shoulders.

I found the situation hard enough to deal with, and it had to be so much worse for Sienna. At fifteen years old, she now had to cope with the aftermath of her mother's death. There was never a good time to lose your mother, but fifteen was especially difficult.

Her anchor, her biggest supporter, the one person who'd shown her unconditional love had been ripped away, and now she had to try and find her own place in the world. She had Steve, of course, but even I could see he was a workaholic. Would he be present enough to give Sienna the stability she needed?

A black Mercedes roared towards us, going way too fast on the winding, undulating hill.

Charlie and I only just managed to scramble onto the grass verge in time to get out of the way as the car zoomed past. I let out a string of expletives and Charlie looked up at me. His surprised expression made me laugh. Before now, I hadn't believed it was possible for a dog to look surprised.

He cocked his head to one side, watching me curiously.

"Sorry about that, boy," I said taking a deep breath and petting him. "Some drivers shouldn't be allowed on the roads."

He dipped his head in such a way it almost looked like a nod of agreement.

We'd just started walking again, when my mobile rang. It was Sienna.

"Hi, I'm just taking Charlie for a walk. Is everything okay?"

"No." She was whispering.

I froze. "What is it? What's wrong?"

"It's that man. The one that was following me. He's here."

I stopped breathing. "Where are you? I'll get there as soon as I can. Call the police!"

Then Sienna said the words that made my blood run cold. "Abbie, I'm scared."

CHAPTER THIRTY-ONE

"It's going to be okay, Sienna. Just tell me where you are." ·

"At the park. We're sitting on the grass, and the man is on a bench near the children's playground. He's watching us."

The fact she said *us* made me feel marginally better. That meant Zach was still with her.

"Okay. I'll be there in five minutes. Stay with Zach."

I hung up and started running. Poor Charlie wasn't used to moving that fast. But he wasn't as unfit as me. By the time I passed the petrol station and the village hall, I was panting, and when we reached the entrance to the park, a stitch pinched my side and I could barely draw a breath.

I leaned heavily on the rough wooden gate at the park entrance, trying to get my breath back and locate Sienna. It wasn't busy and it didn't take me too long to spot Sienna and Zach sitting beneath an oak tree. Pressing a hand to my chest, I breathed a sigh of relief. They were both there. They were both okay.

With a shaky hand, I pulled open the gate and looked around for the man who'd been stalking Sienna. As it was the school holidays, the playground was busy. Small children squealed and kicked their legs on the swings, and there were kids queuing up for the slide.

In front of the play area, there were three benches. Two of them were occupied. An elderly couple sat on one, and on the other a young mum, cradling an infant was calling out instructions to her little boy who was scaling the climbing frame.

Beside her, sat a man wearing a brown jacket.

Although I was still some distance away, I was surprised how old he looked. Sienna had described him as middle-aged, but I'd guess she'd viewed him through the filter of youth where anyone older than thirty was middle-aged. I judged the man to be around sixty. He had light sandy hair, turning to grey, and he wasn't wearing the light trousers he'd worn when he was following Sienna the last time. Today he wore jeans.

It had to be him.

Finally having some air in my lungs, I marched forward, tugging on Charlie's lead. My tunnel vision focused on the man on the bench. I barely noticed a dark-haired woman, pushing a double buggy, shoot me a dirty look.

"You're not supposed to bring dogs into the park," she said sharply.

I ignored her and kept striding forward.

When I was about twenty feet away, he spotted me. He'd been holding a newspaper. I supposed that was some kind of ruse to make it look as though he was simply enjoying the sunshine while catching up on the daily news. Or maybe he'd brought it with him so he could hide behind it as he spied on Sienna? I gritted my teeth.

He folded the paper and stood up, his watchful gaze now on me. As I got closer, he tucked the paper under his arm and walked quickly towards the other exit.

"Wait a minute. I want a word with you." I was fuming and didn't stop to think this man could be dangerous. We were in the local park. It all seemed so safe and ordinary.

He didn't slow down, but he did look over his shoulder, and I realised he looked vaguely familiar. He wasn't wearing a plain brown jacket... It was *tweed*.

"If you don't stop walking right this minute, I'm going to call the police."

That worked. He hesitated and then slowly turned around to face me.

If I hadn't been so breathless, I might have gasped.

I *did* recognise him. I hadn't seen him in over fifteen years, but he hadn't changed much, at all. It was Professor Eric Ross.

He smiled politely and rubbed the side of his nose. "Can I help you?"

I was so confused. First off, was he really going to pretend he hadn't been watching and stalking Sienna? And why was Professor Eric Ross here anyway?

As the pieces of the puzzle began to fit into place in my mind, I groaned.

Professor Ross cleared his throat. "If there's nothing I can do to help you, I'll just be on my way."

"Wait." I took a deep breath.

A one-night stand? No wonder Nicole hadn't wanted to tell me who Sienna's father was. It wasn't that she didn't know his name. It was because he was our biochemistry tutor.

He blinked, and I wondered if he recognised me.

"I'm Abbie Morris, Professor Ross. You were my biochemistry lecturer at Southampton."

A pink flush tinged his cheeks. "Oh, I thought you looked familiar. Nice to see you. How have you been?"

I shook my head slowly. We were way past the small talk stage. "You've been following Sienna."

He blinked again and then looked over my shoulder. "Sienna."

I turned to see Zach and Sienna behind me. Sienna was clutching Zack's hand.

Zach stood tall and put a hand on my shoulder. I have to admit, his show of solidarity touched me.

I turned my back on the Professor and handed Charlie's leash to Zach. "Could you please take Sienna and Charlie home? I'll be back soon."

Sienna's face was pale and her eyes were wide. "I don't think we should leave you alone with him, Abbie."

"It's fine. No one is in any danger. I'll sort everything out and explain when I get back."

She tucked her hair behind her ears, shot a wary glance at Professor Ross and then squeezed my hand. "Are you sure?"

"Yes, I won't be long."

Zach put an arm around Sienna's shoulders as they walked away.

I turned back to the Professor. "What have you got to say for yourself?"

His face took on a sulky expression. "Nothing. I was merely spending the morning in the park, reading my paper. I don't have anything to say to you."

"Well, I have plenty to say to you. So you can listen." I pointed at the bench he'd recently vacated. "Let's sit down."

With a sigh, he did as I asked.

When we were sitting down, I turned to him and said, "You've been following Sienna, and I have a pretty good idea why."

He stared down at his lap miserably. "Nicole promised me she would never tell anyone. I should have guessed she'd tell you. The two of you were always so close."

Although he didn't mean it, it was a barbed comment. I couldn't help wondering why Nicole *hadn't* told me. We were close, and if she'd confided in me, I would never have told anyone her secret. But she hadn't trusted me.

"Why have you been following Sienna? You could have reached out to her, instead of scaring the life out of the poor girl."

Professor Ross delved into his pocket and pulled out a piece of paper. "Nicole sent me a letter. She said Sienna had been asking about her father. She wanted to know if I'd like to meet her."

"That must have been quite a shock. When did she tell you that you were Sienna's father?"

"Just after she found out she was pregnant. I gave her some money, but I didn't want another child. I was married with children of my own. I still am." He lifted his head and stared at me intently. "I couldn't hurt them."

"So you gave Nicole some money and left her to bring up Sienna alone?"

"It was what she wanted," he said defensively. "She knew I didn't want a child with her."

There were so many ways I could reply. Most of them included swear words. I decided to take the high ground.

"So I have to ask you again, why are you acting like a creepy stalker? If you wanted to meet her, why didn't you get in touch?"

"You make it sound so easy."

"Isn't it?"

He shook his head. "Nicole's letter made me wonder how she'd turned out. I just wanted to see her, I suppose."

"Did you reply to Nicole's letter?"

"I intended to. But I had a lot to consider. My wife... My children."

He didn't see the irony in that statement.

"Did you hear Nicole was killed?"

He closed his eyes and nodded.

My heart was thudding against my ribs. All I could think about was the note left in Nicole's locker at the health club — *keep your mouth shut.*

"I think the police are going to be very interested to hear about your recent contact with Nicole. It's a good motive for murder, isn't it? Perhaps you were determined to keep the fact you're Sienna's father a secret whatever the cost."

His eyes widened as he turned to me. "Don't be ridiculous. Nicole was very mindful of my privacy. She understood."

"Did you see her before she died?"

He clasped his hands together and shook his head. "No, I wish I had. I needed time to think. After I'd heard what happened to Nicole, I just had to see Sienna." He lifted his head to glance at me. "I suppose I wanted to see if she needed anything from me."

"Why didn't you talk to her?"

He gave a humourless laugh. "I was building up the courage."

Disdain must have shown on my face because he pursed his lips together and slapped his hands on his legs before saying, "I don't think you realise what I'm risking here. I could lose my job, my family, my reputation... Everything."

I folded my arms over my chest, leaned back on the wooden bench and tried to hold my tongue. Giving him a verbal dressing down wasn't going to help anyone. Though, it might make me feel better.

Everything he said focused on how *he* felt, how this situation affected *him*.

"However difficult this is for you, Professor, I think things are far worse for Sienna."

He gave a little remorseful nod and sniffed. "Look, I think I'll leave things for now and wait until things are settled before making any decisions. There's no point upsetting Sienna any more than necessary, is there?"

Was this his way of asking me to keep my mouth shut? No chance. Sienna had a right to know, and right now, I didn't care about this man's reputation at all. He hadn't considered his reputation when he'd taken advantage of his position with Nicole.

"When I go back, I'll tell Sienna what I know."

He pushed himself around on the bench to face me. "You can't do that."

"I have to."

"If you tell her, she'll only be more upset. How could you? You were Nicole's friend. Why would you make things even harder for her daughter after everything she's been through?"

"So you think it's better for Sienna to live in fear because a strange man's been following her?"

His eyes narrowed. "Of course not. You could make up some excuse, say it was all a misunderstanding."

"You mean lie to her."

He rubbed his hand over his face and gave an exasperated sigh. "You'd be doing her a kindness."

More like I'd be doing *him* a kindness. I didn't bother to answer.

"Well, at least assure me you won't tell the police about my relationship with Nicole..." He trailed off and looked into the distance.

I followed his line of sight and saw two plain-clothed police officers walking towards us. I recognised Lizzie, but even if I hadn't, the detectives would have been easy to spot. On this glorious warm day, they wore suits and matching serious expressions.

"Well, thank you very much," he spat sarcastically. "This will ruin me. I hope you're satisfied."

It wasn't me who'd called the police but I didn't bother to tell him that. Zach or Sienna must've called Lizzie.

When the detectives stopped in front of the bench, Lizzie dismissed me with a nod. "Thanks, Abbie. We'll take it from here."

I stood up, trying to ignore the hostility in Professor Ross's glare. If looks could kill…

I walked away, heading back to Yew Tree House. I had to talk to Sienna. Whatever Professor Ross said, she had a right to know the truth about the man who'd been following her.

CHAPTER THIRTY-TWO

ON THE WALK back to Yew Tree House, I called Steve. I was going to have to explain the situation to Sienna and tell her Eric Ross was her father, and I didn't want to do that without Steve's input. He was shocked when I told him what had happened. Nicole had fed him the same story she told me – Sienna was the result of a one-night stand she'd had at university and she'd never known Sienna's father's name.

I clamped the phone to my ear as crows cawed in the trees above me. "If you'd prefer to be the one to tell her, it can wait until you get home."

He sighed heavily. "I'll be home tonight, but I don't think she's going to wait that long for answers. You know Sienna…"

"And you're happy for me to tell her everything?"

"I think it's for the best. Even before Nicole's death, Sienna had been moody and acting up. She'd run off twice. I should have guessed there was more to it, rather than dismissing it as teenage mood swings. I should have been more understanding."

"I'll speak to her and then maybe you can have a chat when you get home."

"I should be home by nine. I wish I didn't have to be here, but things are crazy at work at the moment."

"Anything I can help with?"

"You're doing enough, Abbie. I appreciate the time you're spending with Sienna. I love the kid, but I'm not great at dealing with teenagers. I always seem to say the wrong thing."

"I'm not sure I'm much better. Sienna wasn't talking to me last night because I'd told her aunt something she didn't want her to know. Which reminds me… Should I contact Marilyn and Janet?"

Steve gave another sigh, and I imagined him putting his head in his hands. "I suppose they should be told. Although, I imagine Marilyn will have kittens when she finds out."

I was almost at Yew Tree House so I told Steve I'd contact Janet and Marilyn and would see him later.

When I let myself back into the house, Zach and Sienna rushed into the hall to meet me. I kicked off my shoes and leaned down to pet Charlie.

"I was so worried," Sienna said. "What happened?"

"We have a lot to talk about," I said. "Let's go into the kitchen and have a cup of tea."

I straightened up and followed Zach and Sienna into the kitchen.

"I'll make the tea," Zach said, lifting the kettle and carrying it over to the sink.

I sat down at the kitchen table. Charlie settled by my feet, and Sienna sat opposite me.

"The man's name is Eric Ross," I said.

Sienna twisted a lock of hair around her finger and glanced at Zach. "I don't know who that is. Do you know him?"

"He was your mum's biochemistry lecturer."

Sienna looked even more confused.

Just tell her.

I was making it worse by stretching it out like this. It was hard, though. I wanted to deliver the news in a way that wouldn't cause any pain.

"He's your father, Sienna."

Sienna's jaw dropped open, and Zach dropped a teaspoon on the kitchen counter.

"Are you sure? So why was he following me?"

Because he is a coward too worried about his own career to risk contacting you like a normal person.

Of course, I didn't actually say what I was thinking. Instead, I said, "He has another family and he's worried about how they might react."

Sienna's eyes widened. "Do you mean I've got brothers and sisters?"

"Yes, I suppose so. I don't know anything about his other children."

"So why didn't Mum tell me this?"

"According to Eric Ross, your mother sent him a letter, telling him you wanted to know your biological father."

"She didn't tell me she'd sent a letter."

Nicole would have done anything in her power to protect Sienna from getting hurt. If Professor Ross refused to meet Sienna, Nicole would have wanted to protect her daughter from the pain of rejection.

"Maybe she was waiting to get things set up before telling you," Zach said as the kettle came to a boil.

"She told me she didn't know my father's name. She said it was a one night fling… She *lied* to me."

"She told everybody that story," I said. "I think she was trying to protect you."

Sienna shook her head. "She lied. Did she tell *you* the truth? How do I know you're not lying now?"

"What would I gain from lying to you? I know this is a shock but you don't have to do anything now."

Sienna stared down at the table and a large tear rolled down her cheek.

It was hard to watch. Her emotions were in turmoil. She was angry with her mother for keeping secrets, but at the same time, she was feeling guilty for being angry.

I reached out and placed a hand over hers. "It's a lot to take in. If you're interested, we could look him up on the Internet and find out a bit about him, or if you prefer, we won't mention it again until you're ready."

She was quiet for a long time before finally raising her head. "Okay, let's look him up."

All three of us took our tea upstairs to Sienna's bedroom. She sat cross-legged on the bed and opened her laptop. I perched on the end of the bed, and Zach stood behind us.

Sienna typed 'Professor Eric Ross' into a search engine and then clicked on the link for images. The screen filled with images of four different men. I guessed Eric Ross wasn't an unusual name among professors.

"That's him," Zach said, leaning forward to point him out.

He was right. The photo must have been taken a few years ago. The professor's hair was thicker and he didn't have quite so many lines.

What had Nicole seen in him? Had there been a relationship between them, or was it a one time thing? I tried to remember if Nicole had been acting strangely, or been more secretive than usual during our last term at university. But I came up blank.

Either their relationship had been over very quickly, or I was a terrible person, who didn't pay enough attention to my friends.

Sienna clicked on the picture and then the link below it, which redirected us to his research page. We weren't really interested in his research grants, so I suggested Sienna look him up on Facebook or LinkedIn.

There were even more Eric Ross's on Facebook, and it took us some time to scroll through the list to find the profile we were looking for.

Sienna's fingers were shaking above the keyboard. "That's him, right?"

She turned to me, her eyebrows raised.

I nodded, surprised he had a Facebook profile, but then I supposed almost everyone did these days.

She clicked on his profile and muttered, "This feels really weird."

"There, it lists his family: Charlotte Ross and Malcolm Ross are his children. They're your half brother and sister," Zach said.

Sienna's eyes widened and she pushed back from the laptop. "Do you think they know about me?"

"I don't think they do," I said. "Remember, you don't have to do this now if it's too overwhelming."

I wasn't going to push Sienna into anything but I had to admit I was curious to see if there was a family resemblance.

For a while, Sienna did nothing but stare at the screen. I took a sip of my tea. The man whose profile we were viewing looked very ordinary. He certainly didn't appear to be a killer. But appearances could be deceptive. He hadn't wanted the truth to come out about Sienna's paternity. Just how far was he willing to go to protect his secret?

There was a knock on Sienna's bedroom door and all three of us jumped. Hot tea splashed on the leg of my jeans.

My heart was in my throat as I turned round, but I let out a sigh of relief when I saw Angie in the doorway.

Sienna gave a nervous giggle. "I forgot you were here, Angie."

"I wondered where everyone was, then I heard your voices. What are you all doing up here?"

As much as I liked Angie, this was Sienna's personal life, and so I didn't volunteer any information. But Sienna was happy to tell Angie what had just happened.

The older woman pressed her hand against her chest and blinked in surprise. "Well, that's a turn up for the books," she said when Sienna had finished telling the story. "What a silly man following you about like that, and you said he was a *professor.*"

I smiled. Angie made a very good point.

"I know," Sienna said. "He really scared me, especially after everything with Mum."

"Are you going to keep in touch?" Angie asked.

Sienna bit her lip. "I don't know yet. I haven't decided."

"Is that him?" Angie asked, squinting at the screen and leaning forward.

Sienna angled the screen so she could see better. "Yes."

Angie clicked her fingers. "It's all falling into place now. I wondered what he was doing sniffing around here."

"He's been hanging around the house?" I asked, surprised that he would have gone that far.

"He came to see Nicole a couple of weeks ago."

My grip tightened around my cup. "He came to see Nicole? Are you sure?"

She nodded confidently. "Yes, he'd just arrived as I was leaving for the day."

I was starting to get a very bad feeling about this. I'd asked Professor Ross specifically if he'd seen Nicole before she died, and he'd said no.

He said he hadn't spoken to Nicole since receiving her letter, but that wasn't true.

So why had he lied?

CHAPTER THIRTY-THREE

I CONTACTED DC Lizzie Camden straight away to let her know that Eric Ross had visited Nicole shortly before she'd died. If he'd lied to me, I wasn't sure he'd be completely honest with the police.

After Lizzie had assured me, they would get to the bottom of Eric Ross's lies, I decided to phone Janet and Marilyn.

Sitting at the kitchen table with a cup of coffee, I set my mobile phone down beside my mug and stared at it, trying to psych myself up. There was no point putting it off.

Sienna was in her bedroom, and Angie was vacuuming upstairs somewhere, I could hear the low drone of the vacuum above me.

I sipped my coffee and called Marilyn first, thinking that would be easier, but before I got to the crux of the conversation, I heard Janet in the background, loudly insisting her mother hand over the phone.

"What's happened now?" she snapped.

I rubbed my forehead, trying to ward off the tension headache I always seemed to get when talking to Nicole's sister. "As I was just explaining to your mother, we've found out who's been following Sienna. It's a man called Eric Ross."

"And you've reported him to the police? Do they think he was involved in Nicole's murder?"

"The police came to the park and they've been talking to him."

"The park? What's the park got to do with it?"

I closed my eyes. If she would just let me get a word in edgeways, I might be able to explain.

"It's a long story, but Sienna was at the park with Zach, and they spotted the man who'd been following her. She called me, and I got there as quickly as I could...."

"Why didn't you call me?"

"I *am* calling you, Janet."

"*Actually*, you were calling my mother. When did this happen?"

"Not long ago. I..."

"You should have called me *immediately*. You know Mum is under a great deal of stress."

"Look, Janet, I need you to be quiet and just listen for a minute. There's something I've got to tell you."

"Well, go on. I'm not stopping you."

"I recognised the man at the park. He's a biochemistry lecturer, who taught me and Nicole when we were at university."

"So he knew Nicole?"

I hesitated. "He's Sienna's father, Janet."

"Christ. Are you sure?"

"Yes, he admitted it to me, and Nicole had sent him a letter shortly before she died, telling him Sienna was interested in meeting her biological father."

There was silence on the other end of the phone. For once, Janet was speechless.

"I know this must be a shock."

"You're not kidding. Look, I'm with Mum now, but I can drop her off and be with you in ten minutes."

"That's really not necessary…"

Janet grunted. "I think it is."

I opened my mouth to try to persuade her not to come but she'd hung up.

As good as her word, Janet was at Yew Tree House within ten minutes. I opened the door and she pushed past me.

"Where's Sienna?"

"Upstairs. She is feeling a bit fragile. Why don't you come through to the kitchen and I'll make a cup of tea?"

"*You* can make some tea if you like. *I'm* going to talk to my niece."

She kicked off her heels and then marched upstairs. I wondered if I should follow but decided to give them some privacy. Janet already felt I was sticking my nose where it didn't belong.

I'd had too much tea and coffee and didn't need any more caffeine. Although I'd had a late breakfast, it was now way past lunchtime, and I was feeling hungry. After examining the contents of the fridge, I decided to fix some sandwiches for lunch.

Sienna should eat something and maybe sharing a meal with her aunt could ease Janet's temper. I needed to go grocery shopping at some point, but there was sliced turkey, tomatoes and a cucumber in the fridge. That would do for lunch.

As I buttered the bread, I heard the vacuum stop. I'd finished the sandwiches and was arranging them on a large plate when I heard Janet yelling. I rolled my eyes. So much for treating Sienna with kid gloves.

Their voices were raised but muffled, and I couldn't work out what they were saying. It was just as well. I shouldn't be eavesdropping.

Angie entered the kitchen, with a tin of old-fashioned, beeswax polish under her arm and a yellow duster clutched in her hand.

"I've made some sandwiches if you'd like some," I said and put the platter down on the table together with some smaller plates.

"Thanks, lovey. But I've already had lunch."

"Do you think it's safe to go up there and offer them some lunch?" I asked, raising my eyes to the ceiling.

Angie pulled a face. "I wouldn't. They're going at it hammer and tongs up there."

I thought Angie was probably right so I sat down at the kitchen table and helped myself to a sandwich.

I'd just taken a bite when Sienna stormed into the kitchen. "She just won't listen."

Before I could agree, Janet followed Sienna into the kitchen. "I've decided I'd better stay here. Sienna needs a *responsible* adult around, and if Steve's away…"

I shook my head quickly. "You don't have to do that. Steve is back tonight."

Janet's eyes narrowed. "Oh?"

I let out a sigh of relief. Crisis averted. Thank goodness. I didn't think I could stand a night under the same roof as Janet. "I've made some sandwiches. You're welcome to join me."

Janet and Sienna both sat down at the table and helped themselves to a sandwich, while watching each other warily. Zach edged into the room. I guessed he'd been laying low and I couldn't blame him.

We'd just polished off the last of the sandwiches when the doorbell rang. I had a feeling it wasn't going to be good news. When nobody else moved, I pushed my plate away and went to answer the door.

I took a quick peep through the spy hole and saw Toby Walsh standing on the doorstep, looking even more pissed off than the last time he'd visited.

Taking a deep breath, I opened the door and smiled. "Toby, nice to see you. Is everything okay?"

"No, it's not." He walked inside without an invitation, but at least he didn't barge me out of the way like Janet had done.

"What's wrong?" I asked, keeping my tone light. I didn't really want a rundown of his business problems right now. I had more important things on my mind, but it seemed only polite to ask.

"I can't get hold of our IT guy, and Steve still isn't replying to my messages. Is he here?"

"No, but he's back home tonight, I think."

Toby's face was flushed. He raked his fingers through his hair before letting out an exasperated sigh. "It's doing my head in. I just want to know where I stand. I've been locked out of the accounts and my password doesn't work."

"Computer problems are such a pain," I commiserated.

He looked at me as though I were stupid. "I don't think it's the computer that's at fault."

"What are you doing here, Toby?" Janet asked rudely as she walked up behind me.

"I've come to see Steve."

"Well, he's not here."

Toby narrowed his eyes. "I gathered that, thank you."

"Why are you still hanging around then?"

Shocked, I looked at Janet. What did she have against Toby? Did she like anyone? Or was she this rude to everyone?

"I'm about to leave," Toby said coldly. "But first I just need to check some paperwork in Steve's office."

He took a few steps closer to Steve's office door, but Janet quickly stepped in front of him, blocking his path. "Oh no you don't. That's Steve's *private* study. You're not going in there when Steve isn't around."

Toby clenched his teeth, and his face turned bright red. "Get out of my way, Janet."

He growled the words and sounded so angry I took a step back. But Janet stood her ground. "No, come back when Steve's home."

"Toby was breathing heavily, and I suspected he might manhandle Janet out of the way, but at the last minute, he just turned on his heel and stalked out of the front door, slamming it behind him.

I let out a sigh of relief. "What was that all about?"

Janet folded her arms across her chest and looked at me through narrowed eyes. "I can't believe you were just going to let him barge into Steve's office."

I frowned. *What was I? A guard dog?* "Toby Walsh is Steve's business partner. He could have had a legitimate reason for needing some paperwork from Steve's office."

Janet shook her head. "Are you really that naive?"

I stared at her.

"He's been locked out of his accounts. Steve isn't returning his calls... He's obviously trying to push him out of the business for some reason. Our loyalty should be with Steve. I mean, I know you had that thing with Toby a while ago but-"

"A thing? I didn't have *a thing* with Toby."

She raised her eyebrows. "If you say so."

I opened my mouth, ready to argue, but then snapped my lips shut. Just let it go, I told myself. This isn't important.

At that moment, Sienna and Zach walked past us to the stairs. "We're going to my room to listen to some music," Sienna said.

"Well, make sure you keep your bedroom door open," Janet said, watching them climb the stairs with her hands on her hips.

Fortunately, after spending ten minutes telling me everything I was doing wrong with respect to Sienna, Janet decided to leave. The rest of the afternoon was peaceful. Angie left about an hour later, and I fixed Sienna and Zach some linguine for dinner.

I set some of the pasta and sauce aside for Steve in case he hadn't eaten.

He didn't get home until just after nine p.m. He and Sienna had a lot to talk about, so I left them to it and went to bed early. After everything that had happened that day, I knew it would take ages for me to fall asleep. I couldn't stop thinking about that note — *keep your mouth shut* — and the fact Eric Ross really didn't want his family to find out about Sienna.

Could the mild-mannered, academic be responsible for Nicole's murder?

CHAPTER THIRTY-FOUR

The following day, Lizzie turned up when we were having breakfast. Steve had woken early and gone shopping, and I'd cooked the three of us a full English breakfast. When the doorbell rang, I wondered if it was Angie, but then remembered it was her day off.

Steve let the family liaison officer in, and she joined us in the kitchen, sniffing the air. "Oh, that bacon smells amazing!"

"There's some more in the fridge. I could make you a bacon sandwich, if you like?" I offered.

Lizzie shook her head and patted her stomach. "Thanks, but I'm on a diet. No processed meat for me."

She did accept the offer of coffee though, and the four of us sat down around the kitchen table.

"I've just popped by to give you an update. We had an in-depth conversation with Professor Ross. At this stage, we don't think he was involved in your mother's death." Lizzie looked directly at Sienna. "But, we're still looking into his whereabouts when Nicole was shot and examining the communications he had with her. He seems to realise he went about contacting you in the wrong way, Sienna. He is very remorseful."

I took a sip of my coffee. He hadn't seemed very remorseful when I'd spoken to him.

"How are you doing?" Lizzie asked softly, looking at Sienna.

"Okay, I guess. It was a bit of a shock."

Lizzie nodded. "I think you're coping brilliantly." She turned to Steve. "Did you know Eric Ross was Sienna's father?"

I felt bad for Steve being put on the spot like that in front of Sienna. He bristled and looked coldly at Lizzie. I couldn't blame him. The police had carted him off to the police station as a suspect in his wife's murder. It was no wonder he wasn't on the best of terms with them.

"No, Nicole simply told me Sienna was born after she'd had a brief fling. To be honest, it's not important to me. I see Sienna as *my* daughter. Eric Ross has had no role in her life so far."

He reached out and put his hand over Sienna's.

She looked up at him and pushed her wavy hair back from her face. "Steve's been my dad for years. He's been there whenever I needed him. I'm not interested in getting to know Eric Ross."

Lizzie looked surprised, and I had to admit I'd assumed Sienna would want to get to know her new family, especially since she'd just lost her mother. She'd obviously been pushing Nicole for details about her biological father. Perhaps Eric Ross had been a disappointment.

"Are you sure, Sienna? Because he's told his family about you now. I understand his wife is a bit reserved, but his children are keen to meet you."

Sienna shook her head vigourously. "No. I thought about it last night, and I don't want to meet them. They're not my family, not really."

Lizzie nodded slowly. "Of course, I'm just passing on their message. I'm sure they'll respect your decision."

After Lizzie left, Steve retired to his study to do some work, and I suggested Sienna and I take Charlie for a walk. It wasn't as warm as yesterday, but it was the perfect temperature for Charlie. While walking beside the road, we kept him on his leash, and he trotted happily between us.

"Do you want to talk about what happened yesterday?" I asked, glancing sideways at Sienna as we walked along Fleet Hill towards the village.

She tugged her hoodie closed and raised the zip. "Not really. I really wanted to know who my father was. I thought it would give me some answers, make me feel… whole, I guess. But Steve was right, he's my father. That man didn't want anything to do with me, so why should things be different now?"

"It's no reflection on you. He just put his own needs first."

"I know," she said, nodding. "I was so angry with Mum for not telling me who my father was. I knew she was lying. I skipped school, and a few times, I just didn't come home at night… I wanted to make her feel guilty, to force her into telling me."

"It can't have been easy for either of you," I said.

It was so quiet out here, with only the sound of birds singing, insects buzzing and leaves rustling.

"I wish I hadn't done all that now," Sienna said, her eyes glassy with tears.

"It must have been difficult for your mum. She must have had reasons for keeping it secret. She probably wanted to protect you."

"Did she really never tell you?"

I shook my head. "No, and I never guessed. I've been thinking back, wondering if there were any signs I missed, but I can't think of anything."

"Do you think she regretted it? Maybe she was ashamed."

"I don't think she could have regretted it. You were the best thing in her life. You know that, don't you?"

Sienna rubbed her eyes and sniffed before looking up at the sky. "I just wish I could go back in time and be nicer to her."

I reached out and put an arm around her shoulders. "We all have things we wish we'd done differently. I wish I'd made more time for her. I wish I'd come back and seen you both more often. But we can't change those things. No one's perfect, but we have a lot of great memories."

"I made her so sad. I came down for a glass of water one night and found her crying. That was my fault."

"When was that?"

"About a week before she died. I think it was a Wednesday because I'd had drama class with Mr Owens."

I pondered that for a moment. "Did you ask her why she was crying?"

Sienna shook her head. "No, I felt guilty so I pretended I hadn't seen her."

Not only was Sienna dealing with intense sorrow, she was also grappling with guilt. That was a lot for anyone to handle, let alone a fifteen-year-old girl.

I was no expert on grief. I wished there was something I could say to make her feel better, but the only thing I could do was listen.

As we walked through the village, she talked in spits and spurts, trying to make sense of her feelings. We both shed some tears, but when we turned around and began to walk back to Yew Tree House, I felt some of the darkness I'd experienced over the last few days begin to lift. For the first time, I could imagine Sienna getting past this and living a full life again.

It would take time for Sienna to come to terms with her loss and her feelings of guilt. Therapy might help. I decided to mention it to Steve. I hoped Sienna would decide to rejoin the drama class, too. I'd never been involved in drama myself, but knew some people found it very helpful in handling their emotions.

Charlie was panting a little when we got back. He needed a drink. It didn't feel very warm today, but thanks to his dark fur he was very sensitive to the heat.

As I was removing Charlie's lead, Sienna opened the front door. I wasn't really paying attention and almost walked into the back of her. She'd stopped dead in the hallway.

"What is it? What's wrong?"

"Somebody's been in our house."

I walked past her and instantly saw what she meant. From where we stood in the hallway, we could see into the sitting room. The television had been overturned and was on the floor. All the drawers in the cabinet were open.

What had happened while we were gone?

My mind immediately went to the possibility that Toby had turned up and had some kind of altercation with Steve.

"Where is Steve?" I asked, glancing towards his office.

Sienna made it there before me. "He's not there." Her voice was high, verging on hysteria. "Steve! Where are you?"

Charlie let out a low whine. I wondered if he could sense something we couldn't.

I entered the study, not because I didn't believe Sienna, but I wanted to see if Steve's office was in the same state as the sitting room.

It was worse.

His expensive leather chair was on its side. The computer

monitor had been pushed from the desk to the floor. Papers were scattered everywhere.

Who had done this?

I turned in a slow circle, taking in the devastation and then realised Sienna wasn't by my side.

I walked quickly into the hall. "Sienna?"

She was halfway up the stairs. "Come back down." My voice was harsher than I'd intended.

"I'm going to see if Steve is upstairs."

"No, come down here now." My voice was firm. It needed to be because it had only just occurred to me that whoever had ransacked the house might still be here.

Sienna looked torn. She stood in the middle of the stairs gazing upwards and then glanced back down at me. "But what if he's hurt?"

"Come downstairs. We'll go outside and call the police. Then I'll look for Steve."

Finally, she did as I asked. From outside, everything looked perfectly normal. I dialled Lizzie's direct number with a shaking hand and quickly told her what had happened. She promised to send an urgent response unit, and said she was on her way, too.

I promised Sienna I'd go back inside and look for Steve, just in case he was hurt and needed first aid. After taking a deep breath, I told her to look after Charlie and then went back inside Yew Tree House to find Steve.

I stepped into the hallway and paused, listening.

Silence.

That didn't necessarily mean there wasn't anyone here. I did a quick circuit of the downstairs first. I checked the dining room, then the kitchen and utility room. I'd just turned away from the utility room, when I caught sight of something through the kitchen window.

There was a lounger in the middle of the lawn and someone was sprawled on it.

Was it Steve?

The back door was open, so I stepped out onto the patio.

It *was* Steve. He was wearing the same clothes. He had one of those old-fashioned straw hats pulled over his face and he wasn't moving. One arm flopped over the edge of the lounger.

"Steve?" I called out, my voice wavering.

He didn't answer and he didn't move.

Oh, please, let him be all right. Sienna wouldn't be able to handle losing both parents.

My muscles were stiff, seized up through fright, but I forced myself to walk closer.

"Steve?" I said again, louder this time.

When he sat up, blinking in the bright sunlight, I almost fell over.

My hands flew up to my face. "Oh I'm so glad you're okay... I thought."

He frowned and rubbed a hand over his sleepy face. "What's wrong?"

"The house... It's been trashed."

Abruptly, he got up to his feet and threw his hat down on the lounger. "What? That's not possible. I've only been out here for half an hour."

"Sienna," I called, walking away from Steve towards the garden gate at the side of the house.

It was locked, so I slid the metal bolt free and pulled it open. "Sienna! Steve is okay. He was in the garden."

After a moment, Sienna and Charlie walked down the path at the side of the house and joined us in the garden.

Sienna flung herself at Steve, sobbing.

Charlie looked as confused as I felt. I filled his outside drinking bowl with water from the external tap and watched as he lapped it up.

"Did you see anyone when you were walking back," Steve asked, putting his arm around Sienna's shoulders. "Whoever did this could have passed you on the road."

"Not that I noticed," I said. "A few cars passed us, but I didn't pick up on anything unusual. I looked around downstairs, so I think whoever did this has gone, but I suppose they *could* be hiding upstairs."

Sienna gripped Steve's arm.

"Did you call the police?" Steve asked.

"Yes, they're on their way."

I looked back at Yew Tree House as the sun slipped behind a cloud. I shivered. Had they been looking for something, or did they simply want to scare us?

Because if frightening us was their aim, they'd succeeded.

CHAPTER THIRTY-FIVE

WE STAYED in the garden while the police searched the house and conducted various forensic tests. Steve pulled some more garden furniture from the summerhouse, and we settled in the padded chairs, looking like a group of friends relaxing and enjoying a pleasant summer's day in the garden. Only, none of us were feeling relaxed.

Sienna was very quiet, and I worried this was a big setback after all the talking we had done earlier. Steve was tense, and I couldn't help glancing at him every now and again, wondering if he thought the same as I did… That this had to be down to Toby Walsh.

In some ways, I hoped it was Toby. His temper had been scary to witness yesterday, but being able to put a face to your adversary helped to humanise them.

After all Angie's talk of evil, the idea of an unknown person rummaging through our personal possessions made my skin crawl.

I wasn't sure how much time had passed but it felt like hours when Lizzie finally came out to give us an update.

"It looks like nothing else was touched. Whoever was here focused on the sitting room and the study."

"Did they go in my room?" Sienna asked, her eyes red and her cheeks pale.

Lizzie shook her head. "It doesn't look like it. If it is all right with you," she said, looking at Steve, "I thought it might be a good idea for me to stay with you for a couple of days. Nothing to worry about, but just so I'm on hand if you need anything."

"Do you think they'll come back?" Sienna's voice shook.

"I doubt it," Lizzie said, smiling reassuringly.

I can't say her smile helped make me feel any better. My stomach was twisting and churning, and my pulse rate still hadn't slowed to its normal level.

"That's fine with me," Steve said. "I still can't believe I slept through everything."

Lizzie gave him a tight smile. "Yes, that is quite *unusual*."

We heard Janet before we saw her. She was yelling at one of the officers at the front of the property.

I rolled my eyes and looked accusingly at Steve. It was his fault. He'd decided it was a good idea to let Janet and Marilyn know what was going on so they could take Sienna home with them.

Janet strode into the garden closely followed by Marilyn. Sienna stood up to hug her grandmother.

"Sweetheart, are you okay? Do the police know who broke in?" Marilyn asked.

Sienna shook her head. "They're still inside the house, but I'm not sure if they know who did it."

"You'd better get your things," Janet said. "I'll drive you back to Grandma's."

Sienna took a step back and shook her head. "Thanks, but I want to stay here." She looked at Steve.

He sighed and stood up, the lounger creaking when it was free from his weight. "I think you'll be safer at your grandmother's."

Sienna shook her head again, more vigorously this time. "No. It's not fair. I want to stay *here*."

"I don't even know if we will be allowed to stay, Sienna. The police might not be finished with the house for some time."

"Well, where are you going to stay?"

Steve lifted his palms. "I don't know. I'll stay here if they are finished, or I'll have to check into a hotel."

"Then I'll do that, too," Sienna said firmly and then glanced at me. "I want to stay with Abbie and Steve."

Sienna wanted to stay in familiar surroundings. That was understandable. She wasn't as scared as she had been when we'd first got back to the house and discovered the break-in. I wondered if that was because she'd guessed, as I had, it was Toby Walsh behind the break-in.

Marilyn's eyes filled with tears at the rejection, and my heart went out to her. She only wanted to protect her granddaughter.

Janet turned on me, her eyes flashing angrily. "Well, thank you very much, Abbie," she said sarcastically.

"What have *I* done?"

"You've turned Sienna against her family. It didn't take you long. What stories have you been feeding her?"

Stories? I had no idea what Janet was talking about. This was nothing but irrational jealousy. Sienna didn't want to stay at Yew Tree House because of me. She wanted to stay here because it was her home and she felt safe with her stepfather.

"Don't, Janet," Marilyn said putting a hand on her daughter's arm. "This situation is bad enough without us getting into an argument."

Janet shook her head slowly and her eyes narrowed as she glared at me. "You may have fooled the rest of them, Abbie, but I've got the measure of you." She looked at her mother. "I'll wait in the car."

Janet turned and marched across the lawn towards the garden gate.

Marilyn dabbed her eyes with a handkerchief. "Are you sure Sienna, darling? I'd feel so much better if you were safe with me for a few days."

"Thanks, Grandma. But I'd really prefer to stay at home. The family liaison officer is going to stay with us for a few days, so we're going to be safe."

Marilyn drew her granddaughter in for a hug. "Okay, darling. Let me know if you change your mind."

"I will. Love you."

"I love you, too, darling, very much." Marilyn kissed her on the cheek and then turned to Steve. "Keep a close eye on things, won't you?"

"Of course. I'll let you know how things go here. Fingers crossed we'll be back in the house in a couple of hours and be able to clear up."

"I hope so. It was lucky only a couple of rooms were affected, I suppose." Marilyn struggled to smile. Then she turned to me. "Abbie, I do appreciate you keeping an eye on Sienna, and I know Nicole would be very grateful."

She'd surprised me. I'd been feeling so defensive after Janet's attack, and the frosty way both Marilyn and Janet had treated me over the past week or so. It hurt me more than I'd realised.

I was touched and my eyes filled with tears. "Thanks, Marilyn."

She kissed me on the cheek and then said, "I'll be getting home now. Let me know if there is anything I can do to help."

Sienna linked her arm through her grandmother's and walked her around the side of the house towards Janet's car.

I let out a deep breath and sat back down on a garden chair as Steve reclined on the lounger.

"What is it between you and Janet?" he asked me.

That was a very good question. And one that was hard to answer. The difficulties in our relationship went back years and were tied to Janet's strained relationship with Nicole. Janet had been jealous of her sister, and that jealousy had eaten away at her and left her a bitter shell of a woman.

"When we were younger, there was a bit of rivalry between Nicole and Janet. Obviously, as I was Nicole's friend, Janet saw me as the enemy. I suppose it's something most sisters grow out of, but Janet seems to hold onto that bitterness."

I squinted in the sun and then turned to face Steve. "Were Janet and Nicole getting along better recently?"

"Not really. I suppose I only ever saw it from Nicole's point of view. She did make an effort. She included Janet in all family plans. We invited her to every barbecue, all of Sienna's birthday parties... But Janet was always quick with a sarcastic comment, and I think it really hurt Nicole. But no matter what, she never lost her temper with her sister. I think she'd come to accept that was who Janet was."

"It's almost like she can't help it, as though it's out of her control."

"Yes," Steve mused. "It's like they fit into those roles when they were children and never managed to break free."

That was true. Janet was always second best. She'd never been as pretty or as clever as Nicole. And that ate into her when we were still children. Nicole's death must have turned Janet's mind topsy-turvy. Now she no longer had anyone to compete with or put down in order to make herself feel better.

We were quiet for a few moments, enjoying soaking up the sun before we had to go inside and deal with the mess the intruder had left behind.

Sienna would soon be back after waving Janet and Marilyn off, and I needed to ask my next question while Steve and I were alone.

"Do you think it was Toby who broke in?"

Steve didn't answer straight away. He sat up and turned, placing his feet on the floor. "I don't know. But it does seem likely."

"What's going on with him?"

Steve groaned. "I don't really want to talk about it, Abbie. It's nothing personal, just business."

I tried to pretend that Steve's words hadn't stung. Maybe it was just business, but I couldn't help feeling personally involved. I made the decision there and then to tell Lizzie about my suspicions.

If Toby Walsh was responsible for the break-in, the police needed to know.

CHAPTER THIRTY-SIX

AN HOUR after Marilyn and Janet left, Lizzie came out into the garden to tell us we could go back inside. The police had finished examining every nook and cranny for evidence, and now we had the unenviable task of clearing up. Steve focused on his office, while Sienna, Lizzie and I tried to clean up the sitting room.

The television was damaged beyond repair. The screen wasn't cracked or smashed but it wouldn't turn on. But surprisingly, nothing else was broken.

Steve brought down an old television from one of the rooms upstairs. Although it was smaller and slightly thicker than the old one, it worked perfectly. When he carried the old television into the garage, I suggested Sienna make some tea.

While Steve and Sienna were out of earshot I took the opportunity to tell Lizzie I suspected Toby Walsh had been the one who'd broken in. She listened carefully and made me feel like she was taking me seriously then promised to look into it.

Once we'd finished, it was impossible to tell anything had occurred in the sitting room. Notebooks, pens and odds and ends were back in the drawers of the cabinets. Everything was back in its rightful place.

Now I was feeling a little calmer, I worried about Janet. She could be an impossible, irritating, sarcastic cow at times, but I knew she was only doing it because she was so unhappy.

The only thing I could do to repair the rift between us was speak to her to clear the air. That's what Nicole would want me to do. No matter how mean Janet was to us when we were young, Nicole always forgave her sister.

I knew Sienna would be fine because Steve and Lizzie were staying at Yew Tree House. On my way out, I stuck my head into Steve's study. He was shuffling papers together on his desk.

"I'm heading over to see Janet," I said. "I don't want to leave things as they are between us."

Steve raised his eyebrows. "You're brave."

"Not really," I admitted. "I'm dreading it, but I'll apologise if that's what it takes to make her feel better."

Steve shrugged and I got the sense he didn't think treating Janet with kid gloves was the way to go. I wondered if he and Nicole had argued over the matter in the past, but it wasn't my place to ask.

It took just over fifteen minutes for me to park in Rose Street car park in Wokingham, and a couple of minutes after that, I was ringing the buzzer at Janet's flat.

I imagined Janet rolling her eyes when I spoke into the intercom, but she did buzz me in.

As I walked up the stairs, I mentally prepared what I was going to say. I would apologise for not keeping Janet in the loop as much as I should have done, and then I would try to reassure her I wasn't attempting to come between Sienna and her family. Would it work? Unlikely. Janet and I would never be best friends, but I owed it to Nicole to try and smooth things over.

Janet opened the door to her flat before I had a chance to knock. "Yes."

She kept one hand on the door, and positioned her body to block the doorway. She wasn't even going to invite me in. This had been a waste of time.

"I've come to apologise, Janet. Can I come in?"

She stared at me for a few seconds before stepping aside. "Go on then, but make it quick. I'm busy."

We walked into her open plan living area, and I sat down on the sofa without being invited. If I waited for an invitation, I'd be here all day.

"I'm sorry for not involving you with things. I should have called you when I first spoke to Eric Ross. You're Sienna's aunt, and you're right, you should have an important role in her life."

Janet, who had remained standing, crossed her arms over her chest and stared at me. She had a talent for getting under my skin and making me feel uncomfortable.

I swallowed nervously and then continued, "I don't want to come between you and Sienna. Sienna should have a good relationship with her family. I want her to be happy."

Janet surprised me by not responding to what I'd said. Instead, she offered me coffee.

"Oh, yes. Thanks. Coffee would be lovely." I stammered and blinked in surprise.

Janet moved into the small kitchen area to fix the coffee, and I put my handbag on the floor beside me and stood up.

"Could I use your bathroom?"

"Yes," Janet said, flicking a switch on the coffeemaker. "But you'll have to use the en suite. The toilet in the main bathroom isn't working. The flush is broken."

"Right. Thanks."

I walked along the hall and opened the bedroom door. It felt strange to be in Janet's bedroom. It smelled faintly of Chanel No5, and there was an ashtray on her dressing table, which didn't smell as pleasant as the perfume.

My fingers grasped the handle on the en suite bathroom door, but I paused. In the middle of Janet's double bed was a box of photographs. Intrigued, I walked over to the bed to take a look.

It was filled with photographs of Janet and Nicole as children. Most were still in the box, but some were scattered on the duvet. There was one that had been taken at the Tower of London as the two girls stood beside a Beefeater. Another, was of Nicole standing beside a large raven. She looked nervous and was watching the bird warily.

I reached for another photograph, this one showed Nicole blowing out candles on a birthday cake. Janet stood by her side, her face lit up by the candles as she watched her sister enviously. I stared at the picture, feeling uneasy. The expression on Janet's face was… unnerving.

I grabbed another and gasped. In this one, Nicole and Janet were in their early teens, standing side-by-side on the deck of a boat, leaning back against the rail. Both girls had permed hair and braces. But the horrifying thing about the photograph was that Nicole's eyes had been scratched out.

I heard footsteps, and flustered, I dropped the photograph.

Whirling round, I was just in time to see Janet enter her bedroom. "Are you all right? I wondered what was taking you so long."

My mouth opened but no sound came out. My gaze dropped back down to the photographs on the bed.

Janet walked closer to me and stopped, her face inches from mine. "Been having a nose, have you?"

"I saw the photographs and…" I looked back down at the photograph of Nicole with her eyes scratched out.

Janet saw what I was looking at and picked up the photo. "I was angry with her. It was ages ago. Don't get your knickers in a twist."

"It's not normal."

"Of course it's normal," Janet snapped. "Sisters are supposed to fight. Don't look at me like that. Have you any idea how prissy and judgemental you sound?"

I took a step away from her but conceded she had a point. Family relationships could be complicated. After Nicole had died, everything seemed to take on a more sinister meaning.

"Well, are you going to use the toilet, or not?"

I managed to nod and quickly scurried into the en suite bathroom, locking the door behind me.

I took a deep breath and pressed a hand against my chest, trying to slow my breathing. What was wrong with me? It was only Janet. I didn't really suspect Janet could have done anything to hurt her sister, did I?

I took my time in the bathroom, and when I finally emerged, Janet had left the bedroom and the photographs were nowhere to be seen.

When I entered the sitting room, she handed me my coffee as though there were nothing wrong.

I perched on the edge of the sofa, wishing I hadn't come. Now I would never be able to scrub the image of Nicole with her eyes scratched out from my mind.

"So, what's wrong with the other toilet?" I asked, wanting to change the subject and not think about that photograph any more.

"No idea. It just won't flush. I've called a plumber, but he can't come until the middle of next week."

"Do you want me to take a look?"

Janet frowned. "You? What do *you* know about plumbing?"

"I'm no expert, but I've had to fix a few issues when we were out in the sticks. We couldn't call out plumbers, so we had to do things ourselves."

She shrugged and put her mug down on the coffee table. "Knock yourself out."

She followed me into the main bathroom, her sceptical eyes on me as I lifted the lid off the cistern and set it down on the toilet seat.

"The floatation ball still raised," I said. "But the cistern is empty."

"And what does that mean?"

"Usually, when the water level drops in the cistern, after you flush, the floatation ball drops and signals more water is needed to fill the cistern. In this case, the flotation ball isn't dipping down and sending a signal that more water is needed."

"Will that be expensive to fix?"

"I doubt it." I took a closer look. "It looks like the valve and connection here is just clogged with limescale. If we clean that, chances are it will be good as new. If not you might have to buy a new floatation valve, but you could fit it yourself."

Janet looked horrified at the idea.

I set about cleaning away the limescale with a cloth and the edge of a screwdriver Janet had managed to find for me. The floatation ball dipped down to the water level when I was finished, and the cistern began to fill with water.

I smiled. "That should do it, I think."

Janet looked grudgingly impressed. "Thank you."

After I replaced the cistern lid, Janet tested the flush, and it worked perfectly.

I washed my hands, and Janet asked, "When did you learn how to do that?"

"On my last placement, with the help of YouTube videos."

I followed her out of the bathroom and she said quietly, "I know that photo freaked you out. I'm not going to deny Nicole and I argued and fell out from time to time, but she's my sister, and I loved her." Her voice caught at the end of the sentence.

I welled up but quickly blinked away the tears. The last thing I wanted was Janet spotting a weakness. "I know you did. And I know she loved you."

Janet didn't meet my gaze as she picked up our coffee cups and carried them to the kitchen. "I'd never hurt her."

The photograph had scared me. There was something menacing and ominous about scratching someone's eyes out in a photo, but deep down, could I believe Janet hated her sister enough to kill her?

I watched Janet as she stood with her back to me at the sink. No, I didn't believe she shot Nicole. To the best of my knowledge, Janet had never even fired a gun.

CHAPTER THIRTY-SEVEN

THE NEXT MORNING, I was woken by loud voices. Bleary-eyed, I squinted at my mobile on the nightstand. It was seven thirty a.m.

I sat up in bed and yawned. Ideally, I'd curl back under the duvet and get another few hours sleep. I'd been restless last night. Every time I closed my eyes I saw the picture with Nicole's eyes scratched out.

The loud voices carried again up the stairs. One was Steve's, his low, rumbling voice seemed to permeate the walls. The other voice was female, and I wasn't sure whether it was Sienna's.

I got up to investigate, dressing quickly and then padding out into the hall. The argument was getting very heated now. Then a door slammed downstairs.

Should I go downstairs and find out what was going on? Or should I leave them to it?

It wasn't really any of my business, but curiosity got the better of me.

The door to Steve's study was closed. When I walked into the kitchen, I saw Lizzie sitting at the table with a cup of coffee in front of her, tapping away on her mobile phone. She looked up and her normally open, friendly face looked tense.

"Morning," I said, heading for the coffee machine. "Is everything all right?"

"Toby Walsh seems to have disappeared."

"Disappeared?" I froze, my hand in mid-air, reaching for a mug in the cupboard.

"Yes, our investigation has revealed he's been embezzling money."

"From Steve?"

"From Steve *and* from their clients."

I leaned back against the kitchen counter. Poor Steve. He really didn't need this on top of everything else. How could Toby do something like this to him?

"What does that mean for Steve's business?"

Lizzie shrugged. "Well, it's not *good* news."

I looked around the large kitchen and then through the window to the beautiful back garden beyond. This house had to be worth a fortune. And its upkeep couldn't be cheap. I wondered how this would affect Steve financially. Would he be forced to sell Yew Tree House? Would he struggle to provide for Sienna?

I slid my mug beneath the coffee machine and waited as it growled to life, pouring rich, dark coffee into my mug.

It sounded like I might have to change my plans. Then a more serious thought occurred to me. "This embezzlement… It won't get Steve into trouble, will it?"

"There's no evidence Steve was involved."

I carried my mug over to the kitchen table. "What happens now?"

Lizzie looked up from her phone. "We're trying to locate Toby Walsh. He can't hide forever."

"I heard raised voices earlier. I guess Steve hasn't taken the news well."

Lizzie tilted her head to the side and then sighed. "Yes, I had to give Steve some bad news this morning. We've been trying to trace Toby, and one of their mutual friends has reported his yacht is missing. It could be a coincidence... But it also could be Toby took the yacht and is trying to escape to the continent."

I could see why that would make Steve angry. Not only had Toby been cheating him and stealing from him, now he was trying to flee, and to make matters worse, it looked like he might get away with it.

"Angie won't be in today," Lizzie said. "Steve told her not to come to work this week."

"Oh, I see."

Was that because Steve was worried about paying Angie's salary, or was he worried she might spread gossip? If that was the case, I thought he underestimated her. I was sure Angie Macgregor was a loyal woman.

I finished my coffee and conversation with Lizzie, and then went upstairs to check on Sienna. I was surprised she hadn't been woken by Steve and Lizzie discussing the Toby Walsh situation.

I knocked softly on her bedroom door, but there was no answer. I pushed the door open and saw her bed was unmade, but there was no sign of her. The door to her en suite bathroom was shut, so I guessed she was in there. I'd turned to leave when I heard the sound of retching.

My first thought was that the stress of the situation had raised her anxiety levels to such an extent it was making her physically ill, but that thought was immediately followed by another.

Morning sickness.

I waited until she came out of the bathroom, feeling like I was spying on her, but unable to walk away. If I was right, she was going to need my help.

Sienna opened the bathroom door, and when she spotted me, her eyes widened.

I got straight to the point. "Is there something you should tell me?"

The guilt on Sienna's face convinced me her sickness wasn't down to anxiety.

"When was your last period?"

Sienna gasped. "Oh my God! I'm not talking to you about this!"

She marched over to her bed and climbed under the covers.

"You don't have a choice. Is it Zach's?"

Fat teardrops rolled down Sienna's cheeks, making me feel like a bully, but she couldn't just ignore this. It wasn't going to go away.

"We're going to have to tell Steve and your grandmother and Aunt Janet. They need to know as soon as possible."

"They do not! And you can't tell them if I don't want you to."

I sighed and ran my hands through my hair. "You're under age, Sienna. This is serious. If the baby is Zach's, then he could be in real trouble."

"It isn't! And I don't want to tell anyone yet."

I tried to talk to her and get her to open up, but she buried her head beneath the duvet and refused to respond.

In the end, I left her in her bedroom and went back downstairs. Steve's office door was still closed, and I hesitated in the hall. Should I tell him now? He already had a lot to deal with this morning, and I wasn't sure how he would take this news.

I made a snap decision and told Lizzie I was going out for a little while.

I had a plan.

* * *

I drove to Zach's parents' house on Barkham Road. There was only one car on the drive – Zach's old Renault Clio. His parents had probably left for work already, luckily for him.

I rang the bell and waited, but Zach didn't answer quickly enough for me, and I hammered on the door.

Eventually, he opened up. His eyes were like slits as he squinted against the bright sunlight. He wore a crumpled black T-shirt and black sweatpants, and his normally carefully-styled hair was shooting up in all directions.

"Have you only just got out of bed?"

"It *is* the school holidays, Abbie."

"I had a job in the holidays when I was in school," I said, regretting the words as soon as they left my mouth. I was nagging him already, and I hadn't got to the main point of my visit yet. "Can I come in? We need to talk."

"Um, okay." He shuffled backwards and I stepped into the hall. The stairs were immediately in front of me, and to the left, was a large sitting room.

Zach led the way and sat on a grey two-seater sofa beside the window.

Instead of sitting in one of the armchairs, I sat beside him on the sofa, looking him directly in the eye. I wanted to study his facial expression when I asked him about Sienna's pregnancy. That way I'd be able to tell if he was lying to me.

"Sienna is pregnant, Zach," I said. "Did you know?"

His sleepy eyes widened, and he shook his head. "Are you sure?"

I nodded and repeated my question. "Did you know?"

He shook his head vigourously. "No, she didn't tell me. I had no idea. Poor Sienna. She must be so stressed right now."

"So what are you planning to do about it?" I asked, leaning back against the cushions and crossing my arms.

"What am *I* planning to do about it?"

"Yes, this isn't just Sienna's problem. It's your responsibility, too, plus we can't forget the fact that Sienna is underage, Zach. You could be in trouble."

"But... You don't think..." He stared at me in horror. "It's not my baby."

He was so convincing it made me pause. "But..." I trailed off. Now it was my turn to be confused.

Zach leaned forward, resting his elbows on his knees. "I did try to tell you before. Sienna and I are just friends."

"I just thought you were keeping things secret."

Zach rolled his eyes.

"Are you absolutely sure?" I hadn't been involved in Sienna's life as much as I should have been over the past few years. Since coming back to the UK, I'd never heard her mention anyone apart from Zach.

"Of course, I'm sure. Look, Abbie." He linked his fingers together and stared down at his hands. "I'm not really into girls."

"Oh." I let his words sink in for a moment, digesting the implication of what he'd just said. If the baby wasn't Zach's, then whose was it?

Had Nicole known about this?

Zach knew Sienna better than anyone. Surely he would know who Sienna had been seeing recently.

"If you're not the father, Zach, then who is?"

He frowned and shrugged. "Honestly, I don't know."

"She can't be that far along," I said, thinking aloud. "It has to be somebody she's been seeing over the last few months."

"I didn't think she'd been seeing anyone, except…"

I turned to him. "Go on. Except what?"

"Well, before the summer holidays started, she was in a really good mood, really happy, and I thought maybe she'd met somebody, but she just laughed it off when I asked her."

I put my head in my hands. This was getting worse. I was going to have to tell Steve, Marilyn and Janet as soon as possible.

If I'd discovered Sienna's secret a couple of days ago, I would have gone straight to Janet, but after finding that photograph of Nicole with her eyes scratched out, I didn't feel like confiding in Janet about anything. Then again, I couldn't deal with this alone.

I said goodbye to Zach. Sitting in my car, I used my mobile to dial Steve's number. There was no answer.

Swearing under my breath, I called Janet.

When she answered, I told her everything, and Janet listened in utter disbelief as I told her I suspected Sienna was pregnant.

"Steve doesn't know yet. I can't get hold of him." I felt guilty saying that. I probably should have spoken to him before I left the house. "I'm going to pick up a test, just in case it's a false alarm."

"I really hope it is," Janet said. "I'm not going to tell my mother until we know for sure. I'll meet you at Yew Tree House."

I thought about objecting and then changed my mind. Sienna would be angry with me for telling Janet, but she'd soon need her Aunt's support and be grateful she had a family to rally around her.

CHAPTER THIRTY-EIGHT

I PICKED up a pregnancy test from Jats Pharmacy opposite Creswell's garage on the way back to Yew Tree House. When I put the bag on the passenger seat, I wondered if it was a false alarm. Had I jumped to conclusions? Maybe Sienna had eaten something that didn't agree with her. She wasn't showing yet…

Then I remembered the guilty look on Sienna's face and sighed. No, I hadn't been mistaken. I drove past the doctor's surgery. We'd soon be making an appointment there if my suspicions turned out to be correct.

When I finally arrived back at Yew Tree House, I parked between Lizzie's Volvo and Janet's Mazda and noticed Steve's Mercedes had gone. Where was he? Had he spoken to Sienna and stormed off to cool down?

I let myself in and found Janet and Lizzie talking urgently in the hallway. They looked agitated.

Janet's face fell when she saw me. "I thought you were Sienna."

"Isn't she upstairs?"

"No," Janet said coldly, shooting a fierce look at Lizzie. "She's gone off somewhere."

"On her own? Where is Steve?" I asked.

"Steve left first," Lizzie explained. "He's determined to find Toby Walsh. He thinks looking through Toby's London office might provide answers. Sienna left shortly afterwards."

"You just let her go?" I asked in disbelief, putting the paper bag containing the pregnancy test down on the hall table.

"She is not under house arrest, Abbie!" Lizzie said defensively.

I was being unfair. She didn't know about Sienna's pregnancy. Neither did Steve. I should have told them before I left. I'd handled this badly.

With a groan of frustration, I fished my mobile out of my bag and phoned Zach as Lizzie wandered off to the kitchen, muttering, "I'll make us all a cup of tea so we can calm down."

When Zach answered, I asked, "Where's Sienna?"

"Um, is this a trick question?"

"Zach, she's not here. I'm worried. Just tell me if you know where she is."

"I don't. I sent her a text message after you left, but she hasn't replied yet."

"If you're lying to me—"

"I'm not. I swear."

"Do you have any idea where she might be?"

"Maybe the park. She likes it there, says she feels safe."

Okay. I could check there. It was a start. A plan of action.

"I'll come with you," Zach offered.

"There's no need. But let me know if you hear from her."

I hung up and gave Janet a quick summary of the situation, then said, "I'll go to the park and look for Sienna."

Janet gave me a brusque nod, but I could tell from the tense way she held herself that she was as worried as I was. "I'll stay here, in case she comes home."

I drove to the park and left my car parked in the lay-by. My stomach was in knots as I walked briskly to the entrance gate. I paused just inside the park to scan the playing fields.

The park covered a large area, and today, I couldn't help wishing it was a bit smaller. To my left, were the tennis courts and the Memorial Hall. To my right, was the playground for small children and the bench where Eric Ross had sat and watched Sienna. Today, the bench was empty. Directly ahead of me, were playing fields and a large cricket pitch. I didn't immediately spot Sienna so I started to walk slowly around the perimeter. Kids were hanging around in small groups, enjoying the last days of the summer holidays.

In the furthest playing field, a large tractor-mower chugged along with a low rumble, and the sweet smell of cut grass surrounded me. A few feet away a group of teenagers squealed with laughter.

I stared at them, but didn't recognise any of their faces. Sienna's coppery hair, *should* stand out and be easy to spot.

Come on, come on. Where are you?

As the minutes passed, my panic grew. I couldn't explain it...but I had a gnawing fear something terrible was going to happen if I didn't find Sienna soon. My mouth was dry and my heart was fluttering in my chest as the sun beat down on my head.

After fifteen minutes, I reluctantly left the park. She wasn't there, and I had no idea where to look next.

I tried to think through the options logically as I made my way back to the car. Perhaps she'd gone to hide out in Zach's grandmother's shed again... But that seemed unlikely now. I'd found her there once, so if she really didn't want to be found, she wouldn't use the same hiding place. Had she gone to the river where Nicole had been shot? I shivered. I really hoped not.

I was almost at the car when I spotted a familiar figure.

It was Sienna's friend, Jessica Richardson, walking along the pavement on the other side of the road. She was wearing small, fitted, denim shorts and a tight, cropped, white T-shirt.

Calling out, I ran across the road to talk to her. "Jess! I'm looking for Sienna. Have you seen her?"

When I got closer, I saw Jessica had been crying. Her eyes were bloodshot and watery. Tears had smudged her eyeliner, and her nose was bright red.

She sniffed and shook her head. "No, not today."

"What's wrong?" I put a hand on Jessica's shoulder.

She looked down at the floor. "I can't tell you. It's too embarrassing."

I looked into Jessica's red rimmed eyes. "You can trust me."

Smiling reassuringly, I gave her hand a squeeze.

She blinked at me and her lips quivered. I wasn't sure what had upset her, but it looked like something major. Then again, teenage girls could overreact to drama.

I was worried her tears could have something to do with Sienna. "Maybe I can help."

"I feel stupid," Jessica said, dropping her gaze down to the floor.

"I'm worried about Sienna, Jess. Does this have anything to do with her?"

Jessica's forehead puckered in confusion. "Oh, no, it's nothing like that." She took a deep breath in, then said, "I went to see Mr Owens. He told me to come to his house today to pick up a copy of a play…but then he…" She trailed off and wouldn't meet my concerned gaze.

That probably wasn't a bad thing because my concern must have been written all over my face. The mention of Jason Owens had set off alarm bells.

If Sienna was pregnant and Zach wasn't the father... Then who was? It wouldn't be the first time a teacher had used their position to take advantage of a student.

I felt sick. I tried to swallow but my mouth felt too dry.

Focusing on Jessica, I asked, "It's okay. Tell me *exactly* what Mr Owens did?"

"He said I was special," Jess said in a shaky voice. Her lower lip wobbled as her tear-filled eyes met mine. "You think I'm stupid, don't you? It's just he made me feel so important. Like I really was something special."

"You are, Jess. You don't need me or Mr Owens to tell you that. Has he ever tried anything with you?"

Jessica's cheeks flushed scarlet, and she looked at me wide-eyed and horrified. "No! I mean, all the girls in our drama group have a crush on him, but... I just... It made me feel important when he asked me to come to his house..."

I looked down at her tight fitting T-shirt, and her extremely short denim cut-offs. She had a tell-tale line of foundation at her jawline where she hadn't quite mastered blending her make-up yet. She'd been out to impress.

Had she gone to see him and found herself out of her depth? Had he scared her? Or done something worse?

"What happened when you went to his house, Jess?" I asked gently.

Jessica put her fingertips to her forehead and sighed before shaking her head. "I can't tell you. It's too embarrassing."

Frustrated, I tightened my hold on her shoulders, and she flinched.

"You're hurting me."

Instantly, I released my grip. "I'm sorry. It just makes me angry that you're feeling guilty about something that isn't your fault."

Jessica sniffed, wiped her nose on the back of her hand. "He asked me to go to his house. I didn't just turn up unannounced… But when I got there, he was acting really strangely and ordered me to leave."

I frowned. This hadn't been the explanation I'd expected. "So you didn't even go inside his house?"

Jess shook her head forlornly. "No, he told me to go away." A big tear rolled down her cheek. "It was so humiliating. When I reminded him he'd asked me to come, he said I was being ridiculous and then shut the door in my face."

My mind was working overtime. Was Sienna with him now? Was that why he didn't want to be disturbed? "Did you get the impression there was someone else in the house?"

Jessica thought for a moment. "I don't think so… Do you think he had somebody else there with him and that's why he didn't want to let me in?"

That was *exactly* what I was thinking.

My stomach churned. Just how close had Sienna been to her teacher?

Without evidence, I didn't want to say too much to Jessica. But as I stood there with my arm around the young girl's shoulders, I couldn't help thinking how this was an echo of what happened to Nicole when she was just a few years older than Sienna. Professor Ross had been Nicole's lecturer. He'd held the same position of trust when he'd had a relationship with his student.

I felt stinging bile rise in my throat as I considered the possibility that Jason Owens had been taking advantage of Sienna and goodness knows how many other young girls. If this was true, he would lose his career and could go to prison. Was he deluded enough to believe no one would discover what he'd been up to?

If there was the slightest chance Sienna was there, I needed to go to Jason Owens's house now. There was a chance my suspicions were wrong. Was I leaping to conclusions?

Why hadn't I told Steve or Janet this morning that I suspected Sienna was pregnant? If I had, they wouldn't have let her out of their sight, and she wouldn't be missing. I'd screwed up. Now, I had to find her and make this right.

"Listen, Jess, I need you to do something for me."

She looked up at me and blinked, before hiccuping.

"I need you to go to Yew Tree House and speak to Sienna's Aunt Janet. I want you to tell her everything you've told me."

"But I can't," Jess said in desperation. "She'll know I had a crush on him. It's too embarrassing."

"Please, Jessica. It's important."

"Why can't you do it?"

"Because I'm going to go and see Jason Owens and get to the bottom of this."

Jess shook her head frantically. "Please, don't. He'll think I'm such a baby."

Jason Owens's view of Jessica Richardson was the least of my concerns right now, but I patted the girl on the arm and said, "Don't worry. I won't mention you unless I have to. But this is important. I need you to go and speak to Janet, okay?"

Reluctantly, Jessica nodded.

"There's a police officer at the house as well. Tell her if you can't find Janet."

Jessica looked alarmed, and I thought she might be about to bolt, but instead she wiped the smudged mascara from beneath her eyes.

"I need to speak to Mr Owens because I think he's been using his position to get close to a number of young girls. Is that right?"

She shook her head. "No, he's always been really nice to me before. He really listens, you know? He said I was talented."

As Jessica defended him, I felt my blood boil.

"That's what predators say, Jessica. They butter you up so you feel compelled to do what they ask."

Jessica looked miserably at the black smudges of mascara on the backs of her hands. "I'm an idiot."

"No, you're not. You're a good person and you trusted somebody who is meant to be there to help you. None of this is your fault."

She sniffed again and fresh tears glistened in her eyes.

"Will you go and tell Janet and the police officer where I'm going, please?"

"All right. Are you going to talk to Mr Owens now?"

I looked along the road running through the village in the direction of the primary school and Jason Owens's thatched cottage and nodded.

"Yes, I am."

CHAPTER THIRTY-NINE

SIENNA

SIENNA WHIMPERED and closed her eyes, trying to picture herself safely back in her bedroom at Yew Tree House. Why had she left? What a stupid thing to do. She'd been safe there with Steve, Abbie and the police officer. Now she was in serious trouble.

Her eyes snapped open. She heard footsteps. Her body flooded with adrenaline, making her tremble uncontrollably.

Her instincts were screaming at her to run and hide. But she couldn't.

He'd tied green garden string around her wrists and looped it through the arms of a heavy wooden chair, making escape impossible.

The string had rubbed her skin red and raw as she pulled and yanked her arms, struggling to get free.

She took a shaky breath and tried to calm down. If she panicked, she would never get away. She looked slowly around the room, her gaze focusing on everyday objects.

A fireplace. Brass ornaments. Paintings on the walls. Normal. Everything was normal. This was just a mistake. He was trying to scare her into keeping quiet. If she was good and promised to do as she was told, he would let her go.

But then her head shifted to the right and she gave a sob of despair when she saw the mangy, stuffed fox with its dark, glass eyes. It seemed to be staring at her, taunting her.

She screwed her eyes shut and murmured a prayer.

Please, let somebody help me. Please, I just want to get out of here. Please.

Then the door opened.

Sienna's body was rigid with fright. Her eyes opened wide, and she recoiled at the sight of the figure in front of her.

It took all her courage to say, "Please, let me go. I won't tell anyone what happened."

"It's too late for that," he said, looking at her in a way that filled her heart with terror.

He was evil. Nasty. It was hard to believe she'd seen him as anything else.

Sienna shook her head, and as her hair fell forward, covering her face, she whispered, "It's not too late. Please."

"Shut up," he said viciously. "You're so boring. All you ever talk about is yourself. Such a pathetic little girl."

"But... You said that you loved me."

He laughed then, an emotionless, cold, wicked bark of laughter that made her stomach tighten with fear.

"I'd never be interested in you," he taunted. "Why would I be? Just a pathetic little girl?"

"Why are you doing this? I did everything you asked. I didn't tell anyone. Not even my mum."

"Yes, you did," he snarled. "And it's your fault she died. If you'd kept your mouth shut, none of this would have happened."

The lump in Sienna's throat made her feel like she was choking. She couldn't breathe. What did he mean? She hadn't told a soul. Not even Zach.

"Are you the one who shot her?" Sienna asked with a sob.

He smiled. A wide smile that showed all his teeth.

CHAPTER FORTY

WHEN I ARRIVED at Jason Owens's thatched cottage, I was shaking with rage. I hammered on the door, not caring if any of the neighbours heard me causing a scene. I couldn't believe he'd been carrying on like this under everyone's nose.

He didn't answer straight away. What was taking him so long? If he had Sienna in there, he was going to wish he'd never been born.

I used the side of my fist to hammer on the door again, only just resisting the temptation to kick it and unleash some of my anger.

As I'd walked to his cottage, I'd tried to call Steve but he didn't answer his mobile. He was probably still driving to London, so I left a message. Of course, I hadn't been able to say everything I wanted to tell him. It was hardly the sort of thing I could leave on voicemail, but I asked him to call me back as soon as possible and told him it was about Sienna.

I banged on the door again. There was still no answer. Stepping over the flower beds, I peered into the leaded windows at the front of the house but saw nothing.

Where was he?

When I'd seen Jessica, she'd come straight from his house so he must still be here. The only possibility was that he was hiding from me.

The idea made me feel even angrier and I rapped on the door again.

This time the door opened, just a crack.

It was bright and sunny outside and very dim and dark in the cottage. I could only see a fraction of Jason's face and most of that was in shadow.

"Can I come in?" I asked bluntly. "I'd like a word."

I stepped up and put my hand flat against the door, but to my surprise, he didn't let me in.

Instead, he bolstered the door with his weight. "It's not a good time, Abbie."

His voice sounded odd and strained. Like he was hiding something.

My eyes narrowed as I studied him.

"I'm sorry if you're in the middle of something, Jason, but this is actually very important, and I need to speak to you *now*."

His eyes widened in surprise. Did he really think he was going to be able to keep his disgusting secret from me now? Even now, as he was about to be caught red-handed, he thought he could fob me off.

"Please, Abbie. I'll speak to you later, I promise. But now really is a bad time."

"Just let me in, for God's sake," I hissed at him. "I'm perfectly prepared to make a scene out here if I have to. But I don't think you want me to do that, do you, Jason?"

His face was blank as he stared at me, and I couldn't work out what game he was playing. It was all over now. Surely he could see that?

He was much stronger than me, and there was no way I was going to be able to barge my way inside his house. But if he wanted to do this on the doorstep, that suited me just fine. It was his reputation that would suffer, and news would soon spread anyway.

I wouldn't mention Jessica or Sienna by name, but I'd say enough to get the neighbours talking.

"I've heard some extremely disappointing things about you today, Jason."

He stared at me, horrified, but said nothing.

"I wonder what the school governors will make of you inviting young girls to your home. Is Sienna here? Just how far did your inappropriate behaviour go?"

That did get his attention. He was so shocked, he stopped leaning his weight against the door, and as my hand was flat against the wood, I pushed it open wider and got a better view of Jason's face.

What I saw made me feel sick.

On the left side of Jason's face was a long red mark.

A scratch mark? He'd been hit by someone. Sienna? Had she fought back and this animal…

Why hadn't I just phoned the police after speaking to Jessica? I should have trusted my instincts.

By that point, I wasn't thinking logically. I was so furious and scared that Sienna was still in his house and in danger that I gave the door a tremendous shove, putting all my body weight behind it.

He wasn't expecting it, and the move made him stumble backwards into the hall.

I took my chance, darting inside.

Even then I knew it was reckless. A little voice in the back of my mind was warning me to be careful, but I didn't stop. Yes, I was taking a risk and could get hurt, but I was driven by fear, worrying that Sienna was somewhere inside the house, hurt and needing my help.

But as I rounded on Jason Owens, ready to give him a piece of my mind and demanded he tell me where Sienna was, I felt a rough shove from behind. Something hard hit the centre of my back, propelling me forward.

I fell awkwardly. My outstretched arms failed to break my fall, and the side of my head hit the edge of the door frame. Everything went grey and hazy. Then I fell flat on my face on the floor.

* * *

JESSICA RICHARDSON WALKED SLOWLY ALONG FLEET HILL. SHE HAD no idea what sort of trouble Sienna was in this time. For the past few months, Sienna had been moody and distant.

Jessica had tried to be a good friend. She'd tried to get Sienna to talk about whatever was bothering her, but she seemed to prefer Zach's company these days. Not that Jessica cared. Why should she? She had plenty of other friends. It didn't matter that Sienna was her oldest friend, the girl she'd known since nursery school. Things changed, people moved on. Jessica wasn't a child. She understood that, but even so, it hurt a bit.

She shivered as she walked in the shade of the oak trees and wished she'd worn something warmer. What had she been thinking? God, everyone would hear about how she got tarted up and went to see Mr Owens. It wasn't fair. Why couldn't Abbie mind her own business?

Everyone was so worried about Sienna all the time, and Jessica knew she was supposed to feel sorry for her old friend, especially as she'd just lost her mum, but Sienna had been acting up for a few months before that, and Jessica couldn't help resenting the fact she never got into trouble.

If she'd tried Sienna's antics, she wouldn't be allowed to leave her room for the next month! The one time Jessica had spoken back to her mother, only to tell her she didn't want any more piano lessons, she'd had to do the washing up every day for a week!

She did feel sorry for poor Mrs Carlson, though. Sienna's mum had always been so glamorous and interesting.

Jessica yanked down her white T-shirt, which was riding up her stomach as she walked. All this effort for nothing. Mr Owens couldn't get rid of her fast enough. Her cheeks flushed as she remembered him ordering her away from the house.

Abbie seemed to think Sienna's disappearance had something to do with Mr Owens. Jess wouldn't be surprised if Sienna had been in the house when she'd called round. She'd probably been crying on his shoulder as he stroked her hair and whispered kind words. Had they both had a good laugh after she'd left?

Jessica clenched her fists. It really wasn't fair. Sienna got everything she wanted. No one even looked at Jessica when she was around.

It was out of order. Why should Jessica have to go and speak to Sienna's Aunt Janet while Sienna got nice and cosy with Mr Owens?

She'd never really liked Sienna's aunt very much. Janet was always pulling sarcastic faces and making mean comments. Jessica was never sure what to say to her and ended up tongue-tied whenever she was around.

The breeze whistled through the tree canopy overhead, and Jessica's skin prickled with goosebumps.

Did she really have to do this? Couldn't she just go home? It had been a bad enough day already, and this was all Sienna's fault for going missing again.

All she wanted to do was go home and curl up on her bed, feeling sorry for herself. If she got home soon, she'd have time to polish off the rest of the chocolate ice cream before her mother came home and gave her a lecture about saturated fat levels.

As she reached the driveway entrance to Yew Tree House, Jess sighed and sulkily looked at the cars parked outside. She folded her arms over her chest and debated whether to tell Janet or keep walking.

CHAPTER FORTY-ONE

THE WOOL CARPET was rough against my cheek and smelled old and musty. My arms trembled as I tried to push myself up from the floor. I didn't understand what had happened. Someone had hit me... but it wasn't Jason... he'd been standing in front of me.

I pushed myself to my knees and tried to get my bearings.

Just ahead of me, Jason sat on the stairs. He was looking at me in a very strange way. His head dipped, and his eyes narrowed.

In my dazed state it took me a while to process the expression on his face. Then suddenly it clicked. Fear. Jason Owens looked afraid.

I tried to turn my head, but my neck felt stiff and my head was banging. I sensed a movement behind me but didn't move fast enough to see who was there.

"What's going on?" I asked. My voice was thick and slurred and didn't sound like my own.

"You could let her go?" Jason said. "She hasn't seen you. She doesn't *know* anything."

I blinked in confusion, wishing my brain would work properly, but the pain behind my eyes was blinding. I put my hands against my temples and squeezed. When I lowered my hands, one was covered with blood.

A harsh laugh sounded behind me, and I turned quickly, so fast the room seemed to spin.

"It's too late for that," the voice said. "She knows far too much. You all do."

I blinked into the dim light of the hall and flinched back seeing a tall figure towering over me.

Toby Walsh.

What was he doing in Jason's house? What was going on? Had he pushed me? I reached out to steady myself against the wall and tried to stand up.

"What's going on?" I asked again, this time angry.

That's when I saw the gun.

A short, stubby rifle. It looked antique. In fact, it looked like one of the matching pair Jason had hanging on the wall in his sitting room. But this gun wasn't harmlessly decorating a wall. It was pointed at my chest.

Toby cocked his head and smiled at me, and I felt my blood run cold.

"Sorry to interrupt, Abbie. You wanted to have a conversation with Jason. Please, go ahead. It was most amusing."

I turned back to Jason, and he shook his head almost imperceptibly.

"Go on," Toby prompted again. "You were about to ask Jason if he'd been having his wicked way with young girls, weren't you?"

I swallowed hard, feeling very out of my depth. Toby had shifted his position so now his body blocked the front door. Rushing inside hadn't been the most intelligent decision I'd made recently.

I needed to get out of here, but first I needed to find out if they had my goddaughter.

"Where's Sienna?"

"She is waiting in the sitting room," Toby said pleasantly, as though we were having a polite conversation at a dinner party.

I started to stumble towards the sitting room, searching for her, half expecting Toby to stop me, but he didn't.

I put out my hands to stop myself from falling as I shakily entered the sitting room. There at the far end of the room was Sienna.

I gasped in shock. She had material tied around her mouth, acting as a gag, and she was tied to a chair.

"You animal," I spat over my shoulder at Toby, forgetting for a moment he was holding a gun.

I rushed to Sienna's side, dropped to my knees and tried to free her arms from the coarse green string, which was biting into her delicate, pale skin.

Behind me, Toby and Jason entered the room.

Toby held the gun against Jason's ribs.

"Stop that, Abbie, unless you want me to shoot Jason." His voice mocked me. He was enjoying this.

Sienna let out a muffled sob, and I stopped trying to undo the string, and instead, put my arm around her shoulders.

"It's okay," I muttered. "Everything is going to be okay. I promise."

"You shouldn't make promises you can't keep," Toby said dryly, indicating with the rifle that Jason should move closer to us. "Pick up the chair and carry her into the kitchen. I want everything contained in one room."

Contained? What did he mean by that?

Jason's face was tense, his jaw clenched as he lifted the large wooden chair and Sienna. As Jason struggled towards the kitchen, I noticed the empty spot on the wall where the antique rifle had been displayed. Its partner was still on the wall. Maybe if I could just grab it...

"I'd shoot you before you crossed the room," Toby said, with a huff of impatience. "Now move."

I followed Jason into the kitchen, acutely aware of the rifle Toby kept trained on us.

Toby pulled out a chair and sat down beside the kitchen table. He smiled at me again as though we were all just having a polite chat in a friend's kitchen.

"What the hell do you think you're doing?" I demanded. "Put down that gun and untie Sienna right now. You're going to be in so much trouble."

Toby said nothing, and maddeningly, just smiled. I'd had this all wrong. I'd put two and two together and come up with five.

What I couldn't figure out was why Toby was in Jason's house. The police were looking for him. Why was he *here*?

"You've given me an idea, Abbie, so I have to thank you for that. Unfortunately, there's no way I can let any of you get out of this alive."

Sienna began to cry loudly.

"You're crazy if you think you're going to get away with this," I said. "The police are looking for you. They know you committed fraud. There's no way you'll get out of the country."

He grinned. "The police aren't quite as smart as you think. I arranged for a boat to go missing and now they think I've run off to the continent. They're looking in the wrong place."

"Not all of them," I said. "I just spoke to Jessica Richardson, and she's going to tell Janet *and* the family liaison officer at Yew Tree

House. So you should stop looking so smug, Toby, because the police will be here at any moment."

The smile dropping from Toby's face gave me a brief moment of satisfaction. But it didn't last long. A second later, Toby began to laugh. The sound echoed through the kitchen, and I felt Sienna's body tremble beneath my arms.

I turned to Jason for help, but he seemed distracted.

"You're not going to be laughing when the police get here," I said, hoping that Jessica had gone straight to Yew Tree House as I'd asked.

"I'll be long gone by the time they arrive," he said. "And thanks to you, I now have a scapegoat. I have to give you credit for that brilliant idea. Of course, everyone will assume the teacher was overcome with guilt and turned the gun on himself after killing you and Sienna." He turned to smile at Jason. "It's perfect."

Toby turned, walked over to the draining board and picked up a red plastic container.

I knew what it was even before he unscrewed the cap, but when the smell of petrol filled the small kitchen, I thought I was going to throw up.

I needed to keep him talking until the police got here. That was our only chance. Toby was obviously crazy. He'd stolen money from Steve's company and thought somehow he was above the law.

"So I take it you were the one who took advantage of Sienna and not Jason?" I said scornfully.

Toby walked towards me, holding the petrol. I breathed shallowly so I didn't inhale the fumes.

"You've got no proof," he said.

"She's fifteen. That's sick."

"It only happened a couple of times," Toby said, shrugging as though it were no big deal.

I swallowed my anger. I needed to keep calm and make him see reason. "This is totally over the top, Toby. Yes, the police will charge you for the fraud and your relationship with an underage girl, but murder is on another level. You'll probably be in prison for the rest of your life. That doesn't have to happen. Just let us go."

"It's gone too far."

"It hasn't. Not yet. You haven't killed anyone. Hand yourself in, get a good lawyer and you could be out starting a new life in a few years." I had no idea if that was true, but I tried to sound convincing.

"I wish that were the case, Abbie. But sadly it's no longer an option for me. It's not my fault. It's hers." He waved the gun in Sienna's direction. "The stupid girl couldn't keep her mouth shut and told her mother."

Sienna shook her head vigorously from side to side.

"Nicole knew?"

The pieces of the puzzle slid into place. How could I have missed it? Nicole would have been furious when she'd found out Toby had been taking advantage of her daughter like this. She would have confronted him.

It wasn't just about the money and his predatory relationship with Sienna. The man had murdered my friend.

I shook my head, not wanting to believe it. "Did you kill Nicole?"

Toby glared at me. "I warned her. She said she was going to tell Steve. She knew what would happen if she did. I told her all she had to do was keep her mouth shut, but it was like she was on some sort of crusade. The stupid woman. I told her it wasn't me. It was Sienna. She was always coming on to me, throwing herself at me like some tart, and I'm only human."

I couldn't reply, I could barely even draw another breath into my lungs. The man standing in front of me had abused Sienna and murdered her mother.

"I didn't intend to kill her," Toby said, frowning at the petrol container. "I took the shotgun along to frighten her. It was her fault. If she'd just agreed to keep quiet, I wouldn't have had to do it."

My breathing was ragged, and my skin was sweaty and cold. I wanted to scratch his eyes out. I wanted to see him suffer a slow, torturous death.

I looked around the kitchen for a weapon. There were no knives on view. The only thing that looked like it could be used as some kind of weapon was the bright orange cast iron pan sitting on the stovetop, but it was too far away.

He began to splash petrol around Sienna's feet. She wriggled in the chair trying to get away from him.

Think, Abbie. Think.

If I didn't keep him talking, it was going to be all over before the police got here.

CHAPTER FORTY-TWO

JESSICA RICHARDSON KNOCKED on the door. She did it tentatively, hoping no one would hear her, she'd be able to run off home and lick her wounds. But within seconds, the door was yanked open and she was face-to-face with Sienna's aunt.

"Jess? Is Sienna with you?" She stuck her head out the door and looked around at the driveway as though Sienna might be hiding behind one of the cars.

Jessica took a step back. Sienna's aunt was very odd.

Jessica shook her head. "No, she's not with me. Abbie asked me to come." She linked her fingers and cringed. It was so humiliating.

"Well, what is it? Abbie's not here," Janet said, irritably, preparing to shut the door.

"I went to Mr Owens's house earlier, and he sent me away." She shrugged. "It's not a big deal, but Abbie was going to go to his house, and she asked me to tell you that is where she was going."

"Why on earth has she gone there?" Janet said, huffing and tugging at the sleeves of her green jumper. "She told me she was looking for Sienna. For goodness sake, if she's been distracted by some man candy when she is supposed to be looking for my niece, then I won't be responsible for my actions."

Jessica opened her mouth to say something else, but Janet closed the front door, and she was left staring at the polished oak.

* * *

"Why did you do it?" I asked. It wasn't the most inventive question, but it was all I had.

My pulse raced, and my mouth was so dry I could barely talk.

"Quite simply because she wouldn't keep her mouth shut. Much like her daughter," Toby said.

"But what I don't understand is why you're in Jason's house." I shot a glance at Jason, who was staring at the gun in Toby's hand. "What's Jason got to do with all this?"

Toby shrugged. "You're not very bright, are you? He doesn't have anything to do with it. I followed Sienna. I couldn't leave any loose ends. Eventually she'd tell someone else. When I saw she was coming here, I knew she was about to confide in her favourite teacher, weren't you?" Toby turned to look at Sienna.

Her tear-stained face crumpled.

There was a sudden movement to my left as Jason pushed himself off the kitchen counter and launched himself at Toby, making a grab for the gun. The petrol can went flying, hitting the edge of the table and then righting itself.

I used my body to try and protect Sienna, bracing myself for the gun to go off at any moment.

Then there was a sickening crunch. I turned. The base of the shotgun was bloody and Jason was lying motionless on the floor.

Rather than shoot him, Toby had knocked him unconscious. "That's your fault," Toby snarled at Sienna.

I wanted to shout back and tell him a few home truths but silence was a better option now that our lives were hanging in the balance.

He took a menacing step closer to us, but I didn't move. If he was going to kill Sienna, he needed to go through me first.

"You can't kill us both," I said. "You're not evil. You should just make a run for it. The police are going to be here at any moment. If you leave now, you still have a chance to get away."

I tried to sound confident, but I had to admit I was getting more and more frantic by the second. Surely Jessica must have told Janet and Lizzie by now. Why weren't they here yet? Why weren't they banging down the door?

Toby narrowed his eyes and slowly lowered the shotgun until it was pointing at my chest. Then he inched forward until the barrel was pressed against my breastbone.

CHAPTER FORTY-THREE

I'D ALWAYS ASSUMED DESCRIBING knees knocking together was an inaccurate cliché, but at that moment, I understood how the phrase had originated. My legs were shaking so badly, I wasn't sure I'd remain upright for much longer.

Don't panic, Abbie. What were the chances he just took the gun from Jason's wall and hadn't loaded it with bullets? I hung onto that thought as my only hope to get us out of this alive.

Jason hadn't moved, and I was starting to think maybe the blow to his head *had* killed him. His face was covered with dark red blood.

I licked my lips and shook my head. "You haven't thought this through, Toby. Things will be so much worse if you kill us."

"But I have to kill you, don't you see? I have to make it look like this was all down to Jason," Toby said, jerking his chin toward poor Jason who was sprawled across the kitchen tiles.

I wanted to check his pulse and move him into the recovery position but the gun was digging into my chest, reminding me any sudden movements were a very bad idea.

"Why did you kill Nicole? She'd never done anything to hurt you." I wasn't thinking logically now and was just saying the first thing that came into my mind. Anything to stretch out the time we had left before he shot me.

"But she was about to hurt me, Abbie. I couldn't let that happen. I don't want to do this. I'm not a monster. There really is no other way."

He smiled at me, and I realised then he was quite mad. I had zero chance of reasoning with him or making him see sense. I closed my eyes and took a shallow breath.

Why hadn't I given more details on the voicemail message I'd left Steve? If Toby killed us here no one would know who really committed the murders.

But surely the police would work out Toby was behind this. They wouldn't pin it on Jason, would they? I'd been stupid enough to jump to the wrong conclusion, but the police were trained to handle this. They were professionals. Forensic officers must be able to prove Toby had been in this house... He wouldn't get away with this. I had to believe that.

There was a muffled sound in the hallway, the creaking of old floorboards, and I saw a flash of green in the dim hall beyond the kitchen.

Toby, who had his back to the hall, turned quickly, lowering the gun so it was no longer pressing into my flesh. "What was that noise?"

"I didn't hear anything."

Toby turned back to me and raised the gun. I could push the barrel away and run, but even if I did, he would overpower me within seconds.

And Sienna couldn't run. I wouldn't leave her.

Again a flash of green crossed the hallway. There was someone else in the house. I forced myself to look away, only because I didn't want to alert Toby. I hoped it was the police. I hadn't heard any sirens, but maybe they didn't want to signal their arrival. Maybe they had a SWAT team and a gun trained on Toby right now.

God, I hoped so.

I wondered if these were the same thoughts that flooded Nicole's brain in the moments before she died.

The flash of green came again, this time closer, and for a fraction of a second Janet's face appeared in the doorway.

My body tensed. What was she doing in the house? Surely she hadn't come alone?

Toby put the antique rifle on the kitchen counter, and pulled a box of matches out of his pocket. Sienna began to sob again.

He smiled as he struck a match and then threw it on the floor. The effect was instantaneous. With a whoosh, the petrol ignited and flames rushed along the rug before catching the kitchen counter.

The petrol around our feet hadn't yet caught light, but it would soon. I could already feel the heat of the fire, and the air was thick with fumes.

"Would you rather be shot? Burning to death won't be a pleasant way to go." He smiled at me as he picked up the gun again. In his sick mind he really thought I should be grateful for him giving me a choice.

I swore at him, and his smile turned into a snarl as he reached up and slapped me across the face with the back of his hand.

It was just the distraction Janet needed. She stealthily crept into the kitchen. I held my breath.

She grabbed the cast-iron pan from the stove, but it scraped against the hob.

At the sound, Toby quickly turned, but he was too late. With a shrill scream, Janet smashed the cast-iron pan against the side of Toby's temple.

He stumbled then fell hard, landing beside Jason Owens on the floor.

Frozen, I stared down at him, watching his blood ooze out onto the floor.

"Well, don't just stand there," Janet snapped. "Help me get Sienna out of here."

Her words spurred me into action, and I pulled the gag free from Sienna's mouth, and then began to work at loosening the string around her wrists.

"There's no time for that, Abbie. Help me lift her." Janet strained as she yanked up one arm of the chair, and I understood what she was trying to do.

I slid my hands under the other arm and between us we shuffled out of the kitchen carrying Sienna on the chair, staying as far from the flames as possible. The bottoms of her legs were saturated with petrol.

I hit my elbow and knee on the walls as we passed but we kept heading for the front door.

Janet pulled open the door. The bright sunlight was a welcome sight. We dragged the chair along the garden path, only stopping when we reached the pavement at the front of the house.

Sirens sounded in the distance.

"Finally," Janet said.

"Untie her," I said and jogged back towards the front door.

"Where do you think you're going?" Janet shouted.

"Jason is still in there."

"For goodness sake, Abbie. Don't be such an idiot," Janet said, but I was already inside.

It shocked me how quickly the fire had taken hold. The hall was rapidly filling with smoke. Fortunately, I could still see, though the smoke stung my eyes and made me cough. I reached down to pull my T-shirt over my mouth, but it hardly made a difference.

Tears streaming from my eyes, I held up my hands in front of me and felt my way along the hall towards the kitchen. The smoke was stronger there, so I dropped to my hands and knees, crawling forward. It was impossible to keep my eyes open for longer than a second before being forced to shut them again by the stinging smoke.

More by feel than sight, I located the bodies on the floor and unless one of them had moved, I knew Jason was the body closest to me. I gripped his ankles, and with all my strength, I pulled.

It was slow work. He was a big man and I only managed to pull a few inches at a time.

I tried to hold my breath as the smoke was travelling upwards, thick and dark above my head, and it was difficult to breathe without choking. I grunted with the effort of pulling him along the hallway.

By the time, I reached the front door, the air was clearer. I'd left it open behind me, which was a stupid mistake. I remembered reading that oxygen fuelled the fire and that doors should always be shut to slow the hungry flames.

It was too late to worry about that. I took a full breath for the first time since entering the house again and then began to splutter and cough as I pulled Jason through the door.

Above me, the thatch had already caught and smoke was streaming into the sky. There were no flames yet, but it wouldn't be long before they consumed the cottage.

I felt hands, pulling me to my feet. "Is there anyone else inside?"

I turned. Through stinging eyes, I saw a fireman looking intently at me as he repeated his question.

It was tempting to say no one else was inside, very tempting to let that man burn, but unlike him I wasn't a cold-blooded killer.

"Yes, there's another man inside," I spluttered.

Lizzie appeared over the fireman's shoulder, and I recognised another officer behind her.

"Who is inside, Abbie?" she asked sharply.

"Toby," I said. "Toby Walsh. He killed Nicole and he just tried to kill us, too."

* * *

THE NEXT FEW MINUTES WERE A BLUR. I WAS BUNDLED INTO THE BACK of an ambulance and treated at the scene. My eyes were still streaming, and I couldn't stop coughing. Fire officers from three fire engines battled the blaze as I sat inside the ambulance.

"Is everyone else okay?" I asked between hacking coughs.

The female paramedic treating me exchanged a look with her colleague. "Let's just concentrate on you for now."

Shouts and orders came from outside, then the sound of more sirens.

I wished I knew what was happening. Was Toby Walsh still alive? Had they managed to get him out in time?

The ambulance door opened, and Janet stuck her head in. "Oh, there you are."

"I'm sorry but you can't stand there unless you're family. We're in the middle of treatment," the paramedic said sternly.

"I am family," Janet lied smoothly and turned back to me. "Sienna has been checked out and she is well enough to go home. I've called my mother and we'll go to her house until Steve gets back from London. You're welcome to come with us."

I blinked in surprise. By Janet's standards, that was rolling out the red carpet.

The paramedic shook her head. "We need to get you checked out at the hospital, Abbie. You've inhaled a lot of smoke, and I'm worried about your breathing."

"Sorry," I said to Janet, not quite sure why I was apologising for having to go to hospital. "Thanks for coming to help us."

Janet shrugged. "Of course, I helped. What did you expect me to do? Twiddle my thumbs?"

"What happened to Toby?"

"They got him out of the house."

"He's alive?" I managed to croak.

"Yes, although for how long is anyone's guess. He's badly burned. No less than he deserves. With any luck, he won't make it."

"Is Jason okay?" I wheezed.

"Looks like it. When Lizzie told him you'd pulled him out of the house, he acted like you were the second coming or something." She rolled her eyes. "Isn't Abbie wonderful? So Brave!" Janet mimicked, pulling a face. "I'm sure he wouldn't be singing your praises quite so highly if he'd seen the clumsy way you pulled him down the front steps, hitting his head. Still…" She paused and looked down her nose at me. "I suppose it was quite brave." She shrugged.

Then she disappeared, leaving me and the two paramedics alone.

"Is she always like that?" The male paramedic asked as he packed up the box of sterile wipes he'd used to clean my head wound.

"Yes," I said shaking my head and smiling.

Despite her prickly, obtuse nature, Janet had some good traits. Unfortunately, she hid them well.

"She's not really a relative, is she?" he asked.

I shook my head and winced as the throbbing at the side of my skull intensified.

"Is she a friend of yours then?" the female paramedic asked, raising an eyebrow.

I hesitated, before finally saying, "Yes, she is."

EPILOGUE

TWO MONTHS LATER

I DROVE THROUGH THE VILLAGE, slowing as I passed Jason Owens's cottage. It was in a sorry state. The thatched roof had burned quickly, despite the efforts of the fire brigade. The fire had swept through the interior, causing major damage, but the renovation work had started. A transit van belonging to a local building firm was parked outside.

I'd seen Jason a few times since the fire. He thanked me profusely for coming back to save him, but there would always be an awkwardness between us. The drink we were meant to share didn't get mentioned again, and we'd never be more than acquaintances now.

I'd suspected him of a terrible crime, and I couldn't blame him for being unable to get past that. I tightened my hands on the steering wheel and pressed down on the accelerator, heading through the village towards Fleet Hill.

A job at the Royal Berkshire Hospital had been advertised six weeks ago, and I'd decided to apply. I was thrilled when I got the job. It was only a temporary role, working shifts as a staff nurse on the general medical wards, but it was just what I needed. I was tired of running away.

I wouldn't be going back to India any time soon. After everything that had happened, Sienna needed her friends and family around her. The last two months had been a time of adjustment. Sienna had decided she wanted to keep the baby, and everyone was trying to get used to the idea. It was hard to see Sienna as anything other than a child herself.

I turned into the driveway, and the large yew tree towered over me. Its boughs stretched out, shading the gravel, but it no longer seemed threatening. The evil and menace Angie spoke of had dissipated.

The exterior of Yew Tree House now appeared welcoming and homely, rather than ominous. I heard Charlie's familiar bark before the door opened.

Steve answered the front door with a smile. Slowly, day by day, I was noticing an improvement. He no longer appeared to have the weight of the world on his shoulders. At times, he would seem lost, looking off into space, perhaps remembering happier times with Nicole, but he'd taken the news about Sienna's pregnancy relatively well once he'd overcome the initial shock.

He'd converted one of the guest bedrooms into a nursery and was full of plans to baby proof the house.

Charlie trotted over to me, wagging his tail manically as I reached down to pet him.

"I've come to take Charlie for his walk," I said, grinning at the Labrador's enthusiastic welcome.

"Have you got time for a cup of tea?"

"That would be lovely." I followed Steve inside and sat down at the kitchen table as he busied himself making the tea.

"Where's Sienna?"

"She's gone out with Zach. They've gone into Reading, shopping. He needs some new jeans, apparently."

I'd never seen Zach wear anything but black. At least he wouldn't have to worry about colours clashing.

"Excuse the mess," Steve said, nodding to a collection of small biodegradable garden pots. "I was just about to take them outside when the doorbell rang."

The last time I'd visited, Steve had told me his plans to build two large greenhouses on some land he owned in Crowthorne and how he intended to set up a nursery business.

If it were anyone else, I would have thought they were over-reaching by jumping so quickly into a new business, but something told me Steve would be successful. He was a hard worker, but more importantly, he seemed to have an enthusiasm he'd never had for his investment business.

"Is it planting time now?" I asked. "I would have thought this was the wrong time of year."

"Depends what you're planting," Steve answered with a wink and pointed at the garden seed catalogue on the kitchen table.

I flicked through it until he sat opposite and set a mug of tea in front of me.

"So how are things with you, Abbie?"

"Pretty good. Work is going well. Although getting used to the shift pattern is taking a bit of time." I smiled, picked up my cup and took a sip before tentatively asking, "Has there been any news on Toby?"

A flash of anger passed across his face. "Still the same," he said, staring down at his tea.

Toby's burns had covered most of his body, and he'd been in intensive care for the past two months. I hated him for what he'd done to Nicole, and every time I thought about what he'd done to Sienna, it made me feel sick.

Sometimes I'd lie awake at night thinking about what would be an appropriate punishment for a man like Toby Walsh. If he died, that would be an eye for an eye, a tooth for a tooth, a death for a death, but if he lived, he would suffer disfigurement and endure a trial and then imprisonment. Maybe that was more fitting?

"Any news on the investigation?" I asked, referring to Toby's embezzlement.

Steve shook his head sadly. "It looks like the investigation will be ongoing for some time."

Their business assets and accounts had been frozen. Fortunately, Steve had a diverse portfolio of investments, and my concern he could lose Yew Tree House was unfounded. It turned out Steve was far wealthier than I'd realised. Money was one thing that wouldn't be a problem.

But money didn't make losing Nicole any easier to bear.

As I was draining the last of my tea, Charlie nuzzled my leg.

Steve laughed. "I think somebody is telling you he'd like to go for his walk now."

I smiled. "I think you're right."

After saying goodbye to Steve, Charlie and I walked down Fleet Hill, sticking to the grass verge. Rather than walk into Finchampstead village, we headed the other way, towards Eversley.

The October air was crisp. It was a bright sunny day, but there was a nip in the air, which was invigorating. I'd taken to walking Charlie at least once a week. I loved dogs, and as I didn't have one of my own, I liked to borrow Charlie.

We'd almost reached the junction where Fleet Hill met the A327 when I heard a car slow as it approached us from behind.

I turned and saw Angie Macgregor's, silver mini. Angie was behind the wheel waving at me. When she pulled up beside us, I leaned down to look in the passenger window.

"I thought it was you," Angie said. "Everything all right?"

"Yes, thanks. I'm just taking Charlie for a walk."

"Fancy a drink?" Angie gestured to the pub just in front of us, The Tally-ho.

"Sure," I said.

Angie pulled in to the car park, and I followed on foot with Charlie. When she got out of the car, Angie suggested we sit outside so we would have some privacy, and she went into the pub to get the drinks.

No one else was sitting outside on the chilly October afternoon. So we had the garden to ourselves. I sat down at one of the wooden benches, and Charlie settled beside me. Before long, Angie came out with a soda water and lime for me and an orange juice for her.

"I'm glad I caught you, Abbie. There's something I've been wanting to say," she said, setting the drinks on the table.

"Oh?"

"I wanted to thank you for listening to me. Most people would have dismissed me as a daft, superstitious, old woman. I'm so glad you came back when I called. I didn't know who else to turn to. Even after Nicole died, I sensed the danger hadn't left us. If you hadn't come back, that evil man would have killed Sienna, too. I'm sure of it. And who knows if the police would ever have linked him to their deaths."

"I'm sure they would have done."

I felt uncomfortable. I hadn't done much at all. I still had dark moments when I wondered how I could have done more. Should I have paid more attention to the things Nicole said during our weekly conversations? If I'd come back regularly to see her and my goddaughter maybe I would have been able to help.

Toby Walsh saw himself as the victim. The way he'd described having no alternative other than to shoot Nicole… and his need to tie up loose ends by killing me, Jason and Sienna made my blood run cold.

To think Nicole had once tried to set me up with that man... I shivered.

"Are you all right, lovey?"

I nodded and reached down to pet Charlie. His warm, solid body pressing against my leg was comforting.

"Yes, sorry, I was just thinking."

"I can tell by your expression you're thinking about that awful man," Angie said and then pursed her lips together. She couldn't even bring herself to utter Toby's name.

The police had found the murder weapon. Toby had stashed the shotgun he'd used to kill Nicole in his flat in Reading. He must have been extremely confident he'd get away with it. So confident, he didn't even try to get rid of the incriminating evidence.

Had he really just meant to frighten Nicole that day? Had she believed he was bluffing? Had she laughed at him? Was there a moment just before she died when she realised she was dealing with a madman?

Sienna had kept the letters Toby had written to her and they made sickening reading. Leaving evidence like that was yet another example of his arrogance. He thought he was too clever to be caught. We assumed the letters were how Nicole found out about Toby's relationship with her teenage daughter. Sienna insisted she'd never told anyone. The theory made sense, but we would never know for sure.

"Did you hear Sienna is having a wee girl?" Angie asked, her cheeks dimpling in a rare smile.

"Yes," I said. "Marilyn went to the scan with her, didn't she?"

Angie sighed. "Aye, though I think she found it difficult. Very emotional. Sienna told her she's going to name the baby Nicole."

I'd been impressed with how Marilyn had handled the situation. It seemed she was taking the news of Sienna's pregnancy better than she had Nicole's.

It was as though she wanted to draw a line under what had happened and move on, think about the positive things in the future, not dwell on the tragedies of the past.

I was glad Marilyn was embracing the idea of becoming a great-grandmother. She'd even started knitting booties and a little cardigan for the baby.

And Janet and I…well, we'd never be bosom buddies exactly, but we had an understanding. We both wanted what was best for Sienna.

"I hoped to see Sienna today when I picked up Charlie, but she's gone shopping with Zach," I told Angie. "Do you know what she's decided to do about Eric Ross?"

Angie gave a disapproving sniff. "She doesn't want anything to do with him, and I can't say I blame her."

That was exactly what Sienna had said when I'd asked her last week. I wondered if she would change her mind eventually. In time, she might want to get to know her half brother and sister.

"Did you ever find out why Eric Ross lied about coming to the house to see Nicole?" Angie asked.

"Apparently, it was because he thought it might make the police suspicious."

Angie's eyes widened. "How did he get to be a professor with such a total lack of intelligence?" she asked sharply with a disapproving shake of her head. "Surely it's more suspicious that he lied about it!"

"That's what I think, too, but people do strange things under stress."

I asked after Jock and then Angie checked the time. "Oh goodness me! I'd better get back. He'll be wondering where I am. We were supposed to be doing some gardening this afternoon."

After Angie left, Charlie and I resumed our walk, walking over the bridge which sat at the borderline between Hampshire and Berkshire. I gazed down into the dark, gurgling water.

Charlie stood patiently beside me on the bridge, watching the river. He'd perked up a little these past few weeks, as though, in his own way, he was slowly coming to terms with Nicole's death. I supposed we all were.

Charlie bumped my legs gently with his head. It was his signal he was ready to continue our walk. I looked up at the bright October sky and took a deep breath. I'd always miss my beautiful, kind-hearted friend, but it was comforting to imagine Nicole was up there somewhere, looking down on us.

I smiled down at Nicole's dog. "You're right Charlie. It's time to head home."

* * *

THANK YOU FOR READING!

AN EXTRACT FROM LOST CHILD

CHAPTER ONE

I think about the day I lost Jenna all the time. It's always with me.

People say the pain lessens over time, but I'm not sure that's true. Every time I remember, my stomach twists as I'm reminded of how I let everyone down, my sister most of all. I only took my eyes off Jenna for a second. But a second was all it took to lose her.

The day it happened, the twenty-fifth of May, was a bank holiday. The weather was sunny and warm in the small market town of Woodstock, in Oxfordshire, a hint that summer was finally on its way after a cold and rainy spring. I had grown up in Woodstock. The town seemed so ordinary and safe. Perhaps, that was why I'd let my guard down. Nothing bad happened in Woodstock. It was a quintessentially English town, a safe haven.

My father had died suddenly five years ago, shortly before my sister, Kate, had fallen pregnant with Jenna. As Mum wasn't keen on rattling around the big house on her own, and Kate and her partner, Daniel Creswell, were living in a one-bedroom flat, it seemed logical for them to move in with Mum for a while.

Kate and Daniel married the year after Jenna was born, and Daniel progressed well in his career as a graphic designer. I was sure they could have afforded to buy their own place after the first year, but there was no need. The arrangement worked well for everyone. The house was large enough for Mum to have her own sitting room, and she was tolerant, easy to live with and adored Jenna.

Kate liked to joke she had a live-in babysitter. When I look back at that time now, I wish I had appreciated it more. We had so many happy memories.

Although I'd moved away from Woodstock, I hadn't gone far. I had a one-bedroom flat in Oxford, near the train station. I enjoyed living in the hustle and bustle of the city, but I came back to Woodstock every weekend. Sunday lunch at my mother's house was a ritual I didn't want to miss.

It was a good job Mum was easy-going because I'm sure living with Daniel Creswell would have driven most people to distraction. It wasn't that he was a nasty man, and he didn't treat my sister or Jenna badly, but he could be condescending and always wanted to be the subject of the conversation.

If you told him you had a pet elephant, Daniel would have a bigger one and the box to put it in. The constant one-upmanship irritated me, but Mum and Kate didn't seem to notice. The simple truth was they were nicer than me.

On the day it happened, my patience was already wearing thin with Daniel. He'd dominated the conversation yesterday over Sunday lunch, droning on about how successful he was and describing his recent business trip to Barcelona. When I asked whether he'd gone to see any sights, he informed me he wasn't there as a tourist and was far too busy to explore the city. I hadn't done anything more than roll my eyes, but that was enough for Mum to send a chastising look in my direction. I was very familiar with that look.

One day a week in Daniel's presence, I could tolerate, but because today was a bank holiday and it was the Woodstock spring fête, I was in his company for the second day in a row, and he was starting to grate on my nerves.

The fête was held in Woodstock primary school's playing field. There weren't a huge number of attractions, but I'd been doing a pretty good job of avoiding him, slowly walking around the make-shift stalls that sold homemade jam, fragrant candles, tea and small cakes.

The smell of freshly-cut grass carried on the breeze, and the sun was warm on my skin. Children's excited laughter came from the stocks where they were pelting one of the female teachers with sopping wet sponges. Her once wavy hair hung in lank, dripping strands.

She caught me watching and grimaced. "Do you want a turn?"

I shook my head, grinning. "No, thanks!"

They were raising money for a good cause, maintaining the communal gardens. I stopped to watch for a while, laughing when one small boy grew sick of his poor aim and rushed up to squeeze water from his sponge onto the teacher instead.

When a few sharp words rose above the general chatter around me, I turned to see Daniel had his hand on my sister's arm. The rigid way my sister stood next to her husband made me think they were arguing. Her body was tense, and she held Jenna's hand tightly.

My niece, Jenna, like most three-year-olds, didn't like to stand still. She was tugging Kate's hand and bouncing on the balls of her feet, eager to participate in the fun.

There were children running everywhere, laughing with delight. The fête was set up for young children. Face painting, a bouncy castle, balloons, an ice-cream van, and for the older children, there was tinny music blaring out from one of the stalls with a minor local celebrity, Robin Vaughan, holding court.

Robin Vaughan wore a garishly-bright Hawaiian shirt and dark skinny jeans. Not a good look for a man in his fifties. I didn't understand the attraction, but the kids seemed to love him.

I dragged my gaze away from Robin and his cringe-worthy attempts to impress the youngsters gathered around him and turned back to my sister. I didn't want to listen in on their private conversation, so I waited until Daniel turned and stalked off before walking towards her.

"Is everything all right?" I put my hand on her shoulder.

Kate blinked and smiled brightly. "Of course, everything is fine. Isn't the weather amazing? I can't believe the sun is shining on a bank holiday. Wonders will never cease."

She was babbling and talking about the weather, so I knew something was wrong, but whatever it was, she didn't want to confide in me. At the time, I thought it was only a minor tiff between husband and wife.

I smiled down at Jenna who had progressed to whining and yanking on her mother's arm. "I want the bouncy castle."

I ruffled her soft blonde hair and looked at where she pointed to the inflatable, red bouncy castle and frowned. It looked very big, and I worried it might be a bit too rough for a child Jenna's size.

"I think that's for bigger boys and girls, Jenna," I said and watched her small face crumple. I should have used the distraction technique.

"We'll see what Mummy thinks," I said, turning back to Kate, but she wasn't paying attention. She was looking over my shoulder, watching her husband, Daniel, talking to one of our friends, Pippa Clarkson. Pippa was in charge of a stall selling handmade candles. She'd been in Kate's year at school and was a couple of years older than me. She'd made quite a success of her candle business, even managing to employ Kate part-time to help fulfil orders. Pippa's husband, Mark, was nowhere to be seen.

Next to Pippa stood Phil Bowman. He was supposed to be helping but he looked blankly down at the table, his arms hanging by his sides.

"God, he looks awful," I muttered.

"Hmm?" Kate sounded distracted and kept her gaze on Pippa and Daniel.

"Phil Bowman," I said and felt my chest tighten. "How long has it been now?"

Kate sighed. "Eight months."

"Poor bloke."

Phil had lost his wife and daughter in a car accident on the A44. He'd been driving but survived without a scratch. His wife and daughter hadn't been so lucky. Today, he looked grey, worn out and out of place. The people surrounding him were smiling, joking and laughing, but Phil looked like he was using up all his energy just to stay upright.

He was only a few years older than us. I'd dated his younger brother, Luke, for a while. It was years ago, but I could remember how I'd been so impressed by Phil. He went to music gigs, wore a leather jacket and seemed so mature and exciting. When I was sixteen, he'd bought Luke a bottle of Strawberry 20/20, and we'd sipped it while sitting on the bench behind the cemetery. I'd been slightly easier to impress when I was sixteen. These days, I preferred wine to fruit-flavoured alcohol.

Phil had been one of life's successes. He'd had it all. After studying Chemistry at Oxford, he had settled into domestic bliss with his wife and daughter. That all ended eight months ago.

He kept his gaze lowered, avoiding all the curious glances from locals. It was hard to keep things private in a small town where everyone knew each other's business. It was to be expected, I supposed, but I found it claustrophobic and stifling at times. I looked around, wondering where Luke was. He'd been his brother's almost constant companion since the accident, but today he was nowhere to be seen.

Kate's face tightened and she reached down to stroke Jenna's hair, as though reassuring herself her daughter was still safe. "I can't imagine how you can get past something like that," Kate murmured.

Frustrated at her mother and aunt, Jenna stamped her foot. "Mummy," she said, drawing out the word to pronounce every syllable.

"Just a minute, Jenna. Mummy is talking," Kate replied. Her voice was calm as it always was when she spoke to her daughter.

Jenna could be headstrong and was prone to tantrums, but it all washed over Kate. She patiently dealt with every one of Jenna's outbursts, calmly explaining to Jenna why she couldn't do all the things she wanted to.

I'd tried the logical conversations Kate was so fond of with Jenna but found they didn't suit me. I preferred the distraction technique when it came to dealing with my three-year-old niece.

But today, it was Kate who seemed distracted and impatient. It was very unlike her. I reached out for Jenna's hand. "Why don't I take Jenna to the bouncy castle?"

Kate smiled gratefully at me. "Thanks. You're an angel."

Jenna bounced along beside me, her tiny hand warm in mine. She had so much energy she found it impossible to walk in a straight line. She swung our arms, giggling and skipping beside me.

I've replayed that moment in my mind a thousand times since then, wondering if someone was watching us, waiting for the perfect time to strike.

Lost Child

A NOTE FROM D. S. BUTLER

Thank you for reading Her Missing Daughter!

Please give the book a review on Amazon if you have the time. I appreciate your kind words and encouragement, and honest reviews help other readers find books they'll enjoy.

If you like standalone psychological thrillers, you might also enjoy Lost Child.

Next up for me, is a Dani Oakley novel, and after that, I'll be working on another D. S. Butler book. I also have a new police procedural series coming out in Oct 2018!

If you would like to be one of the first to know when my next book is available, you can sign up for my new release email:

www.dsbutlerbooks.com/newsletter

All the best,

Dani

www.dsbutlerbooks.com

Or you can connect with me on Facebook, Twitter or Instagram :)

facebook.com/D.S.Butler.Author

twitter.com/ds_butler

instagram.com/dsbutlerauthor

ALSO BY D S BUTLER

Lost Child

Deadly Obsession

Deadly Motive

Deadly Revenge

Deadly Justice

Deadly Ritual

Deadly Payback

Deadly Game

If you would like to be informed when the next book is released, sign up for the newsletter:

http://www.dsbutlerbooks.com/newsletter/

Written as Dani Oakley

East End Trouble

East End Diamond

East End Retribution

ACKNOWLEDGMENTS

I would like to thank my readers for their support and encouragement.

My thanks, too, to all the people who read the story and gave helpful suggestions (especially my mum!) and to Chris, who, as always, supported me.

To Nanci, my editor, thanks for always managing to squeeze me in when I finally finish my books!

And last but not least, my thanks to you for reading this book. I hope you enjoyed it.

Printed in Great Britain
by Amazon

50969452R00199